Allison
2024

The NOISE

ALLISON A

The Noise © 2023 by Allison A

Cover and internal design by White Petal Press

All rights reserved. No part of this book may be reproduced in any form or by any electronic or mechanical means including information storage and retrieval systems—except in the case of brief quotations embodied in critical articles or reviews—without permission in writing from its publisher, White Petal Press.

The characters and events portrayed in this book are fictitious or are used fictitiously. Any similarity to real persons, living or otherwise, is purely coincidental and not intended by the author.

All brand names and product names used in this book are trademarks, registered trademarks, or trade names of their respective holders. White Petal Press is not associated with any product or vendor in this book.

Published by White Petal Press

Cataloging-in-Publication Data is on file with the Library of Congress

Printed and bound in the United States of America.

This book is for my dad, Andrew J. Nazzaro.
Here's to your next thirty years.
And for Tom.
I'm sure.
I will always be sure.

"A thing of beauty is a joy for ever:
Its loveliness increases; it will never
Pass into nothingness; but still will keep
A bower quiet for us, and a sleep
Full of sweet dreams, and health, and quiet breathing."

John Keats

ONE

His face is unnatural—gaunt and twisted in a way it wasn't when he was alive. I know enough by now to say this with certainty.

Decaying gray skin hangs from claw-shaped hands as they stretch into the stream of moonlight shimmering through the curtains. If I wasn't so unfortunately acquainted with the sight of rotting flesh, I'd think his fingers had been mangled by some kind of machinery, leaving the thumb and index of his right hand suspended by nothing more than a deteriorating tendon. A pebble of light flickers within his deep-sunken eyes glaring from the corner of the living room where he's crouched.

He lets out a small noise. A kind of guttural growling. This is new. I've never heard them make sounds before.

Air from the vent shifts the curtains, causing light to ripple over the white fabric and reflect onto his purple lips as they

THE NOISE

peel back from putrid teeth. The growling grows louder, as if to match my building fear, rumbling like thunder from deep within his gut.

My whole body is paralyzed, fighting through pins and needles just to allow my chest to rise and fall with my begging breaths. The only movements I can manage are blinking and chattering my jaw in an effort to tell him to get out. Saying those two words is the only thing that makes them leave.

"Ge…et…" I stammer, as if I've awoken from a coma to find I've lost my ability to speak.

He stumbles a step closer, hands grasping for me in what might look like a plea for help if his fiendish features didn't reveal his true intentions.

"Ge...t *out*."

I jolt free, wobbling unsteadily atop the air mattress in a sad attempt to regain control.

Just as I manage to lift myself up onto my elbows, I'm shoved back down. The silky sheets offer no traction whatsoever, rendering what little fight I have inside of me useless. I can't see him, but I feel his pressure on my chest and throat, pinning me tight. I try to scream, but his hold around my neck is too strong and my attempted call for help morphs into muffled weeping.

And then, just like that, just like always, the pressure releases.

ALLISON A

Before I have a chance to embrace relief, large hands clasp my shoulders and shake me violently.

Taking advantage of the freeness of my lower limbs, I push through the arthritis in my knees and kick as forcefully as I can at the air, at the mattress, at anything within range, hoping to strike one good blow.

My feet don't connect with anything solid, but the more I kick, the more the pressure releases, and I waste no time rushing to get up before just as swiftly falling to the hardwood floor. The stiffness in my bones after a night of rest is too great to be mobile right away. I should know this by now.

There's a hard thump on the floor beside me. I can feel the movements of whoever they are as they wrestle to get closer, but I can't see anything in the dark.

The hands return, grappling to catch hold of my arms as I thrash about, screaming for him to get off.

"It's me!"

Can they talk now?

"It's me. It's Jack. Stop it," he demands. "Calm down."

I stop fighting long enough to smell his sweet cologne—Endymion. It *is* him, I realize, huffing as I relax onto the cold floor.

Jack releases his grip long enough to turn on the lamp, illuminating the living room in a soft amber glow. I don't bother protesting as he lifts me back onto the mattress, half

THE NOISE

because I don't have the energy and half because my focus is fixed on the corner of the living room.

I don't see the man anywhere. The only other person here is Jack. Jack, with that heartbreakingly familiar look of worry on his face.

Before I can alert him to the intruder, he pulls me close and tugs the blanket up to my shoulders.

"It's okay," he hushes me as he brushes his fingers through my hair, something that has always helped me fall fast asleep. He knows the routine by now. "You're alright. You're safe."

It's only a matter of time before the man returns, and I want to stay alert, but I'm so tired. I'm so very tired. I can't remember the last time I slept through the night.

The seductive thought of sleep swarms my brain, rapidly infringing on my sensible instinct to stay alert. Jack is awake now, I tell myself, so maybe I can close my eyes for a minute. A minute would be enough.

No. Focus.

I know the man is still here, somewhere. They're all here somewhere. But as Jack's fingers gently massage my scalp, I give in to the appeal of rest. My eyelids flutter closed, then burst open before fluttering closed again.

I just want to sleep.

I jump awake. A bolt of adrenaline rips through my body, as if someone used a jumper cable on my chest. My eyes instantaneously bolt to the corner. It's still empty.

ALLISON A

I can't do this all night. I can't.

I burrow my face in the side of Jack's hard chest, and close my eyes. If I can't see it, it's not there.

TWO

The living room is freezing. It's been such a warm October that this sudden blast of chill is unexpected. My skin actually hurts from the sharp goose-pimples standing at attention, and I fear my teeth may break from their violent chattering.

I look to the corner. The man isn't there.

Of course he's not there. Get a grip, Angela.

To be certain, I carefully scan the room, searching for any sign of him and his sunken eyes. I inspect the gray armchair to my right, the kitchen to my left, and the enclosed porch ahead of me, searching every corner within view. I can't see the entire porch from here, but I can see enough to know it's empty. If someone was there, they'd have to be crouched down low enough to hide behind the four-foot-high half wall. The man I saw last night looked as though his back would snap in two if he bent that far.

ALLISON A

The house is empty. At least, from what I can see. But something still isn't right.

Wind billows through the curtains, sending them swirling like white tornados, but it isn't the air vent that's animating them this time. The windows are all open.

It's possible I dreamt this, but I could swear I saw the man's backside reflected in a *closed* window pane last night. I remember, because the back of his head displayed a vicious gash, one that dripped gooey blood and matted white hair to his sagging scalp. Like most dreams, though, it fades the more I try to hold on to it. In these early morning hours, it seems less tangible than it did last night.

I swallow past the soreness in my throat, and am reminded of the man's hands wrapped around it. *I couldn't have dreamt that.*

Or, I consider as I trace ethereal dust particles floating through the glow of the lamp Jack left on, I spent the night inhaling sawdust, leaving my throat raw and irritated.

As the rational part of my brain wakes up, I consider that the most reasonable explanation for the windows is that Jack opened them after I fell back asleep. The more I think about it, the more that makes sense. He loves sleeping in the cold, a mountain of blankets piled high on top of him.

I look at Jack, sleeping soundly beside me, breaths puffing from his lips like the intermittent chimney of a train. He looks so tired, even as he sleeps. He's been working on renovations

THE NOISE

non-stop these past few months, not to mention he's had to go into the shop from time to time, and then there's his volunteer work. No wonder he's exhausted. I'm sure being jolted awake nightly by his loving wife hasn't helped. The least I can do is leave the windows open and let him sleep comfortably for the rest of the morning.

Careful not to make too much noise, I crawl off of the air mattress and limp into the kitchen. The bones in the tops of my feet splinter with each step, like a cinder block was dropped on them. I know it'll ease up the more I walk around, so I circle the kitchen island a few times until the pain is bearable.

The coffee pot would be too loud, but I need something in these ungodly hours. There's coffee left over from yesterday, so I pour myself a cold mug full and head for the porch, collecting a red flannel blanket from the couch on my way and wrapping it around my shoulders.

As I cross the threshold, a blast of cold air encases me. I tug at the blanket while cursing myself for convincing Jack that we could wait to get a new front door, one that doesn't have an inch of empty space at the bottom. Worse than the cold, the porch is pitch black, making it impossible to see out of its eight windows.

My heartbeat quickens as I imagine potential intruders. The man from the living room corner coming back to finish his attack. Or that shady teenage kid from down the street who always rides his bike too slowly past our house. *Yeah, I see you*. Or an axe murderer wanting to squat in our dilapidated, and seemingly abandoned cape, only to discover his next victims.

Jesus Christ, Angela.

I flip the switch to the outside light. *Nothing. There's nothing.*

My fingertips linger over the switch as I try to decide whether I should leave it on, whether I *can* accept that there's nothing. Leaving the light on means giving in to my fears, but allowing the darkness, especially after what happened last night, might not be best for my mental health right now.

I decide to leave it, convincing myself it's because I never get the chance to admire our front yard this early in the morning. *Is it even morning?* More like really, really, really late night.

After tightening the blanket around my shoulders, I ease my stiff body into the wooden rocking chair and set my attention on the small scene of light just outside.

When we first toured this house, I imagined spending my mornings sipping warm coffee on our sunlit porch with a book in my hand, gazing now and then at our quaint street, and thanking my lucky stars for getting such a great deal on a house that would otherwise be unaffordable.

I struggle through the weakness in my hands to lift the cold mug to my mouth, teeth rattling against the ceramic as I take a sip, and I feel anything but lucky.

THE NOISE

I close my eyes and try to imagine the warmth of sunlight on my cheeks, try to picture the black asphalt sparking like onyx in the day, and taste the comfort of fresh coffee on my tongue. But I can't hold on to any of those images any more than I can stand this thick sludge. I thrust my mug aside in revulsion and push the liquid down my throat, wincing from the bitter aftertaste. I'll make a fresh pot once Jack wakes up.

Unsure what else to do with myself, I grab my journal from the table beside me. I need to record last night's event at some point, anyway.

I flip through hundreds of pages in search of a clean one. Past the clown, past the bloody teenage greaser, past the disembodied brown trousers, past countless accounts of shadow people—I learned that term from sleepparalysisnightly.com. I'm not sure how credible that site is, but it basically says the same thing as all the others. Really, there are no credible sites on the topic, because it isn't considered to be a credible topic. As a former librarian, I know where to look for reputable information, and I know that what I have been able to find is the best I'm going to get.

I touch my pen to a crisp page.

I still don't know what to call this one—old man? Old hag? Rabid old man? He was standing in the corner of the living room again, which is somehow more disturbing than the woman three nights ago who crawled onto the air mattress and got so close to my face that I nearly choked on her rancid breath. He's different. More unnerving. He's unnerving in the sense that

Unnerving in the sense that he seemed hesitant? That he didn't seem totally evil, but willing to do something evil? I drop my pen, unsure how to proceed.

My attention drifts to the windows in search of inspiration, landing on the yellow light of the lamppost in the center of the yard, encircled by a vignette of dusk. It casts a perfect autumn glow on the stone pathway leading to our front door, and my skin crawls. I've never noticed before, but it looks like the perfect opening scene of a horror movie. If someone was standing in the middle of the path holding a knife, it'd be nothing more than fitting.

Maybe I shouldn't do this right now. It'd be better, healthier, if I waited until daylight to finish the entry.

Good. Keep yourself in check.

Despite what I saw last night, or what I *thought* I saw, I feel proud of myself in this moment. This is more willpower than I've had in a while, and I'm sure it's because I'm reaching my limit of seeing that look of worry on Jack's face. I never want to see it again.

THE NOISE

Without coffee or my journal, I have no idea what to do for the next few hours. I'd rather not hobble back into the living room and risk waking Jack, and I certainly don't want to sit staring out of these windows.

I glance at the moving boxes piled high in the corner. I wrap my long red hair into a ponytail, roll up the sleeves of my gray knit sweater, and climb down from the rocking chair.

These boxes have been here since we moved in six months ago. With the state of the house, it's been impossible to unpack anything other than the living room and the kitchen, and even the kitchen was a mess until Jack finished it last week. Well, nearly finished it. It still needs backsplash and a sink disposal, but then we, *he*, can move on to the bathroom.

We knew this house needed work when we bought it—anyone would know that by looking at it—but we didn't know *how* much work. It's needed everything from wallpaper removal to a new roof. Thankfully, the living room wasn't too bad. After we slapped some wispy white on the walls, we set up our temporary bed in front of the fireplace, where it'll remain until we can refinish the bedroom upstairs.

Who knows when that'll be. We can't even use the stairs to the second floor because they're rotted. You couldn't tell by looking at them, but Jack is pretty handy, and he says we'd fall right through if we climbed even halfway up.

Despite the seemingly endless list of TLC, this house is stunning. Or, it will be, once Jack finishes with it. Either way,

ALLISON A

it's a big step up from our cramped apartment with loud neighbors who stole countless packages from our front door. I think it was just hard for other buyers to see this house's potential, like Jack could. Even when the Realtor told us other buyers dropped out when they discovered new information about the house, Jack was persistent in his ability to fix whatever came up. So far, he has. I just wish I could do more to help.

I quietly tug at the tape on the box marked "Bedroom."

I'm reassured to find my books are still here, packed away as neatly as they were that scorching April afternoon when we left our apartment. *The Woman in the Window* by A.J. Finn—the first book I ever read in a day flat. *Old Country* by Matt Query—that bear chase will haunt me forever. The list goes on: *Voices in the Snow*, *A Head Full of Ghosts*, *The Shimmering Ghost of Riversend*. I'm ashamed to say I stole that last one from my middle school library eighteen years ago, well before I knew I didn't just like books like these, but that I would end up needing them. In some way, they help me make sense of the things I see and experience.

The things I think *I see and experience.*

There was a time when I toiled with the idea of turning my journal entries into a book of my own. I imagined putting a desk under the window in the bedroom upstairs and spending my afternoons there, fingers dancing across the keyboard. But the room hasn't been touched, let alone the stairs to get to it.

Besides, I don't know how healthy it would be to indulge myself with a book of my own delusions.

The tape on the next box is much easier to open, as the adhesive is barely clinging to the cardboard. I must not have taped it correctly.

A few more books, though these are more necessities than treasures. *Beating Ankylosing Spondylitis Naturally* by Dr. Scott A. Johnson. *Kicking My AS* by Kip Jennings, and so on and so on. As helpful as these books are, they're *too* uplifting. Sure, I know I need to look on the bright side of things; I get it, but I can't do that all the time. No one can. Where's the chapter on no longer being able to drive, or only being able to have sex once in a while because it takes days for your body to recover? Where's the paragraph about how you can't carry shopping bags anymore, or help your tired husband with renovations you both probably never should have gotten yourselves into?

Casting the books aside with a bitter grimace, I uncover some picture frames I wrapped as poorly as the box itself. The weight of the books seems to have cracked a few of them.

After brushing bits of glass back into the box—I'll deal with that some other time—I stare down at the picture in my hands, the sight of which hurts more after sorting through those stupid AS books. It's a picture of Jack and I during our first vacation to Disney World, me sipping a Lapu Lapu from a pineapple and him smiling wide with his arm around me. We walked eleven miles that day. During dinner that evening, Jack

ALLISON A

confessed that was one of the reasons why he loves me—because I pushed through the blisters and threats of plantar fasciitis. If we ever go back, I'll need a scooter.

I place the picture back in the box, this time on top of the crushing books, and pick up another.

I hate that this has been in a box for months, but I'd hate even more for it to be covered in sawdust or paint. As soon as we're finished with the first floor, I'll display it front and center atop the fireplace mantel, beside his urn.

There's a sharp crack in my hip as I lift myself from the floor, accompanied by a searing pain that sweeps down to my feet and back up through my shoulder blades. I taste warm blood on my tongue as I bite through the pain and slither into the rocking chair, one hand gripping the handle, the other clutching the frame.

It's always worse in the morning, I tell myself. Remaining immobile for any period of time, especially overnight, is the worst thing for AS. It'll be better once Jack wakes up and I can move freely around the house.

I run my fingers over the scratched glass, half to reminisce and half to distract from the pain blooming in my spine.

I wonder if he even remembers this note. It must have been fourteen or fifteen years ago that we wrote it to each other. I know what I must look like, body contorted in a rocking chair, surrounded by darkness, laughing to myself, but I can't help it.

THE NOISE

Dad,

I went to Philly with my friends Chris, Ben, and Justin. I probably won't be back until late Sunday night. I haven't told mom, but I'm sure she'll be fine with it. I didn't do my homework. I'm bringing it with me, but with the party going on, I don't know how much I'll get done. I can always do it when I stay home from school on Monday. My phone is also dying, so I guess I'll talk to you Sunday night because I don't know the number to Chris' apartment. -Ang

P.S. I'm really at the movies with Alice. I won't be home late. I did my homework and cleaned up the kitchen. Love ya.

In the top right corner, he wrote back, "VERY FUNNY" with a circle around it. Then, "Love you too. -Dad."

I wish I knew what exactly it is that brings him here. If I did, I'd ask him to come right now.

THREE

Someone grips my shoulder.

I bolt up from the chair before just as soon melting back into it. It's Jack. He's practically glowing in the yellow sunlight.

I try to sit up again, but it seems the adrenaline is gone and pain and stiffness have taken its place. A wooden rocking chair isn't the best choice for someone with my condition, but it's not like there are many other options in this house at the moment.

Jack takes the framed note from my lazy hand, and I hear a gentle clink as he places it on the ledge separating the porch from the living room. He collects the blanket that slipped halfway onto the floor and wraps it back around my shoulders before helping me up, nice and easy, like the old woman I am.

"Have you been out here all night?"

A nod is all I can manage.

THE NOISE

"Why didn't you wake me?" He asks as he presses his lips to my forehead, bracing himself as my body lists into his. His sweatshirt somehow feels both rough and soft on my cheek.

As his lips tend to my head, it almost feels as if the pain has disappeared. Maybe it's the distracting warmth of his skin, or maybe I've convinced myself over the years that his kiss is actually capable of relief.

"Please wake me next time," he requests, pulling away. The pain immediately returns.

"I will," I lie.

After easing me onto a stool at the kitchen island, he swiftly turns and heads for the bathroom. It must be seven o'clock, I realize, as I hear him open the medicine cabinet.

He returns, pill bottles in hand, then goes for a banana and a glass of water. I'm far from hungry, but I peel the banana anyway, half out of habit and half because he's watching me. If he didn't always remember my medications, I don't think I'd *remember* them either.

After the last bit of banana slides down my throat, I reach for the handful of medication.

First, Sulfasalzine, for inflammation. It's a burnt umber horse pill, but its smooth texture allows it to slide down my throat without issue.

Next is Meloxicam, for pain. This one isn't as smooth. It has rough edges, kind of like Smarties candies, edges which have caused me to choke many times. I've since learned the right technique: place it at the back of my throat, gulp, let the water wash it halfway down, then swallow the rest of the way.

Third and fourth are Vitamin D and a multivitamin. Pretty boring, but nonetheless prescribed.

Last, and worst of all, is Flecainide. I've been taking this little black box pill for the past five months to rectify heart palpitations brought on by incessant inflammation. It's the smallest pill of the bunch, but it's packed with the most awful bitterness. Unless it goes right down, its rancid aftertaste gets stuck on my tongue for hours. I toss it back and take a swig of water, feeling grateful as it trickles into my stomach without a fight.

No matter how bloated it makes me, I have to finish all the water in one shot to help flush the medications through my system. My stomach balloons from the waterfall cascading down my esophagus, but I push through, then slam the glass down on the counter like I've just done a shot of whiskey.

It could be worse.

Last year, my rheumatologist put me on biologics. I couldn't bring myself to do the injection, so Jack did it. Every Sunday, I'd pull my pants down for him to clean the chosen area on my thigh, then I'd nearly bite through my tongue from the anticipated sting of the needle. He would smile at me, tell me he loves me, and press the button. The injections were incredibly painful, but they relieved almost all of my symptoms, leaving me feeling somewhat normal.

THE NOISE

AS already compromises your immune system, though, and the biologics further destroyed it. After my third overnight stay in the hospital for pneumonia, my rheumatologist took me off the injections.

Now I'm left with these tablets, which barely touch the pain.

The coffee pot revs as Jack starts it up. At last, something to cleanse my palette of pills and the mud I drank hours ago.

He spins around to collect my glass, almost knocking over the crystal vase of white roses he picked from the garden yesterday. He catches it just before it falls, a wave of panic rushing red over his face.

"Those look beautiful. Good enough to last a few days," I comment as he awkwardly balances the vase against his forearm before propping it upright.

"You did the hard work by growing them. I just pick them," he says, flashing that crooked smile I fell in love with thirteen years ago.

"Maybe we could give the bushes a break today?" I suggest to his back as he leans over the coffeepot, fiddling with something out of my view. "And let these sit here for a while," I add.

He turns to reveal my favorite mug, steaming with coffee.

I used this mug for everything from hot cocoa to water back when I lived with my mother, and it has stayed with me ever since. It's large enough to fit two cups of coffee, maybe even a little more, but the days when I wanted more coffee are far behind me. I'm allowed one cup of regular in the morning, but then it's decaf for the rest of the day, and coffee just doesn't have the same appeal without all the caffeine.

The mug is white with a red banner and yellow polka dots encasing a quote by Lily Tomlin: "The road to success is always under construction." That used to mean something to me. Now, it sounds so hopeless, as if I'll never get to where I want to be because life is forever filled with barriers. It's the memory surrounding it, the memory of a simpler time when I started a much more productive day with this very mug, that maintains my affection for it.

"Do you want to talk about last night?" Jack bravely asks.

I swallow a hard lump in my throat. "It was nothing. It was just like all the other times."

His eyes narrow in on me, and I can't tell if he's waiting for me to continue or hoping I won't. Jack has never believed in the supernatural. He and I have always joked that his name should have been Doubting Thomas, because he needs hard proof in order to believe in anything. Even then, he still doubts it. He always says the one thing he's never doubted is his love for me. After nights like last night, I worry I'm chipping away at his faith.

Even though I know I shouldn't indulge myself, and even though I know he won't believe me anyway, I concede to yet another chip. "It felt real," I say. "Everything I've read says it's only in a person's head, brought on by stress, or sleeping in a supine position…" I trail off, rolling my eyes. "I fell asleep on my side last night."

"You could have shifted in your sleep."

"I know."

"And, I mean," he hesitates, "you *have* been under a lot of stress."

"I'm not talking about that," I snap, irritated that he's even trying to bring it up.

"I didn't mean *that*," he backs off.

I slouch back on the stool and add an edge of softness to my voice. "I thought you were trying to talk about what happened."

"I wouldn't do that. I know you're not ready to talk about it."

"No," I say, my voice firm. "But I know everything has been worse since then, and I'm sorry you've had to deal with it. I don't mean to put you through this."

He holds my face in his palm, his thumb brushing over my cheek. "You don't have to apologize. A lot has happened. Your diagnosis, leaving your job, all the renovations, and there's that," he nods to the red blinking light on the answering machine. "I understand."

A few months after we moved in, Jack suggested we give up unnecessary electronics. If we are committed to rebuilding this house and being self-sufficient, then we shouldn't rely on meaningless distractions, is what he said. I never used my phone much anyway, but at least a cell phone hides a tiny voicemail icon in the upper left corner, only visible if you're looking for it.

Each time the red light blinks, I can practically smell the cigarette smoke. I feel the moist couch cushions sticking to my thighs, and I hear that cruel tone in her voice, the one that haunts me.

"Why don't we put off working on the house today?" Jack suggests. "We could make a big dinner, like we used to. Maybe roast a chicken?"

A faint smile curls the edges of my lips. I know what he's doing, and it's working. The thought of filling the house with scents that used to comfort us in our old apartment, back when I didn't yet know I was sick, back before the red blinking lights, back when nothing was covered in sawdust, makes me yearn for it now.

"We could build a fire," he goes on excitedly, nurturing my changed mood. "Maybe make peach cobbler for dessert?"

"Okay, yeah, let's do that," I agree, latching onto his optimism.

"It's settled then," he says, relief lighting up his eyes. "I'll have to pick up a few things." He gives a playful double squeeze of my hand, then kisses my forehead as he grabs his keys from the wall hook. "I'll be fifteen minutes."

"See you later," I call to him, engaging in our usual ritual. A goodbye is too final, a sentiment I adopted when my dad passed.

THE NOISE

"See you later."

***

This is what I imagined when we first toured our house—sipping warm coffee on our sunlit porch while gazing at our quaint street. There's no book in my hand, but the flowering crabapple tree sifting leaves and berries throughout the grass is a suitable substitution. I admire a few lingering petals as they swirl through the air in blurs of dusty rose and recall when they were once bright fuchsia, months ago in the spring, for only two weeks.

I needed this. I needed something beautiful to make the horrifying memory of last night feel far away, as forgotten as a bad dream. I don't want to lose this grasp on reality. I want to keep it going, soak it all up, stock up for tonight. Maybe, if I can hold on to this feeling, nothing will even happen tonight. Maybe Jack and I will go for a walk around the river after we eat. Maybe we'll have a nice time. Maybe that will be all that happens.

Content with my plans for the day, I down the last of my coffee and head into the kitchen to rinse my mug, averting my gaze from the answering machine.

Over the gentle stream of our new stainless-steel faucet, I hear the noise.

It's quieter than usual today, but I consider that's because the sound of flowing water is competing for my attention.

ALLISON A

Wondering whether I'm hearing the noise at all, I reach to turn the faucet off.

Don't give in.

I breathe in, pulling from the good feelings I gathered back on the porch, and find the strength to leave it on, instead turning my attention to scrubbing at the polka dots.

The noise grows louder, as if it's angry with me for ignoring it.

It's not real.

I turn the faucet up to drown it out. The force from the nozzle sprays my sweater with cold water, drenching me through to the skin.

Stomping now.

Warm coffee. Sunlit porch. Leaves and berries.

The noise stops.

To be certain, I turn the faucet down and listen.

Silence.

I dry my mug and place it on the dish rack, balancing it between a small white plate and a spatula.

You should be proud of yourself.

A crash from upstairs sends my hand jolting and the plate shattering against the floor. A stray shard strikes the ball of my ankle, instigating a fierce sting that flourishes over the area. I dare to look, fully expecting to see blood pouring from a gaping wound, and am relieved to find only a scrape. Shock made the pain seem worse, I'm sure. Yet another example of how my mind can betray me.

While patting the scrape with a damp cloth, I listen for the noise, wondering if the crash was even real or if my mind has found new ways to torment me.

As I feared, the noise resumes, steady and structured, back and forth, back and forth.

I follow the noise from one end of the house to the other and back again, all while telling myself I'm not giving in to my delusions. I'm searching for a plausible explanation, that's all. *Right. Exactly.* By the time I'm back where I started in the kitchen, I have nothing to show for this field trip around the first floor. Wondering whether I missed something, I step back into the hallway, preparing to follow it a second time, and I'm echoed by two steps from above. Three more steps from me, followed by three more steps from them, and I realize I'm not the one doing the following.

Curious, I step back a few feet into the kitchen. The noise does too.

I know what Jack would say, but Jack isn't here. I could test the stairs, assess how far I can get, and what I might see. After all, I don't weigh that much.

I tread gingerly. The first step seems sturdy enough. I test the second, then the third, my heart pounding from this breach of his trust, yet I can't stop. Not until a loud creak springs from the fourth step. *This is what you get. The only way down from here is by crashing through the basement ceiling.*

The noise carries on, pacing anxiously now, and I can't tell whether it wants me to proceed or if I'm frightening it by getting this close.

I fell in love with the second floor when I first saw it. It had this soft yellow wallpaper that seemed to glitter as sun swept through the oversized windows. I don't know the state of the wallpaper now, but I like to imagine it's still holding on for dear life. The walnut paneling was just as stunning, even though it was loose almost everywhere. It's original to the house, and much of its beauty came from the fact that it has stood its ground for all these years. Jack promised we'd keep it, either by repairs or by using the wood in other ways, like perhaps picture frames or a bookcase we, *he*, intends to build. I hope it hasn't rotted by now.

My affection for the second floor draws me up one more step, then another, and then the front door creaks open.

I turn in time to see the blurred image of Jack dropping shopping bags and rushing toward me.

"What are you doing? Get down!"

"I'm sorry," I apologize, barely easing myself down two steps before he whips me up in his arms and lifts me the rest of the way.

"You could have been hurt," he warns, placing my feet down firmly on the floor. I have no time to speak as his hands roam over my face, my hair, my arms, looking for any sign of injury and finding none. His fingers are featherlight, yet vicious in their search, and his eyes are so wild with fear that remorse quickly seeps into every crevice of my being.

He pulls me in close, his hand cradling my head against his chest. "Why would you do that?"

I can't think of a good reason, because there is no good reason, so I tell him the truth. "I heard it again," I admit, and I brace for his reaction.

The noise has been near constant since we moved in. It happens day and night, for minutes to hours at a time. Jack has never heard it, not even when we're in the same room together. Whenever I'd press him about it, he'd say it was probably an animal, or an old house settling, but he was never concerned enough to check.

I thought the house was haunted. That was the only explanation. After all, what kind of animal mimics the sound of heavy leather boots? I even experimented with recording devices at one point, but I caught nothing. Over time, I started believing I was imagining it, like everything else, and I stopped telling Jack I was hearing the noise. I'm embarrassed that I gave in this morning, even more so because the look of worry on his face feels like someone punched my own.

He sighs heavily and brushes his fingers through my hair. "If it makes you feel better, I'll borrow a ladder from a neighbor tomorrow." He's working hard to keep his voice gentle and steady, each word measured as if I'm a child afraid to go to sleep without a night light. "Can you wait until tomorrow? Or, I can try to borrow one now?"

Borrow a ladder from who? We haven't met any of our neighbors. Am I really going to make him knock on every door, introduce himself for the first time, and then ask to borrow something?

"No, don't do that. I'm sorry, Jack. It was nothing."

He looks to the stairs he just pulled me off of, then back at me.

"It was nothing," I say again. "I'm really sorry."

"You don't have to apologize."

"I shouldn't have gone up there."

He looks seriously at me, like I'm a puzzle he can't solve. "I'll borrow a ladder tomorrow. Can you promise you'll stay off of the stairs until then?"

"You don't have—"

"*Promise* me."

I concede. "I promise."

I can tell he doesn't believe me. Not only am I a child who can't sleep in the dark, but I'm not even trusted to be in a room by myself.

"The stairs aren't safe. You know that, right?"

"Of course I do."

"I don't want anything to happen to you."

"Nothing will happen to me."

THE NOISE

He pulls me back into his chest. "Please stay off the stairs."

FOUR

Jack returns from the bathroom as I clean the last bit of roasted chicken and mashed potatoes from my plate, palm outstretched to display an array of medication. On a full stomach, I down my evening dose.

He sets my empty glass on the fireplace hearth, then leans back in the armchair we found at an estate sale when we first moved in. He reaches an arm out, inviting me to curl up into him.

"I'm glad we decided against a TV," I say, in awe of the dying embers of the fire Jack built before dinner.

"I am too. Everything seems slower without the burden of modern technology."

"Do you ever miss it?"

"Here and there," he admits, "but not enough to go back." He looks down at me. "Do you?"

"Right now, no. But, sometimes. Sometimes it feels like the world is moving on without us."

"I kind of enjoy that. It's like being awake at dawn while everyone else sleeps in. We get to be a part of things we didn't care to, or didn't have the time for, before, you know?"

I nod, though I'm not so sure I enjoy being left behind as much as he seems to.

"That reminds me," he says, brushing the hair away from my face as I tilt my chin up to look at him. "There's a meteor shower tonight. I heard about it on the radio on my way home from the shop yesterday."

"Oh," is all I can manage as I struggle to remember the last time *I* listened to the radio. If we could have kept just one thing besides a landline, one thing I could use to hear the outside world, or play the music I used to love, then maybe I wouldn't be so lonely all day. Maybe my mind wouldn't wander if I wasn't so lonely all day.

"It's late. I bet everyone else is asleep. What do you think? Do you want to see what no one else is seeing?" His gray eyes sparkle.

"Sure," I agree, pushing my bitterness aside.

Standing from a sitting position, especially when I've been sitting for longer than thirty minutes, has always been the most embarrassing part of having AS. It's almost impossible for me to sit straight up, so I usually hunch, because hunching eases the pain. The more time I spend sitting and hunching, though, the more my spine fixes itself in that position. When I finally try to move, my back refuses to move with me, forcing me to walk at a 90-degree angle until it eventually straightens itself. As straight as it can get, anyway.

Jack places a hand on my lower back for support, gently rubbing at my lumbar spine. Inch by inch, we make our way to the front porch.

After helping me into the rocking chair, Jack gets to work setting up layers of blankets on the hardwood floor, to make it more comfortable. When the time comes for me to move onto the mountain of comforters and throws, I do so slowly, his hands guiding me the whole way.

"Is the floor too hard?" He asks, worry thick around his eyes.

"It's fine."

"Are you sure? I can add more blankets."

"Come join me, will you?" I smile up at him.

He covers me with our favorite gray, black, and white plaid comforter, then moves in close, my shoulder overlapping his. He positions his pillow at an angle from which he can see the night sky through the windows. My pillow is his chest.

We would have had a better view from the front lawn, but this evening has become unusually warm, and the thought of sticky blankets and bugs crawling throughout our hair wasn't as appealing as the closed-in porch, however frigid it is. Jack turned the thermostat up to 72, but it feels more like 60. The cooling system has been acting funny since we moved in, and I know it likely needs to be replaced, which we can't afford right now, so I keep quiet about it. The blankets are helping somewhat, at least.

"I think that's the little dipper," Jack points out, but I see nothing. "That's definitely the little dipper."

"Just like you saw it during our first date?" I laugh, rolling my eyes.

"Oh, I saw it," he says, flashing an impish grin. "You must not have known what the little dipper looked like is all."

"Right. It wasn't a ruse for you to pull me in closer so I could *share in your viewpoint*."

"Well, now the magic of our first date is gone forever. I hope you're happy." He tries to remain serious despite the upward twitching at the corner of his lips.

I pull my body in closer to his, just like I did thirteen years ago. "Where is it?" I amuse him, looking up through the windows. "I don't see anything."

His grin widens, followed by a shrug. "The clouds must have covered it."

"Mhm."

"Did you see that?" He jolts up with excitement and I wince from the pain caused by the unexpected movement. "I'm so sorry," he says, easing back down. "Are you okay?"

"I'm fine," I tell him, forcing a neutral expression to hide the agony. It was an accident. No need to punish him by letting him know how bad my spine hurts.

"Are you sure?"

"Of course."

"There was a shooting star. I didn't want you to miss it. I wasn't thinking."

"I didn't see anything," I say, working through the pain.

"I really did see something that time."

"So you admit you didn't actually see something on our first date?" I smirk at him.

"I said no such thing." He says, his former grim returning. "There!" His finger gently points toward the sky this time.

I see it now, a faint light stretching across a black ocean with only a vanishing trail of glitter to prove its momentary existence.

"I heard once that seeing a shooting star means someone's dying."

"Where did you hear that?"

"In a documentary about the Titanic."

"Hm. Do you think that's true?"

"Probably by coincidence. Lots of things die every day. Joy. Passion. Somewhere out there, someone's love is dying. Just one bright burst of light that fades before anyone can remember it was there at all."

He shifts so that the tip of his nose nearly touches mine, his deep eyes boring into me.

"I love you. You know that, don't you?"

THE NOISE

"I've seen it happen before. People swear they're in love. Then they forget. They move on."

"Mm," he utters as he closes his eyes. "Do you remember how we met?"

It was the first day of the spring semester at county college. It was raining outside, and I had to run from the parking lot all the way across campus to reach my class. I had my hood pulled down so far over my face that I could hardly see where I was going, but I eventually found the building and went inside. I paused in the classroom doorway to collect myself before entering, but as I lifted my hood, I saw something that robbed me of every other thought. I saw him.

He was sitting by the window, looking out at the storm. I could only see a sliver of his profile, but it was more than enough. I still can't explain it, but I was drawn to him, as if I knew him, somehow. They say love can sometimes feel like a lightning bolt striking you in the chest, and that's pretty close to what I experienced that day. It was as if everything that had happened in my life was meant to lead me to that very spot, to him.

I sat down in front of him, in the only seat in his vicinity that hadn't been claimed. It wasn't until the instructor took attendance that I realized I was in the wrong classroom, but I decided it didn't matter, because I was exactly where I needed to be.

ALLISON A

I was so desperate to see his face. I thought that if I could just see him, then it would somehow prove this strange familiar feeling I had. Eventually, I worked up the courage to turn halfway in my chair, pretending to stretch, and we locked eyes. I'll never forget seeing his face for the first time, and how striking his stormy blue-gray eyes were against his dark hair. I could only look away from them long enough to bask in the beauty of his plum-colored lips set above a strong jaw, and the small amount of stubble that highlighted his perfectly sculpted bone structure. I adored his tall forehead, which led to dark brown tussles in a messy crew cut with a curl at the front that I was sure was natural. He was beautiful.

He seemed startled at the sight of me, and a bit afraid. I was afraid too, and I turned right back around in my chair. I was afraid because my feelings were confirmed. I didn't know how, but I knew him. It was more than just a feeling that we'd met before at some point during our lives. It was a much deeper, intimate familiarity. That was the first time in my life I ever considered soulmates to be a real thing.

Weeks went by, and I was too shy to talk to him, but I could hardly think about anything else during that time. I went home and cried some days because I felt that I knew him, and yet I couldn't even say hi. It was like we'd known each other for a lifetime, only now he didn't remember me. As crazy as it sounds, I felt homesick.

THE NOISE

I eventually built up the courage to pass him a note. It was like the emotional version of restless leg syndrome—something had to give. I was so relieved when he promptly slid the note back over to me with a "hi" and a smiley face. Before I knew it, we were walking to our cars together.

As we made our way across the parking lot, we talked, and that sense of familiarity only grew. Before we parted ways, he said something I've never forgotten, something that proved to me that everything I'd been feeling was in fact very real. He said, "I hope this isn't weird, but I feel like we've met before." It was then I knew soulmates are real, and that he is mine.

"What happened to your parents…it won't ever happen to us. You know that, right?" He tells me now.

I glance up in time for another meteor to blast into orbit before just as quickly disappearing.

"Are you sure?" I ask, my eyes resting on his, shimmering like blue topaz under the moonlight.

It's what I asked when he first told me he loved me, and again when he proposed. I never meant for that to be my response, but it seemed to be a natural reflex, like my subconscious doubted whether he really meant it, or whether anyone could really mean it. After all, my dad believed in soulmates, and now my mother doesn't remember his birthday, let alone the anniversary of his passing.

I have prepared for the possibility that I've been wrong all along about the existence of soulmates. I've prepared for Jack and me to drift apart, like my parents did. I've prepared for death to leave me as nothing more than the dust of who I once was as I disappear into the night in time for a sparkling replacement. He's never given me any reason to think that would happen, but does anyone?

He tugs at the side of my sweater, pulling me closer, like he did on our first date.

"You're the one thing I don't doubt. I'm sure."

FIVE

It feels like my torso is connected to my lower half by nothing more than a resilient tendon, a tendon that might finally snap if I move another inch. In my sleep-deprived state, I test these limits, sending a pulsating warning throughout every nerve ending in my body.

I remember lying on Jack's chest, his fingers brushing through my hair as shooting stars took off overhead. I told myself we should move back to the air mattress once the spectacle ended, to save my bones from the hard floor, but sleep must have taken us without warning.

I know how this works by now—no matter how much pain I'm in, I need to move. If I don't, then I'll be crippled for the entire day.

In one swift action, I grit my teeth and flip onto my stomach.

ALLISON A

With my lower back raised like a tent, I drag my legs underneath my belly, forming a sort of vertical fetal position. The full weight of my upper body rests on my brittle wrists while I take a moment to huff through the pain. My back hurts so bad I might vomit.

Over the blaring alarm of agony, I'm able to make out a steady battering against the windows. It's storming outside.

A flash of lightning illuminates the room, revealing my reflection in the glass door before me.

I can't stand to look at myself, twisted and hunched like an old hag. Using my own revulsion as inspiration, I force my spine upright with as much strength as one would need to unbend a metal bar. I can't help but release a vicious wail, then draw on every bit of willpower I have to silence myself. Jack is somehow sleeping through everything, even the storm. He must be exhausted.

I slide my left knee out to stretch the joints. That was somewhat bearable.

I pull my left leg back in toward me, then go through the same motions with my right leg. I ease to a standing position while focusing on the storm outside for a distraction.

Something is moving across the street.

All I can manage are excruciating baby steps toward the window, my knees buckling underneath me like a fawn learning to walk. It gives me enough time to consider that it's an illusion cast by the winds and rain, or that my imagination is

THE NOISE

starving in the dark. The more I look, though, the more consistent the shape appears, and the more I believe it to be the shadow of an actual living thing. Whatever it is, it's walking in precise circles, around and around and around.

As my eyes work to adjust in the night, I'm able to make out a female shape—distinct hips paired with straggly hair blowing wildly.

A flash of lightning.

It *is* a woman.

A rumble of thunder vibrates through the floorboards, followed by another flash of light.

She's frail, but she has large hands that hang from her arms like broken tree limbs. She's looking down at something, pacing around it.

Lightning.

A rosebush.

I rest my left hand on the windowsill, my right cradling the burning pain in my spine, and lean in to get a better look, hearing the sill creak with the kind of strain I myself can understand.

It doesn't take long before my tired wrist burns with agony, so I shift my body weight from one side to the other, leaning into my right hand now for support, but support comes with the price of a screaming sill and splitting wood.

ALLISON A

I'm able to catch myself as half of the sill collides with the porch floor, both waking Jack and drawing the woman's attention straight toward me.

I turn away on instinct, but I can see her shadow through the reflection of a side window. She's bending at the waist, trying to get a closer look at our house, at me.

A boom of thunder echoes my racing heart as she steps closer, followed by a powerful flash that momentarily transforms the dark scene into day.

Though her face is back in shadow now, her skeletal features linger vividly in my memory. She looked malnourished to the point that I'm not sure how she could even be alive. Her cheeks were black and sunken in, like cavernous peat moss, and seemed connected to her dark purple lips by only a drooping bit of skin.

"Angela?"

I imagine Jack is sitting up on his elbows while rubbing his eyes, but I won't look away from her long enough to see if I'm right.

You're dreaming. You're imagining this. This isn't real.

I haven't been sleeping, and sleep deprivation can cause hallucinations. I know this.

If I know this, then why can I still see her?

She takes another step forward as her head tilts to one side, as if she's trying to figure out my motives for watching her.

"What's going on?"

THE NOISE

Her eyes never leave mine as she raises a bony leg and stomps it down on the roses. Her foot rises and falls four more times before she evaporates into the darkness, as if she never existed at all.

There's wheezing coming from somewhere in the room.

"What's wrong?" Jack's arm is around me, cradling me. "What's wrong?" He asks again, and I realize I'm struggling to breathe.

I can't stand seeing that look on his face. I don't know whether he's more worried about my health or my mind. I don't know which one worries me more either.

"Angela?"

"I'm fine," I manage.

"You're *fine*?"

"Couldn't sleep. My back." I tell him through gasping breaths. "I got up, and, I don't know—"

Before I can finish my lie, he lifts me from the floor and carries me to the air mattress. He fusses over me, propping my head up with pillows and wrapping a blanket around my shivering body. Then he climbs into bed and pulls me close.

"It's okay," he tells me. "Whatever happened, you're okay."

Endymion wafts from the fabric of his flannel shirt, putting me at ease within seconds. As his fingers labor through my hair, my breathing returns to normal, my eyelids feel dense, and I yearn for sleep. Fatigue grows, and the pacing of Jack's fingers slows, slows, and then his hand thumps to my shoulder, and suddenly I'm wide awake again.

I close my eyes and try to join him. As tired as I am, my mind won't stop racing between the fear that I imagined what I'd seen, and the fear that I didn't.

If she wasn't real, then was I dreaming? If I wasn't dreaming, then did stress cause some kind of hallucination? It certainly wouldn't be the first time for either. If she was real, then what kind of town have we moved to? What kind of people stand outside in the middle of the night, in the middle of a storm, just to kill flowers? What kind of people look like that?

I think back to the first time we learned a town called Hidden Heights exists. We were enjoying breakfast at a local diner when we overheard a couple beside us discussing the next house they would flip.

"There's a fixer-upper, dirt-cheap, in Hidden Heights," the man declared, rather uninterestedly, as he shoveled eggs through his brown mustache.

The woman rolled her eyes and her voice took on a mocking tone. "The *pearl* of the river? It's a useless town well past its potential."

Jack and I grew curious, so we looked into it. By the way the couple spoke about Hidden Heights, we half expected it to be one of those living history places, a town forever stuck in one moment in time, but it was nothing like that. It was beautiful, and it was only an hour's drive from our apartment.

THE NOISE

Through our research, we learned that people in Hidden Heights often refer to it as the pearl of the river it borders because of its picturesque riverside homes and quiet atmosphere. Spanning just eight streets wide, and containing century-old homes with vintage charm, it was a waste of time for this woman and her extravagant leopard get-up and solid gold jewelry. For us, it had the enchantment we'd been looking for, at a price we could afford.

Jack grew excited at the responsibility of restoring an old craftsman, and I admired the idea of breathing life back into something old and forgotten. Now I wonder if there's another reason that couple overlooked this town.

***

My eyes shoot open faster than the time it takes for me to realize I'd been sleeping.

It sounds like the noise.

I wait and listen, refraining from moving, or even blinking, for fear I'll somehow encourage it.

There it is once more. It's in the back den.

I've only ever heard the noise coming from the second floor, which leads me to wonder if there's an intruder.

I consider altering Jack, but I've already woken him two nights in a row. Each time, it turned out to be nothing, or my imagination. I know there's only a slight chance that this is any different.

It's nothing.

ALLISON A

I pull my eyes closed.

It's nothing. It's always nothing.

Louder now.

Jack hasn't moved. He hasn't even stirred. *He's a light sleeper. If someone was in our house and making this much noise, then he would definitely hear it too.*

It *has* to be my imagination, and I conclude that it will only stop once I look and realize there's nothing.

After crawling from the air mattress like an ailing lobster, I limp sluggishly down the dark hallway toward the den, drawn closer and closer by the noise.

I come to a stop in the doorway, and the noise stops too.

A shaking hand reaches into the darkness to turn on the lamp by the door, but there's no power. I glance to the window, past the elusive outline of a workbench and some sheetrock. The storm has subsided, but perhaps a pole is down somewhere nearby.

"Hello?" I whisper.

A shadow shifts.

SIX

"You scared me," I scold him.

He giggles as he takes a seat at a stool under the window, patting the one opposite for me to join him. I stay put, arms folded defiantly across my chest.

"Okay," his face grows more serious. "I'm sorry. I didn't know how else to get your attention."

"Maybe don't choose the middle of the night?"

"It seemed like you needed me."

I yield, appreciation converging over the annoyance I felt mere moments ago. Of course I need him. I always need him.

I surrender my tired body to the relief of the stool. "Am I crazy?"

"Why do you think you're crazy?" He asks, but I can't bring myself to utter the specifics of what happened tonight.

"Just, am I?"

ALLISON A

"How would I know that?"

"I don't know. Don't you, like, know everything?"

He laughs, and I slump back with embarrassment.

"I don't know everything," he says. "But I know you're not crazy."

"How can you say that when I'm—"

"Sitting here talking to me?" He releases a heavy sigh. "Remembering me doesn't make you crazy."

"Remembering isn't seeing."

"Isn't it?"

I release a sigh of my own. "How are you?"

"I'm doing alright."

"That's all you ever say."

"What do you want me to say?"

"I don't know. Are you still gardening? Is there a place where you go fishing? Where do you live?"

He cracks a smile, but gives nothing else away.

"How's Jack?"

"He's doing *alright*."

He ignores my retaliation and moves on. "And the shop?"

"It's going alright," I answer, still being childish as I refuse to give him the same kind of detail he won't give me.

"Did he sell that table yet?"

"Which one?"

"The one he made from salvaged wood."

"Oh. Yeah. A while ago, actually."

"He's always been very creative," he acknowledges. "What about the animal shelter?"

"He's still there. He's volunteering tomorrow."

"And—"

"It's well past my turn to ask a question," I interrupt him, grinning as I warm up to his midnight visit. But my smile is soon overshadowed by the question forging its way to my lips. "Is it all real?"

"My answer depends on yours."

"What does that mean?"

His hazel eyes pierce the darkness, settling determinedly on my own, and I brace myself. "Are you ready to talk about it yet?" When I say nothing, he prods further. "We need to talk about the incident, Angela."

My posture dips, my shoulders drawing in so close they almost touch. "It's not the right time."

"This is important."

I force a smile, pretending this part of the conversation never happened. "Hey, do you remember that note? The one I wrote to you a few years before you passed?"

I can see his energy is wilting as he struggles to consent to this detour. But he does, for me. "What note?"

"The one I wrote you about going into Philly, the night I really went to the movies with Cat?"

His face lights up. "I remember."

ALLISON A

"I found it in one of the moving boxes today," I tell him. "I used to have it on display in mine and Jack's old apartment, remember?"

"In the wooden frame?"

"That's the one."

"Well, let's see it."

After easing my stiff body up from the stool, I creep down the hallway, through the living room, and to the porch where I left the framed note. Cupping it in my hands, I begin my journey back, warily treading on the creaky hardwood floor beside the air mattress where Jack is sleeping.

There's a loud click as I pass by the bathroom door, followed by the rumble of an air vent. Light explodes from the den, and I know the power is back. I realize I must have left the light switch in the on position when I tested the lamp earlier.

"Angela?" Jack's groggy voice calls from the living room. The sounds of the house reawakening must have stirred him.

Hiding the picture frame behind my back, I tip-toe back into the living room.

"Everything's fine," I tell him. "I just got up to use the bathroom."

"Where's that light coming from?" He asks, noticing the dim glow from down the hall.

"The bathroom."

"You're okay?"

I nod.

THE NOISE

He drops back into the mattress and falls asleep within moments.

The revived vents puff warm air over the top of my head as I skulk back to the den, excited to reminisce with my dad.

As soon as I reach the doorway, I make sure to turn off the lamp so as not to disturb Jack again, but now the room is so dark that I can't see anything at all.

"Dad?" I whisper. "Dad?"

I accept the risk and flick the lamp on one more time.

He's gone.

SEVEN

"I'll need to stop by the shop on my way home from the shelter," Jack says. "I should only be gone a few hours."

"Is there anything I can do while you're away?"

"Just rest."

"I'm capable of doing at least *some* things, Jack," I tell him, immediately regretting the edge in my voice, likely due to yet another night of barely any sleep.

"I know," he says, treading carefully. "I just worry when I'm not here."

"You don't have to worry. I'm fine."

He's cautious to say anything further, and I understand why. He doesn't believe I'll be fine, but he's hoping that, as long as he doesn't acknowledge his doubts out loud, he'll be wrong.

He kisses my forehead. "I'll be back by twelve."

"See you later," I call to him as he heads to his truck.

THE NOISE

"See you later," he calls back, his hand wavering over the door handle.

***

I drop my journal to the table with a thud and take a timid sip of coffee. It was scalding when I poured it a few minutes ago, but it's cooled down just enough now for me to wash away the horrid aftertaste of my medications.

I open to where I left off writing about the old man with the intention of finishing the entry, but that's starting to seem easier said than done. The light of day and the early morning breeze wipe away the details of what I experienced, and I struggle to connect with my own words. Like rediscovering a diary entry from long ago, I can understand and sympathize with the intent, but the emotional impact has since vanished.

I suppose this is normal, though. Things always seem clear in the moment, but that clarity never lasts. I wish I could go back in time to when this episode occurred and remind myself that I will feel this way come daytime. That it's not as real as it seems. That it won't last.

When the episodes first began, I was certain they were real. I thought journaling them would help me put the pieces together and finally understand why this was happening to me. The pieces never came together, though, and my original intent is now yet another thing that has faded. Journaling is more of a coping mechanism now, one that serves to remind me the next day, or days later, or whenever the fear has faded, that it probably wasn't real to begin with.

I scribble a few halfhearted words before slamming the journal closed and tossing it to the floor, scooting it aside with my foot.

I raise the mug back to my lips and invite a larger gulp than I intended, burning the roof of my mouth. The coffee has cooled, but not nearly enough to swig it like I did. It stings my throat as I push it down, suffering helplessly as I endure the fiery pit in my stomach.

I exhale heat and breathe in the cold air until the pain resolves, then raise the mug back to my lips as if I've learned nothing. The hot ceramic rim reawakens my awareness enough that I alternate from gulping to sipping before any further damage is done. *I need to get with it this morning.*

I furiously rub at my eyes, trying to wake myself up, as not even the scolding coffee could do. Sleep refuses to leave me, so I rub harder, harder, so hard that I've blurred my vision and all I see are floaters drifting over hazy shapes. I can sort of make out the panes of the French-style front door, and I set out to count each little window one by one until I arrive at twelve, hoping my vision will return in the process.

Gazing through a fog of silhouettes, I try to make out the lettering on some of the moving boxes, and I feel grateful when the words begin to materialize. I can almost see the switch for the outside light, too. I focus more, and I recognize the roses

THE NOISE

poking up below the porch windows, the delicate spectacle becoming clearer with every breeze.

I look beyond the porch, testing my sight on the outside world.

Mom?

There's a woman at the top of the street with eerily similar dirty-blonde hair cut just below her ears. As she strolls closer, I see the same chopped bangs, and my suspicion grows.

She's gripping something, like a handle, pushing something, but I can't make out what it is.

A baby stroller.

As I fixate on this impostor, I realize I can see everything. I can see the baby inside the stroller, dressed in a onesie and wrapped in a blanket. I can see the woman's tidy sweater and jogging pants with bright white sneakers poking out of the bottoms. I wonder if my mother ever looked this put-together, or this happy, when she was younger.

The woman stops in front of our house to tend to her pride and joy, tucking the baby in tighter and giving them a playful bop on the nose. The baby's face lights up with a smile, encouraging the woman to give her another little bop. I can hear their giggles from inside the porch. I can hear the woman saying how much she loves the sound of it.

The woman straightens and resumes her place behind the stroller. She takes a moment to gaze upon her neighborhood, a smile revealing her appreciation for the beautiful town and crisp weather. Then her gaze falls on our house, and all of her happiness disappears. Her eyes harden and her lips form a tight line, her expression so grim she almost looks like a different person. I offer an uncertain wave, hoping she won't think I'm some kind of voyeur, but she doesn't return the gesture.

She doesn't do anything, really. She looks frozen, and disturbed, and I might wonder whether she's disturbed by *me* if I hadn't seen this same look on so many others' faces.

I was embarrassed by the gawking townspeople when we first moved in. It felt as if Jack and I had somehow offended them by buying this run-down house, this sore sight in their perfect suburb. But then shame turned to anger. We worked hard for this, and no one has a right to stare just because it's not pretty at the moment, just because it isn't as perfect as every cookie-cutter house here.

I push up from the chair, wobbling unsteadily as I approach the door with the intention of going outside and telling her to fuck off. To my disappointment, she scurries away before I get the chance, looking over her shoulder as if I would've chased her. As if I *could* have chased her.

I grab my cane from its resting spot against the door and venture outside to see if the house looks more upsetting than it did the last time I saw it. The door wavers before closing softly behind me, and I make my way down the stone walkway and toward the mailbox. I think this is the furthest I've walked in over a week.

THE NOISE

I peek inside the mailbox. Nothing. Jack must have brought the mail in already. I can't remember the last time I brought it in myself, or even received mail, for that matter. Once you go on disability, the world stops sending you things, even junk mail. It's as if an alert went out to let everyone know I'm now useless and not worth wasting their time on. The closest thing I get to mail are my benefits, but they're deposited directly into Jack's bank account because I have no more use for an account of my own.

Turning my back on the disappointing mailbox, I face our house. I can admit it doesn't look great, but it's not as decrepit as these people make it seem. Some things take time and patience.

I imagine what the house will look like when we, *he*, covers the peeling green paint with a fresh coat of white and installs his custom-built cedar shutters. The shutters are, as Jack insisted, one hundred percent operational. He went on for twenty minutes about how useless shutters are if they're only there for show. I didn't care either way back then, but now that they're sitting in the garage, polished and ready to go, I see the beauty in their practicality.

I picture the stone chimney Jack will build in place of the brick one that's been painted white, and I can practically smell smoke mixed with the frosty air during Christmas time. I can't wait to see the white roses showcased against the finished house, especially as the seasons change. The best thing about roses is that they bloom all year round. Well, except for the winter, but they linger a little while past the fall and they always promptly return in early spring, which is more than I can say for most other flowers.

The rose bushes are the only thing we've done to the outside of the house so far, planted at my insistence when we moved in. I grew them to help my dad find his way here, though I would never say that to Jack.

Something shatters inside the house.

Before I have the chance to wonder what caused the crash, another booms in succession, prompting me back up the stairs and through the porch door faster than I knew I could move.

I see shattered bits spread out on the floor before I even step foot in the kitchen, with some pieces having made it all the way into the living room. A few steps closer and I'm met with a cabinet door hanging wide open.

Did I leave it like this?

Did a ghost do this?

My skin is flushed with embarrassment. The fact that I could even entertain a ghost as an option shows how tired and irrational I am.

Think about this.

It's possible I left the cabinet door open by accident. It's also possible the dishes were wet from when we washed them last night and simply slipped off the rack. At least, I think we did the dishes last night. It could have been the night before. Either

THE NOISE

way, they could still have been a little damp, and I'm sure I didn't position them securely enough. Two separate mistakes on my part, nothing more.

I strut over to the broom and dustpan, chin raised with pride over winning this battle in my mind. I embrace the triumph, humming as I sweep up the shards. It feels good to bring myself back to reality. I'm the only one who has control over where my mind goes, and as long as I keep reminding myself of this, as long as I keep thinking rationally, then everything will be okay.

I bind the ceramic bits in paper towels and encase the tightly wrapped bundle within three plastic bags to prevent animals from getting cut, should they be so inclined to dig through the trash. Anticipating the rancid smell of the chicken carcass we discarded last night, I hold my breath and turn my head away as I open the bin. I hope Jack fixes the disposal soon. Or, better yet, I hope we, *he*, can build our vegetable garden and begin composting.

With my head turned, my aim is off, and the bag crashes to the floor, the shards within breaking into even smaller pieces. Thankfully, the layers of bags contain the mess.

The stench inside the can is overwhelmingly offensive, but my twisted curiosity to look at the decaying bits takes over. Only there's nothing there. Jack must have taken the garbage out early this morning. I'm sure the chicken could have left a lingering sour aroma, but I'm realizing I don't *just* smell it inside the bin. With my shirt pulled up over my nose, I look inside the recycling can. Empty. The sink is also empty, but the room smells increasingly of rotting flesh.

I dare to push my nose up in the air to decipher where the putrid smell is coming from.

It can't be coming from outside, because none of the windows are open. Unless we left a window in the den open, I consider, glancing down the hallway.

No. Control your mind.

I don't see this. He's not real.

EIGHT

Gravel stabs through my moccasins with each step I take away from the house. They're meant to be slippers, but I needed to get out and they were the easiest thing to slip into. I thought enough to grab my cane, but even so, taking off like a bullet is jarring on my joints. The pain in my hips and knees is agonizing, but I can't stop. I need to get away from his gaunt and twisted face.

I've never seen the same spirit twice. Yet, there he was, the same man from the living room corner with the same clawed hands and the same dark, sunken eyes. He staggered in the hallway like a puppet who could barely stand without strings to hold him up. His decomposing eyes bulged at the sight of me, as if he was starving and I could somehow satiate his hunger.

In the light of day, I saw deep purple bruises encircling the sagging skin around his wrists, as if he was at one time bound.

ALLISON A

There was a cavernous split down his cheek, exposing the fat and bone below, and a strange cross-hatch bruise covering his neck. I would have seen more, I'm sure, but a crunch emanated from the base of his spine as he moved forward, and I fled.

It could have been some kind of distorted reflection cast from somewhere outside the house. I don't know enough about that kind of thing to understand how it could work, but just because I don't understand something doesn't mean it's not possible. Or, it could have been a hallucination. After all, I'm dead tired. I search the database in my brain for quotes from all the books and articles I've read about sleep paralysis, trying to remember whether daytime hallucinations were ever mentioned. I think they were. I remember something about narcolepsy, but I've never been diagnosed with that. I've also never sought out a diagnosis, so I suppose I can't rule it out.

The more I strive for an explanation, the more I come to terms with the fact that I know nothing. There are too many things fighting for a place in my mind, and it all seems logical and illogical at the same time. I'm too exhausted to determine which is which, and the confidence I felt earlier is absolutely gone.

The further I get from the house, the stronger the wind from the river becomes, and I breathe it in and out, in and out, in and out. Maybe it's because I'm too tired to think anymore, or maybe the white fog escaping my lips is working to erase what

THE NOISE

I thought I saw, one puff at a time. Either way, that man is becoming as distant as an elusive childhood memory.

That's good. Let it drift away. Stop making a mess of things.

When we first drove through Hidden Heights, I daydreamed about walking by this river. I imagined the weather just as it is now—cloudy with no direct sunlight, chilly, but not so chilly that I'd need a coat. Now I'm here. I'm walking by this river in the very same weather I love, and I can't stop trying to take it away from myself.

I take everything away from myself.

I remember standing on the sidewalk and looking at the house we were about to tour for the first time. As I gazed over the yard, I imagined what it could be once I got to work on it. I envisioned a lush garden, a tire swing, and a bird feeder where all sorts of animals would congregate. I hoped the feeder would attract chipmunks, like we had at our apartment. I saw one in the yard last week, but they left once they realized there was nothing to eat except weeds.

I pictured a set of pine Adirondack chairs from where Jack and I would sit and look at the birds and squirrels and chipmunks, and the river in the distance. I dreamt of an apple tree, a firepit, and golden lights strung above a picnic table where we would sit and eat dinner.

All of that could happen, if I let it, but all I've been doing for the last four months is ruining any chance of a future with Jack in our home.

ALLISON A

I make a U-turn at the end of Riverside Drive, my pace slowing as I trace my steps back along the water. I can feel my bones calming along with my nerves, and I rely less on my cane.

The sunfish boats are out racing today. They look like tiny white shark fins in the distance, bouncing up and down with the waves. A few yards in front of me, there's a family fishing from the dock, their lunch set up on a blanket beneath the gazebo. I must have walked by too quickly before to notice the plaque nailed to the front of the pier in memory of Admiral Farragut, a naval academy that was once the heart of this small town.

I learned about Farragut from our Realtor after Jack and I asked why so many houses in Hidden Heights are the same light-yellow color. He explained that the school had buildings spread out around town, and they were painted light yellow to help students find their way. After the academy closed, the town converted the buildings to residential homes. From what I've gathered, most people have forgotten the academy and don't even understand why their homes are yellow. I doubt this tiny plaque makes much of a difference.

I can't help but smile as I watch children chase each other around the playground, maddening elation spread across their tiny faces. Beside the swings, a man holds his terrier back from attacking a squirrel as the dog barks wildly and wiggles to free himself. Nearby, a red SUV stops to allow a row of geese to

THE NOISE

cross safely. Up ahead, there's a beautiful little yellow house with pots of mums adorning the front porch, like a tiny meadow. The wind carries the voice of an older woman as she hums and lugs a tin watering can over to where even more mums are popping up around the base of her mailbox.

Feeling calmed by her delicate symphony, I take a seat on a nearby bench and try to appreciate the beauty of this town and remind myself that this is where I live. *I live here*. My house, in this small and peaceful town, is not haunted.

In the garage attached to the mum house, there's a man with curly silver hair working on an old mustang. I assume he's the woman's husband, as they look to be about the same age.

The man's mustang reminds me of the one my dad had when I was a little girl, the one he would sometimes pick me up from school with. The engine revved loudly, attracting the attention of every kid on the playground, and he'd get such a kick out of it. I don't remember whether it embarrassed me, but I do remember the excited look on his face as he rolled the window down and yelled over the thunderous rumble, "Red, over here!"

He bought that mustang when it was barely a hunk of metal on a frame and fixed it up in his spare time at the mechanic shop he used to own. I remember sitting at the front desk with a breakfast sandwich and a tall chocolate milk he bought me from the corner store, waving my greasy fingers at people who entered and directing them to the workshop, where he had his head buried in the engine of his pride and joy.

ALLISON A

Loud banging erupts nearby, jolting me to a standing position. It sounds like firecrackers.

I follow the sound to the garage, where the man with the curly silver hair is beating a wrench against the mustang's engine. I think little of it, assuming he's frustrated with a failing project, until he bangs the wrench against his head, and then his head against the engine.

I take a cautious step forward, searching for anyone else who might also be witnessing this, but the whole town seems oblivious.

I can hear the banging from where I am, so the man holding back his dog, who is much closer than me, should hear it too, but he doesn't.

A waterfall of blood washes over the man's face as his wife strolls across the lawn, toward the garage.

Move faster!

I consider running over there myself, but no one else is alarmed by this, and I can't stop the doubt from setting in.

I hardly blink as the woman nears her bleeding husband. My breath catches as she peeks in at the mustang, and I wait anxiously, eager for her to rush to him, to call for help. But she only fills her watering can at the spout and heads back to her mums.

I start walking at as quick a pace as I can manage. *This is real. It is. Someone needs to help him.*

The man looks in my direction.

THE NOISE

He seemed so helpless before as blood poured from his scalp, but the look on his face now is enough to stop me in my tracks. He reminds me of the man I've been seeing. The man I *think* I've been seeing. His expression is nothing short of threatening as his lips pull up into his gums, exposing the sharp teeth of a rabid animal.

More worried now for my own safety, I flee, just like I did back at the house. I find myself walking faster than I can handle, so fast that my cane can barely keep up.

It's not real. None of it is real.

The more I walk, and the further I walk away, the more I start to believe these lies.

"You'll hurt yourself."

"The Doctor said exercise is good."

"Yes, but you need to ease into it."

I know he's right, and I give in and slow my pace, if only slightly.

"Where did you go last night?"

"Jack woke up. You didn't need me anymore."

"I always need you," I tell him. "Why did you—"

"It's my turn," my dad reminds me. "How's everything going inside the house?"

I freeze at his use of the word *inside*. If he was asking about the renovations, then he would have asked how everything is going *with* the house. *Was he there this morning? Did he witness what happened? What I* thought *happened?*

"I was wondering what's next after the kitchen," he clarifies.

I peek up at him to see if I can decipher his true intentions, but he gives nothing away.

"The bathroom." I keep my answer short.

"The one upstairs or downstairs?"

"Downstairs."

"Oh."

"What?"

"When do you think you'll get to the one upstairs?"

"Not for a while. The stairs, remember?"

"Right, right."

My knee gives out. I almost fall to the ground, but my cane catches me and I steady myself once again.

"My turn," I announce before he can tell me to slow down a second time.

"Go ahead."

I let out a sigh as I prepare to ask the same question I've asked many times before. I know how this conversation will go, but desperation encourages me to nudge him one more time.

"Are you still in pain?"

"You know my answer."

"Has it changed?"

"No. I'm not in any pain."

"I don't want to be stuck in this body forever, dad." *Or stuck with this mind.* "I want to know death will be the end of this."

THE NOISE

"That will depend on you, and Jack."

Guilt floods the pit in my stomach, turning my face bright red. "You couldn't depend on me."

"Only for six months. Now look at us."

"Did you feel everything for those six months?"

He doesn't respond, and I know I should stop pushing, but I can't. I need to know that AS will die with me.

"Even your COPD? Did you struggle to breathe for six months?"

"Angela, you've asked me—"

"Please, just answer."

"Six months is nothing compared to how long others have been in pain."

"You know others?"

"Of course I do."

"How long have they had to wait?"

"Some for decades, others centuries."

"You must have been so afraid."

"I was, but I knew you'd come around," he smiles down at me. "You've never gone along with what's accepted."

"What do you mean?"

"People have accepted reactions to things, including the passing of a loved one. When someone passes, you mourn for an accepted period of time before you're encouraged to move on," he explains. "They all say the same thing your mother said, that their loved one—"

"That their loved one would want them to find happiness," I finish his sentence, having heard this before.

"Right," he says proudly. "I can tell you with certainty that there are a lot of lonely spirits because of what is accepted."

"It's accepted because people don't want to be alone."

"But you're not alone, are you?"

NINE

I hold the door open with my cane as Jack lugs a rusty metal ladder through the entryway.

"Who did you borrow it from?"

"A woman two houses down," he tells me. "The red brick house. The one with the donkey statue out front."

I step out of the way in time for the door to slam closed. "I don't think I've met her."

"You haven't." He leans the ladder against the wall by the stairs. "She was really nice. Said it belonged to her late husband."

Not only did Jack have to work and volunteer today, but he had to ask a woman to borrow her deceased husband's ladder so he can check the second floor of his house for ghosts, at his disabled wife's request. I'm sure shame is what's causing the sudden rush of heat to my cheeks.

ALLISON A

It would only make things worse if he were to see my shame. He would feel obligated to console me and tell me it's no big deal, that he doesn't mind doing this, that he meant to get around to checking the second floor at some point, all of which would be compassionate lies. Wanting to spare him this responsibility, I keep my attention on the floor so my face doesn't give me away.

He unfolds the ladder and stomps three times on the lowest step to make sure it's opened all the way. It just barely fits, with the bottom straddling the first four stairs and the top only just poking up over the landing, but it fits nonetheless. After shaking it to test its sturdiness, he begins his climb and I follow his lead.

"What are you doing?" He stops me.

"I want to see what's up there."

It's been a long day for him, this I know, and the strength of his sigh reveals the amount of frustration he's working to keep at bay. "I don't think it's a good idea," he says, his voice tight and his words measured. "I don't want you to hurt yourself."

Redness returns to my cheeks, and I step off the ladder without argument. He's probably right. I can hardly climb down from a rocking chair, let alone a ladder.

Based on my memory of the second floor's layout, I'm able to trace his boots as they move from the master bedroom to the second, smaller bedroom, and then to the bathroom. He must be standing near the shower now, because I hear him kick the

THE NOISE

shards from the broken toilet tank I spotted during our initial tour of the house.

As I listen to Jack walking about, I notice how similar the sound of his boots is to the noise I've been hearing. He believes the noise is the house settling, or possibly animals, but this doesn't sound like either. This sounds exactly like what it is—a grown man's boots walking with a purpose.

Out of habit, I follow the footsteps from one end of the house to the other and back again, increasingly amazed by the familiarity. The way the wood creaks under his thick soles, how the bristles of the rug squeak beneath the weight of the leather, is uncanny. I know it isn't Jack who's been causing the noise, but it has to be something very similar.

Finding myself back at the foot of the stairs, I give in to the urge to climb the ladder. I know I shouldn't, but I also know this may be my only chance to see what I've been hearing. If I could just see where he's walking, *how* he's walking, then maybe I can determine the cause of the noise. Maybe it would put my mind at ease.

"All clear," Jack announces, appearing suddenly at the top of the stairs.

I remove my foot from the step I was about to take and grab hold of the ladder to steady it for him. Focusing on the cold metal that rattles as he works his way down is the perfect excuse to avert my eyes, as I fear they may somehow reveal my near betrayal. The closer he gets, the harder I have to work to calm the rapid breaths I didn't even know I've been taking.

"I checked every nook and cranny," he says as his boots touch ground. "The windows are locked, and the attic is bolted. No way for anyone to have been up there."

"Then where is the noise coming from?"

"I don't know, honey. Like I said, it's probably—"

"It isn't animals, Jack. You would have found one, or at least a carcass."

"They could be in the walls, or it could be the house settling. Any number of things, really."

Any number of things is exactly what I'm afraid of.

He pulls me into his chest and rests his lips on the top of my head. "I'm sorry I got frustrated before. I worry about you, and I didn't express my worry in the right way because it's been a long day and I'm tired. I'm sorry for that."

I press my cheek into his sweatshirt to hide my shame. *I* should be the one to say I'm sorry. I'm the reason he's so tired all the time. I'm what's draining him to the point of frustration.

"I—"

"How does pizza sound for dinner?" He asks, stopping my apology before it even leaves my lips.

I could say it still. I could tell him how sorry I am for all the pain I've caused, for being crazy, for making his life so difficult. I could promise I'll change, and that our lives will get better.

"Pizza sounds great," is all I say instead.

After leaving another kiss on my head, he pulls away to fold the ladder. As he fastens it closed, his eyes scan from the ladder to the second floor and then to me.

"I'm not going to use the ladder, Jack."

He stands wordlessly for a moment as he searches my eyes for any hint of something he can believe. "I told her I'd return it tonight," he lies as he hoists the ladder under his arm. He invites a smile to spread across his lips, one that tries too hard to appear casual. "I don't want her to think I kept it."

***

Jack is buried shoulders-deep beneath the kitchen sink, sleeves rolled up to shield his favorite sweatshirt from the plumber's putty he's working with to install the sink disposal. There's a book sitting open on the counter before me, a steaming hot cup of chamomile tea beside it, but I can't bring myself to touch either.

We used to share the workload. We were a well-oiled machine working day and night to renovate the porch and the living room, which is why we finished them so quickly. Then everything changed. One day I was putting up sheetrock, and a week later I was walking with a cane. That's how AS works, apparently. All the physical labor I'd been putting my body through triggered a disease that was lying in wait, hauling its ugly head to the surface. Jack was too afraid to let me help with anything after that. He always says keeping him company is the only help he needs. I doubt that very much.

Heavy metal cracks against the brick floor.

"Is everything okay?" I ask, but he doesn't hear me.

"Jack?" I raise my voice a little louder as I lift up from my chair to check what had fallen, but I can't see anything beyond the edge of the counter.

"Jack?"

He comes up so fast that he bumps his head on the bottom of an open cabinet. "What's wrong?"

"Nothing. Nothing's wrong," the words spill out as I realize I've worried, and injured, him. "I heard something fall, and I was just wondering if you were okay."

"Oh." He drops his wrench and rubs the forming bruise on his head as he stands up. "I could use a break, anyway."

I manage to get up from the stool fast enough to beat him to the refrigerator. "Do you want me to reheat some pizza from earlier?" I ask, handing him a cold bottle of water. He wastes no time raising the bottle to his parched lips, gulping half of it before taking a single breath. It's a small win, but it makes me feel like I'm helping.

"No, thanks honey. I ate enough."

Wanting another win, I ask him how everything went at the shop today. I need him to know I'm not just his disabled wife

THE NOISE

who selfishly steals his sleep and his sanity, or who reads a book while he fixes our house. I need him to know I care.

"It went alright." He downs the rest of the water. "Rob's got a good handle on things."

Rob is Jack's childhood friend turned business partner. He's been managing the shop mostly on his own these past few months, so Jack can focus on finishing our house. Jack goes in once in a while, but it's nothing compared to the long hours he put in before.

"That's good, I'm glad." I answer, struggling to come up with a better response.

Before, when he was working regularly, he'd come home and tell me all about his day. I'd ask questions, like the amount of time that went into each project, if he thought something was coming along well, or if the customer was nice or demanding. But he's been working on projects so scarcely since we bought this house, and I'm not sure what else to say, so I move on. "What about the shelter? How are things there?"

He sets the water bottle down on the counter and crinkles his lips as he gives a sad shake of his head. "A dog was brought in today. She was found in a garbage can."

"What? Who would do that?"

"They did a lot worse before she ended up there, but I'll spare you the details."

"I'm so sorry you had to see that."

"It's nothing compared to what Sophie's been through. Seeing it is the least I can do."

"Sophie?"

"That's what I named her," he says. "Everyone kept referring to her as 'it,' and I thought she deserved better."

"I like the name Sophie," I agree. "I hate it when people refer to dogs as objects."

"Or their parents as *owners*. It makes them sound replaceable."

I think back to when my coworker's dog, Ralph, passed from bladder cancer. Laura ran out and bought a new dog less than a week later. It wasn't that she wanted to give another dog a good life. She was just lonely, and she couldn't stand the grief.

"He would want me to be happy," she said one day while we were waiting in line for the copier. *Would*, as if he no longer existed.

Jack and I have discussed bringing home a dog from the shelter, or at least fostering, but our house isn't exactly dog-ready at the moment. There are too many stray nails and pieces of debris that would endanger a curious animal. Once the house is finished, I would love to fill it with dogs. I grew up with three who I still love very much. Jack's love of dogs is one of the reasons I fell in love with him.

"What?" I ask, realizing Jack said something.

"The screwdriver, could you pass it to me?" He asks again, not trying to hide his concern for where I'd gone.

THE NOISE

I catch my reflection in the stainless-steel refrigerator, staring blankly at the wall like a zombie. *Did I look like this the whole time?*

"Of course, sorry," I apologize, snapping out of it and reaching for the tool beside me.

"Could you also pass me the duct tape?" He asks, clearly testing me this time.

"I'm tired, that's all," I explain as I open the junk drawer and hand him a dwindling roll of tape. It's hard not to notice the red beeping light of the answering machine just above the drawer. It's the fourth red beeping light this week, and probably the hundredth since she started calling four months ago.

I toil with deleting it, but I instead play just the first part of the message, hoping, like always, that this one will start with an "I'm sorry."

"Hi Angela, it's mommy," she begins in a raspy voice. I guess she's still smoking. "I'm doing alright, but I miss you." She always says this, even though I never ask how she's doing, nor do I care.

Or maybe I do, deep down. I don't know. I do worry about her, but I think this worry comes more from knowing how infantile my mother has always been. For as long as I can remember, I've felt like *her* parent. I always had to make sure she ate, slept, went to the doctor when she was sick, and paid her bills. I wonder how she's been getting by these past four months without me looking over her shoulder.

ALLISON A

"I just finished sewing a wedding dress for Irene, the woman I work with. The one who's getting married in April. The one with the pet bird?" She asks, referencing a previous message she left. "Anyway, it's not my taste, but I think it came out nice. I hope she likes it."

My mother made most of the clothes I wore when I was younger, and I always got so many compliments, but I hated wearing anything she touched. She's a talented seamstress, but she has a habit of smoking while she works, leaving everything smelling musty, the kind of musty that never washes out.

She made my dress for my eighth-grade graduation. It was beautiful, but, like everything else, it reeked of cigarettes and it gave me a horrible migraine. The pain became so bad that I could barely stand up without the threat of being sick. She was so proud to show it off, though, that I wasn't allowed to change, even after the ceremony. Eventually, nausea won, and I ruined the dress.

I remember little of what followed, except for the yelling and crying, and I remember us not speaking to each other for over a week.

I press delete.

"Are you okay?" Jack asks.

"I'm fine." *Am I fine?* "She'll never change."

"I'm here if you want to talk about it."

THE NOISE

I know I can talk to him, but if I talk about my mother, then it'll lead us down the road of talking about the incident, and I will not speak about that.

"I'm going to go pick roses for the vase," I say instead.

He sighs, but nods, and returns to the disposal.

A gentle breeze carries the sweet smell of white roses to my nose, and I almost feel bad for picking them. As soon as they're cut, the clock starts ticking on how long that scent will last. To justify my actions, I note how overgrown the bush has become and I tell myself that if I don't trim it now, it'll take over the front steps.

There's a tiny black speck crawling across the petal of a rose I pruned. They must love the scent as much as I do, and I smile at the thought of my favorite flowers being a sanctuary for such tiny creatures. I allow the ant to crawl onto my finger before placing them back onto the rose bush. I wouldn't want to carry them inside and risk their family moving on without them.

I watch them crawl toward the other ants gathered nearby, and I smile at a job well done.

As I aim the sheers at a second grouping of roses, I hear the drill start up inside, followed by a thunderous crash, prompting me to drop my bouquet and start for the house.

I swing open the door to find the drill vibrating across the kitchen floor, flailing about like a fish out of water. Jack stands uninjured nearby, thank goodness, yet he doesn't move to turn it off. He's frozen, staring in amazement at the haywire tool.

ALLISON A

As soon as he sees me in the doorway, he lunges for the drill, harnessing and silencing it.

"What happened?"

"I turned it on and accidentally dropped it. No big deal. Sorry I startled you."

Maybe it's the lingering awe on his face as he stares at the drill in his hands, or maybe it's the fact that I know you don't need a drill to install a sink disposal. Either way, I doubt very much that this was an accident.

TEN

It's happening again.

Please wake up, Jack. Please look at me.

I can't turn my head, so I focus on surveying every inch of the room within my view. I feel dizzy from the rapid movement of my eyes as they dash from one spot to the next.

Are they behind me? Are they crawling over the floor?

I imagine them creeping just out of view, preparing to climb onto the mattress and skulk like a putrid spider over my chest.

I just want to get this over with. Please show yourself so I can stop this.

A creak echoes from an all-too familiar corner of the living room. Someone has stepped on a floorboard.

I change my mind. I don't want to look. I don't want to see him.

ALLISON A

I have no feeling in my face, but I know I must be crying because the taste of damp salt fills the edges of my mouth. The taste grows fierce as the creaking increases, becoming incessant now, as if he's rocking. Or, God forbid, walking toward me.

A loud crack rebounds around the room like a boomerang, and I look toward the source, despite my better judgment.

I could never forget his gaunt face. I could never unsee that decaying skin, or those beady eyes laser-focused on me as he rocks back and forth, back and forth, back and forth on the old wood.

His mouth twists into a scowl, one that contorts more with each passing second, as if the sight of me is maddening to him. I must look like a cornered animal, shaking and whimpering in terror, which only seems to make him hate me more. Every time a moan escapes my trembling lips, his fists clench harder at his sides. Even in the dark, I can see an angry vein protruding from beneath his gray forehead.

"Ge..." I stammer with no effect.

Get out, get out, get out!

I blink to resolve the flood of water clouding my vision and immediately realize my mistake. He's four feet closer now.

I can hardly see anything beyond my tears, only an obscure silhouette crouching in the darkness.

Don't blink.

His crouch deepens into a squat, as if he's preparing to leap at me.

I can't help it. I blink.

A swell of wind as strong as a small tornado rips the blankets off the bed. Before I can react, they're just as quickly thrown back over me, trapping me.

I can't tell whether the blanket is wrapped so tightly that I can't breathe or if my own hysteria is inducing asphyxiation. Either way, I'm drowning in the cloth.

"Angela!" Jack yells as the covers are ripped off.

"Get...out," I wheeze the words as I huff free air. "Get out. Get out. *Get out now!*"

"It's okay." Jack pulls me close to his chest and begins brushing his fingers through my hair in a desperate attempt to stop my manic outburst. I can smell Endymion puffing off of his shirt with each anxious breath he takes.

"Please tell me you saw it," I plead through my sobs, but he only continues to shush me. "Jack, please, please don't do this to me," I wail. "Please admit you saw it!"

"Angela, stop," he begs, losing patience. "All I saw was you throwing yourself around under the blanket. I don't know what the fuck is going on."

He attempts to pull me closer, like I'm a baby he's trying to swaddle back to sleep, but I push at his chest so hard that I fall off the mattress and land on the hardwood, a crack screaming from my hip.

ALLISON A

It shakes the panic out of me straightaway, and as I look back at Jack, his face worn with exhaustion and concern, I sober to the realization of what is happening.

"I'm sorry," I tell him. "I'm sorry."

Guilt swarms his face at the sight of my apologetic body sprawled across the floor. He climbs down, helps me upright, and hugs me tightly. I can feel it in the strength of his arms that he's not only hugging me to calm me, but to beg me to stop this. I wish I could.

His heart is racing so fast that his shirt rattles, and I know my panic is making him panic, but I can't stop. He pulls me in tighter, so tight I can hardly breathe, yet I manage to keep crying. I feel so tired, so worn down, so confused, so terrified. I just want it to stop. I just want to sleep. I just want him to admit he saw something. I just want to know I'm not crazy. *I just don't want to be crazy.*

I've never seen the same spirit more than once, but I've seen this man too many times to count. I can't bear to consider how many more times he will haunt me.

What if he gets closer? What if Jack doesn't wake up in time to stop whatever it is he wants to do to me?

What if he isn't even real?

What if he is?

"I don't want to go back to sleep tonight," I tell Jack as I rub my hip, though it does little to rid the pain.

"It was just an episode. If you don't sleep, it'll get worse."

THE NOISE

Just an episode. That's easy for someone to say who didn't see what I saw. *Didn't he see what I saw?*

"I didn't mean it that way," he apologizes, pulling away to look at me. "I'm worried about you." He draws in a breath. "I'm not going to press you to talk about what happened," he pauses again, taking notice of my guarded eyes, tears sobering as I peer at him through the dimly lit room. "But this has been worse since then—"

"Don't you dare bring it up," I snap. I feel my cheeks burn red with fury, and suddenly all I can think about is moving away from this conversation, away from him.

My pathetic attempt to storm out is halted by my inability to move my hip even a few inches without wincing. Before I even know what's happening, bitterness towards my wretched body cumulates in a vicious punch against the floor.

"I'll get you some ice," Jack surrenders as he lifts himself from the floor and starts for the kitchen.

"I know you didn't drop the drill," I tell him, nursing my fist and not taking a single second to think about what I'm saying, or how much worse I've just made things. "You doubt everything, but you can't doubt that. It started all on its own, didn't it?"

His expression turns from shock to what I can only assume is pity, and I wish I could take my words back. I wish I could hide how absolutely mad I've become.

"If you don't want to go back to sleep, that's fine. I'll stay awake with you for the rest of the night," he says. His words are soft and supportive, yet his exasperation is evident. I know his real intention by staying awake is to keep me safe, from myself. I've worried him to the point that he's afraid to even close his eyes.

I'm just like them—a gaunt, twisted spirit, sucking the life out of him.

"I'm sorry. I don't know where that came from."

His eyebrows crush together with too many reservations for him to count, I'm sure.

"It just took me some time to fully wake up, but I'm awake now. I'm sorry, Jack."

He crawls back onto the floor and gently presses his forehead to mine, our eyelashes nearly tangling. He closes his eyes and exhales long and deep. "You have nothing to be sorry for. *I'm* sorry. I'm so sorry for what you're going through, Ang. This is not your fault. I wish I could make you understand that. I'm trying. If I could, I'd take it all away."

I feel even worse now.

"I love you," he says. He places a lingering kiss on the top of my head. "I'll get you that ice, and make some coffee for both of us."

ELEVEN

I saw a psychologist once. Well, not technically a psychologist. A "Licensed Professional Counselor." The difference, I learned, is that an LPC stops their education at the Master's degree level rather than continuing on to get their PhD. Had I known that when I made the appointment, I don't think I would have cared—I didn't really believe in the process anyway. The only reason I even tried it was because I promised Jack I would.

I raise my polka dot-encrusted mug to my lips, steam encumbering my vision in a French vanilla-scented fog, and I take a tentative sip to test the temperature.

I had previously eliminated therapy as a possibility after seeing the wonders it did for my mother. Her sessions lasted no more than thirty minutes and usually ended with the Psychologist confirming, or upping, her dosage of antidepressants. I can only imagine what took place within that half hour—probably a lot of her feeling sorry for herself and just not understanding why she and her daughter fight so much. It must have been a problem with me. I'm too much like my father.

My first appointment with the LPC went surprisingly well. I'm sure she could tell how guarded I was by my crossed arms and legs, coupled with my refusal to crack even the smallest smile, but she persevered. She listened to every word I said and even repeated my own words back to me, to prove she was listening. By the end of the hour, I had opened up in spite of myself. I talked about my relationship with my mother, and about the passing of my dad.

When I showed up for my second appointment a week later, she didn't remember my name, let alone anything we'd spoken about. Yet, she felt comfortable diagnosing me with an anxiety disorder. That experience nixed any professional help I might have gotten for what I'm currently going through. Maybe, if I had gotten the help I needed, I wouldn't be sitting on our porch hating myself for what I did to Jack last night. Maybe last night would have never happened. If she could have just remembered me, if people could just remember anything, then life wouldn't be the way it is now.

As I lift the mug to my mouth for another sip, I catch sight of a woman walking down the sidewalk. She looks as if she might

THE NOISE

be headed for our house, but I can't imagine why. I've never seen her before.

She's stout. To say she's five feet tall would be generous. Her huge purple glasses add more height than her light gray feminine buzz cut. I can see how full her lips are from here because of the firecracker red lipstick she applied in at least four layers. Her petite legs are encased like snake skin beneath charcoal leggings, and even though she's clearly in her eighties, she walks briskly, determined. I can't quite make out the pattern of her oversized sweater. Perhaps horses, or lobsters.

Chimpanzees.

And on her infinity scarf, red question marks.

What an odd woman.

She comes to an abrupt stop at the foot of the porch steps. I freeze, wide-eyed, hoping she's about to realize she's in front of the wrong house, or that she wants to gawk for a moment before moving on, like everyone else. After last night, I'm not in the mood for visitors, nor do I look like I should be entertaining anyone.

To my great disappointment, she takes a step up, then another.

My nails dig into my palms as she makes her way to the door. I would wonder whether she's waiting for me to greet her, but I doubt I'm even visible in the shadows.

ALLISON A

She takes three deep breaths. I count them with each heave and fall of her chest. Somehow, she looks more afraid than I feel, and I wonder whether it's the house that's frightening her, like it seems to do to so many others.

She knocks—two timid raps on the wood frame, then silence.

I slink back further into the darkness of the porch, confident in my ability to wait her out. She dares to peek through one of the windows, and I pull back until the base of my neck is flush with the wall. Her shoulders shake from the shudder trailing up her spine.

Whether she finally sees me, I can't be sure. All I know is that I'm eternally grateful when she turns to leave.

She swiftly turns back and knocks three more times on the door, hard enough to rattle the frame. It's as if she had to force herself to knock, as if it took everything she had inside of herself to drag her feet to this very spot outside my door. *But why?*

The soles of Jack's boots stamp through the living room, a swarm of sawdust blowing by me as he races to the door.

With his hand on the knob, he pauses for a beat to breathe in and compose himself. I've never seen him rush to answer the door, especially not when he barely slept the night before. I wonder whether he was expecting her, or if he could somehow sense my trepidation from across the house.

THE NOISE

His face falls white when he opens the door, as if he didn't believe a human being would actually be standing there. Understandable, since no one visits us. He promptly softens his expression and turns on the charm I fell in love with.

"I'm glad you decided to stop by after all," he greets the woman. Knowing him for as long as I have, I can tell he isn't that glad. If anything, her visit seems more like a nuisance.

I ease one foot to the ground, then the other, and push myself up from the chair, my spine screaming in protest.

"I wanted to thank you for returning my ladder. I hope you got done what you needed to?"

She's the woman from two houses down, I realize, the one with the donkey statue, the one with the husband who passed.

"I did, and thank you again for lending it to me. I'm sorry I left it leaning against the side of your garage. I planned to stop by later today when you were home and bring it inside for you."

"Oh, nonsense," she says, waving her hand at him like she's swatting away a fly. "Charlie always left his tools lying around the yard. I've gotten used to it."

Charlie.

A pang of guilt shoots through me. I used *Charlie's* ladder to feed my hallucinations, a ladder he used countless times but never once to check for ghosts. I wonder how he'd feel about that. How *Charlie* would feel about that.

"I'll still come by and move it inside for you. It's the least I can do."

The woman smiles as she waits in the doorway, presumably for Jack to invite her in, though he seems hesitant. I'm sure he, like me, isn't ready to entertain visitors in this mess.

"May I?" she finally asks, taking a step inside. I get the sense that if she doesn't coax herself to enter, she'll run away screaming instead.

Jack steps aside as she crosses the threshold, tightening her scarf as though the house has given her a chill.

"Hello," I greet her, figuring it'd be better to alert her to my presence now instead of giving her the fright she seems to be expecting.

She scans the porch, and me, up and down, but I can't tell whether she approves of either.

"It's been a long time since I've stepped foot in this house," she announces, directing her attention back to Jack. "After you stopped by, I wondered whether I could stomach a trip back in time. I hope that's okay?"

"Of course," Jack agrees.

I've never given much thought to who lived here before us. The house was uninhabitable when Jack and I bought it, making it difficult to imagine anyone had ever lived here. Knowing now who once called this place home, the very same person who's trekking through our first floor, feels strange.

THE NOISE

Judging by her fashion sense, I imagine this charming craftsman was once lavished with modern art paintings, bold pops of color, plants on every windowsill, and crystals hanging from ceiling fans. None of that sits right with me. This house, built in 1955, screams for ornate furniture, oriental rugs, and crystal vases filled with fresh flowers.

"It's so cold in here," she comments, rubbing her upper arms. Taking notice of the air mattress at the foot of the fireplace, she laughs and adds, "Good spot to stay warm."

"I'm sorry for the temperature," Jack apologizes. "As I'm sure you know, the heating system is old. We mainly rely on the fireplace, but we haven't gotten it started yet this morning."

"No need for sorries," she says, her smile stretching the glossy red lipstick. Her eyes travel from the sturdy walls to the delicate window panes, to the fireplace and the mantel, to the kitchen and the hallway. As she takes it all in, a look of yearning falls over her. "I had a lot of happy memories in this house," she tells us. "A lot of sad ones, too," she adds, and I catch her glance at the stairs.

"How long did you live here?" I chime in, suddenly curious.

"You must have lived here for a long time," Jack adds.

"Fifty-seven years," her smile returns, however briefly. "Fifty-seven years I spent here with Charlie. Holidays, dinners, blizzards." She chuckles. "He loved the snow, couldn't get enough of it. When we were trapped at home during the blizzard of 1996, he was the happiest I'd ever seen him."

"I'm sorry for his passing," Jack says.

She nods. "I've had time to move on. It doesn't hurt like it used to."

I wonder how Charlie would feel if he heard his wife say it doesn't hurt anymore that he's gone.

"Here, let me show you the renovated kitchen I was telling you about," Jack says, stretching an arm out ahead of himself.

"Well..." a huff of awe escapes her at the sight of the redone room. "I wish it looked this good when I lived here. Those cabinets are absolutely beautiful. I love the color pallet you chose—forest green is very popular at the moment, and it goes so well with the red brick floor and the wood countertop." She stops to reminisce, then adds, "And you fixed the crack in the wall behind the stove."

She runs her fingers over the wall, admiring Jack's craftsmanship. "You know, you remind me a lot of Charlie. He could fix anything. Honestly, I never had to do much for myself. I just left it all up to him. And I don't only mean renovations. He was the man of the house in every sense of the word. All I was required to do was cook and clean, but what woman shouldn't at least do that?" She adds, and I could swear she looks right at me as if she can tell I don't do either of those things.

"Oh my goodness," she gasps from the foot of the stairs.

"What is it?" I ask, taking a cautious step forward.

THE NOISE

"It's still there," she coos, raising a shaky finger toward the second floor. "The wallpaper."

I have to squint to make out even just the edges of it, but I assume her memory is guiding most of what she sees.

Her hand falls over her heart. "Charlie hung that when we first moved in. I hated it. I told him we'd never be able to take it down if we changed our minds. Wallpaper is fussy like that, you know? He swore he wouldn't change his mind, but I knew myself too well. And when *my* mind *did* change, I was right and we couldn't get the damn paper off the walls. My God, I never thought I'd be so happy to see it clinging on for dear life."

I feel it in my chest before I even realize I hear it. The vibration of it taps against my rib cage, like nails on stone. I look from Jack to Charlie's wife, then to the stairs.

Jack glances at the second floor, but I can't tell whether he hears the noise or if he's listening to Charlie's wife go on about why they chose yellow—it reminded Charlie of daisies, his mother's favorite flower.

The noise grows louder and Charlie's wife abruptly halts her story, directing a grimace toward the top of the stairs. She *must* hear it.

"Do you hear—"

"I'd offer you a look around the second floor, but the stairs have rot. I apologize," Jack interrupts me.

"No need," she answers, pulling her scarf tight. "I would never go up there again." She shutters as she turns from the stairs, the warm memory of the wallpaper erased in an instant.

Something happened up there.

No. Nothing happened, I tell myself while the noise persists above my head. *Maybe they had fights upstairs, fights she doesn't like to remember. Or, Charlie passed, after all. Maybe he was stationed up there during a long illness. Maybe—*

"You don't like to go up there either, do you?" She asks Jack, her voice serious.

He steals a glance at me. "Like I said, the stairs have—"

"Rot," she interrupts him. "Right. I'm sorry about that."

Something slams down against the floor above, sending me two inches off the ground.

"Are you okay?" Jack whispers in a low voice so as not to draw attention to my outburst. Mortified, I muster a shy nod and plant my feet firmly down on the floor.

"I think I need to step outside," Charlie's wife announces.

With her hand on the doorknob, she turns back to Jack. "I'm so sorry, I didn't mean to..." she trails off as she looks once more at the stairs, her expression melting into sorrow. "I'm very sorry."

I look to Jack for a translation, but he shrugs to let me know he has no clue what she's talking about either. *Is she sorry we inherited the rot?*

"I'd better go before I wear out my welcome."

THE NOISE

"I'm sorry, I never offered you anything to drink. Are you sure you have to get going?" Jack is convincing, but I know he can't wait for her to leave. He's using the same tone of voice I've seen him employ with Ms. Courtney, a regular at his shop. She never buys anything or makes requests for custom projects; she comes in only to talk with him. I think she's outlived her family and she's lonely. I've seen Jack be very sweet with her, but on busy days, when he's trying to balance being understanding and giving attention to paying customers, his voice takes on a mix of pained remorse. If I look close enough, I can always see his jaw clenching through the head nods and polite replies, just like it's doing right now.

"It's alright. I have a dinner to get to anyway, plenty to drink there," she winks. She takes one more look around and sets her gaze on the vase on the counter. "Charlie loved white roses," she manages to say through the building lump in her throat. "I never cared much for them."

TWELVE

Orange light from the declining sun fills the room and my inner alarm clock buzzes. I stretch out my hand and feel the pills trickle onto my palm like raindrops. Jack places a glass of water and a blueberry muffin in front of me, and I set out for my task.

"So, what did you think?" He asks.

"It's really good," I answer as I peel the parchment paper and take another bite.

The corner of his mouth turns upward in amusement at my misunderstanding. "I meant what did you think of Charlie's wife. We didn't get a chance to talk about her visit earlier. But I'm glad you like the muffin. I made them while you were in the shower."

"That must be why the steam smelled like sugar," I smile at the memory. After downing my medication and a glass of water, I finally answer his question. "I feel bad saying this, since she was kind enough to lend us her husband's ladder, but I don't like her very much."

"Why is that?"

"She barely acknowledged me, and when she did, she was rude."

"She's from a different time."

"That's no excuse."

"No, it's not. I'm sorry she made you feel that way."

"It's not like we'll be seeing much more of her, judging by how quickly she ran out of here," I say, working up the courage to ask him why he thinks she left so abruptly. Because *I'm* sure I know.

"I'm sure you're right. We won't see her again, so it's not worth talking about," he says, nixing my attempt.

Maybe it's for the best. If I were to bring up the noise now, after everything I put him through last night, then he might finally reach his breaking point.

He cups my cheek in his palm, his thumb running over the cloud of color spreading out from his touch. His hands are large, but gentle, and the kiss which ensues is affectionate and unexpected.

I thought he would have questions about my behavior while Charlie's wife was here, or that he'd at least wonder why I didn't answer the door. I never saw this ending with him dismissing everything and instead giving me one of the most tender kisses he's given me in a while. I'm certainly not complaining.

He pulls away, leaving a sweet indigo residue on my lips. My cheek widens against his cradling palm but just as soon shrinks when I see how focused he is on me. I've seen this look many times since I was first diagnosed. He's trying to remember this moment by recording my face in his mind, and I suddenly understand what's happening. Hearing Charlie's wife talk about long-lost memories of her deceased husband reminded him of the reality of my disease, and the fact that he will one day be in her position.

"I will never speak about you that way. I want you to know that."

"I know," I say, fighting back unexpected tears.

He nods, though I sense his desire to repeat those words ten more times to make sure I understand. I do.

I pull him close, wrapping my arms around his lower back. He rests his forearms on my shoulders and his chin on the top of my head, and breathes in deeply.

"I'm sure. You know that, right? I could never doubt how sure I am about you."

"I know."

I hear a sniffle as he pulls away.

The back of his shirt crinkles. He's using the hem to wipe his face. "I'm sorry again that she came so unexpectedly. I had no idea," he says, turning back around, and I see a bit of redness circling the rims of his eyes.

"Let's just forget about it."

He forces a smile. "We have to at least talk about the chimpanzees."

Jack has never been great at expressing his emotions, though he's gotten better since being with me. He and I come from polar opposite upbringings—me from passionate parents who once threw pizza at the ceiling in the heat of an argument, and he from a quiet family who wouldn't share their feelings if someone's life depended on it. I don't think he knew he *could* have emotions until he met me. He's welcomed them little by little over the years. More so since I've gotten sick. I know it wasn't easy for him to show even that temporary burst of sadness, so the least I can do is allow him this reprieve.

"I think her scarf was just as confused," I joke, relieved to see his shoulders melt into a relaxed slouch.

He laughs as he pours a glass of water for himself.

"Seriously, though, I'm sorry," he tells me. "When I invited her over, I was just being nice because she lent us her ladder. I never thought she'd actually come, especially with the way she spoke about the house when I first met her. She seemed like she never wanted to step foot in it again."

"There's that," I say, the words slipping out before I can think better of them.

"What do you mean?"

"I don't know," I begin, "there's so much we don't know about this house."

"Like what?"

I hesitate, wondering how I can explain myself without bringing up the noise and ruining the moment we just shared.

"She was clearly afraid of the second floor," I say. "I guess I never thought about what might have happened here before we moved in."

If I would have blinked, I'd have missed his face freezing for a fraction of a second.

"Do you think something *bad* happened here?" His eyes focus in on mine.

"Forget I said anything," I falter.

"No, it's okay. What do you think happened?"

I realize it might be worse if I said nothing further at this point. Who knows what he might think is going on in my head? I proceed with caution, choosing my words carefully.

"I'm sure it's nothing. If something bad happened, like a violent crime or something, we'd know about it. In this state, a Realtor *has* to reveal that a death occurred in a house if it was violent." I learned this when my mother purchased her most recent home in a fifty-five and up community. She asked her Realtor if "Any old people died in this house." Then she laughed nonchalantly, to the realtor's bemusement, and added, "Probably lots, am I right? But you wouldn't tell me." After nudging the poor man with her elbow and failing to wink discretely, he explained the law, along with a simple "No one, to my knowledge, has died in this house."

"Why did you jump right to a violent death?"

"I don't know," I answer honestly. I don't know why my mind went to such dark thoughts. This all started with a simple question—what do I think of Charlie's wife—and I spiraled to violent murder.

"She could have been remembering anything. Maybe the stairs were a problem even then?" He suggests.

I look at the stairs. He could be right, I guess. And she did seem apologetic about the rot. But it was more than that. If she wasn't able to use the stairs when she and Charlie lived here, it would have been upsetting, but upsetting enough to make her never again want to venture to the second floor? I doubt that very much.

"Hey, did I give you the Sulfasalazine?" Jack asks.

I think back to the pills in my hand. I can't remember.

"Let me check the bathroom. I'll see how many you have left." Before I can protest, or tell him it's not a big deal if I miss one dose, he's already left the room.

He returns with the bottle, tips the pills into his hand, and counts them to himself. "I filled this last month," he says aloud, "so you should have…" he pauses to do the math in his head, "seven left. There's eight. I'm sorry, I did forget." He hands me the pill and I gulp it down if only to rid that remorseful look from his face.

He feels this way because I've given him the burden of taking care of me. I hardly ever remember to take my medications, and when I do remember, I don't *want* to take them. I don't even know when I last filled my own prescriptions. He always gets a jump on it before I have the chance. I'm sure that's because he doesn't trust me to remember to do it myself.

"I'll call the pharmacy tomorrow and refill it," I promise him. I want him to know I don't expect him to do these things for me. I appreciate it, of course I do, but I never want him to feel bad for forgetting to do something he shouldn't even have to remember to do in the first place, that he *wouldn't* have to remember if he had a sane wife who didn't require constant supervision.

"No need. I already refilled it this morning."

He watches me down the rest of the water the same way an orderly examines a patient. I'm surprised he hasn't checked under my tongue. *God, am I really this pathetic?*

He takes my glass over to the sink, washes it, adds it to the stack of dishes he cleaned earlier, then starts on the dish from my blueberry muffin. I have to look away, otherwise I may run straight out of the house and into traffic.

My eyes fall on the red blinking light.

Not wanting to watch Jack do the dishes, but also not wanting to remember the message I heard being recorded in real-time earlier—something about the HOA forcing my mother to remove a paddle boat she's been keeping in her side yard—I instead set out to determine the rhythm of the beeps, hoping it's monotonous enough to numb my guilt-ridden mind.

I've never noticed that they beep in a pattern of three in rapid succession, followed by two moderately paced beeps, and three slow beeps. Curious as to whether this is the only pattern, or if it changes every so often, I stare at the machine, at the three two three, three two three, three two three, and I feel myself slip into a fatigued trance.

Heaviness encumbers my eyelids and I start to trip over my enumeration, unable to tell anymore whether there are three fast beeps and two moderate ones, or three moderate beeps and two fast ones, or maybe three of each. Whenever I attempt to start over, my eyelids insist on closing instead. *It's working.*

My tired gaze floats to Jack's back, to the muscles working beneath his thin white t-shirt.

I want to do something for him tomorrow. I *should* do something for him tomorrow. I consider going food shopping, but I don't drive. Wallace's is within walking distance, but I know he'd get upset with me for walking all the way there and back, while carrying bags nonetheless. I could do the laundry, but the machine is in the basement and he doesn't like me using those stairs either. He says they're too steep.

I can't do anything, because then the burden of worry is all on him, and I can't do nothing, so the burden is all on him.

Am I making sense?

ALLISON A

My eyes fight against the bright light of the kitchen, determined for sleep.

An arm reaches under my thighs. Another arm wraps around my upper back. Before I know it, the hard stool disappears from beneath me.

I peel my eyes open just as Jack eases me onto the air mattress. He tucks the sides of the blanket beneath my legs, encasing me tightly. I can't tell if he wants to keep me warm or make it more difficult for me to run screaming mad from the bed later tonight.

For reasons I don't understand, I push through my exhaustion to murmur, "See you later." *Am I going somewhere?*

Maybe, on some deep subconscious level, I know things would be better for him if I *was* going somewhere.

He kisses my forehead, and I know I don't deserve it.

"You're not going anywhere," he whispers to me.

THIRTEEN

You're paranoid, I tell myself as I hear the noise approaching from behind. *You've never heard it on the first floor.*

I'd like to say I have the ability to calm myself, to pull myself back from the edge of insanity, but it isn't until the breeze from the open window carries Endymion to my nose that I realize it's just Jack, not the noise.

He must have his boots on, which means he's about to head out for the shop. He got a request for a new project yesterday— a custom bench.

I scribble a few last words in my journal and slam it closed, imagining the cover is a door to the memory of my last episode. It helps to think that each word I write is plucked from my mind and planted on the page where it remains trapped, like I'm transferring a curse. When it's all written down, the memory of it can no longer haunt me. That's what I tell myself, at least.

I place my journal face down on the table, as if to prevent the cover from opening on its own and the memory from springing off the page and back into my mind. I use my cane to push myself up from the chair before clambering through the doorway and into the house. My legs feel heavy, and it occurs to me that I was sitting in the rocking chair for far too long, causing my bones to stiffen.

I look down at my aching joints as I put one foot in front of the other, like I can somehow will the pain to disperse.

The top of my forehead crashes into something both hard and soft.

"You okay?" Jack asks, laughing as he rubs my head.

He looks so handsome in his gray Henley and backwards hat. Maybe it's because I grew up in a rural town where there were more tractors on the road than cars, but a backwards hat has always been my weakness. When he first learned this little quirk, back when we began dating, he wore a backwards hat almost every time we were together. Thirteen years later, and it still gets me.

I want to tell him to have a good day, that I'll see him later, that I love him, but he looks so handsome right now that all I can do is stare.

"It's weird, you know that, right?" He jokes, eyes rolling up toward his hat.

THE NOISE

"I like what I like."

He kisses my lips and wraps me in a tight hug, the soft fabric of his shirt warming my exposed skin.

"I should only be gone for a few hours. Four, tops," he assures me.

"Drive safe," I tell him. "I'll see you later."

"See you later," he calls back as he nears the door, tipping his hat with a wink.

I watch from the porch as his truck rounds the corner and disappears from sight, feeling the coolness of the morning dissipate with the rising sun that chases his back bumper. There's something about the ochre glow that stretches over the yard that brings me unexpected peace this morning, as if someone draped a silk cloth over the sun the same way they would a lamp.

I take a sip of coffee as I look out over the hay bales and ginger-colored pumpkins in the neighboring yards, and I breathe in the fallen leaves whooshing across the asphalt. A soft light cast from the house across the street adds a certain ambiance to this morning, and I find myself fascinated with it. I wonder if whoever lives there has woken up early because they, too, couldn't sleep. Perhaps they, like me, find solace in the quiet hours before the rest of the world wakes up.

The light inside the house is at odds with the early morning skies, making it look like a dollhouse, and I can see into almost every room. I know I shouldn't look, because I can't stand it

ALLISON A

when anyone so much as glances at our house, but I know nothing about the people in this town, and the opportunity to peek is too tempting.

It's a simple home. Not in a boring sort of way, but more like whoever lives there hasn't fully settled in yet. The furniture is sparse and consists mostly of muted colors, like browns and grays. The only pop of color comes from a sky-blue throw blanket hanging from the back of the couch. If they're new to the neighborhood, they must have moved in before Jack and I did, because I haven't noticed any moving trucks.

A woman enters the kitchen while cinching a tan robe around her petite waist. She ruffles her hand through shoulder-length brown hair and yawns wide, as if she just woke up and is in dire need of caffeine. I can relate.

I watch her set up the cream-colored Keurig as a man walks in. He's shorter than her, but his pin-straight posture and ironed black suit makes him an imposing presence. I wonder if he's a lawyer, or works in finance, or some other bigwig job. Whatever he does for a living, it can't be local because no one around here dresses like that.

To match his fitted suit, his hair is so perfectly in place that I can almost see the streaks of gel from here. Not even a strong wind could dishevel what he likely spent an hour crafting.

A light turns on in the back corner of the house. Curious, I peer closer, expecting to see children waking up for school, but instead I see another adult female stumble out of the doorway as if she's drunk.

She nearly falls over, clutching the molding in time to save herself. She grips her stomach with her other hand and bends at the waist. I gag just thinking about the idea of her vomiting, but instead of looking away, I lean in. It's like I'm watching a movie, or reading a book, and I wonder which character she'll turn out to be.

She's too old to be their teenage daughter who's sick to her stomach after sneaking out to party the night before. She could be a family member with a drug problem who this couple is helping get back on her feet. Or a mistress the woman in the robe has no idea about.

Her hands drop to her sides and she stands upright, her attention captured like a dog who hears the refrigerator door open. She stands still as a statue, like she's in some kind of trance. I might think she fell asleep if her eyes weren't wide open, blinking and widening by the second, as if she can't believe what she's hearing.

In her stillness, I'm able to see her in more detail. Her clothes are dirty and tattered, her hair a black nest, teeth framed in a scowl.

Maybe she's homeless, I consider. Maybe they don't even know she's in their house.

ALLISON A

Her spine snaps into a hunch and she skulks down the corridor, toward the couple. Something doesn't feel right. I take a step back, preparing to run for the phone and call 911.

But then I stop. I force myself to pause and assess whether I'm overreacting, a thought process I am still perfecting.

I can see it now—the police knocking on my neighbor's door to tell them the lady across the street, the recluse they've never met before, called because she was spying on their house in the early morning hours and saw someone hunched over while walking down a hallway.

I can't ignore the feeling in my gut that this isn't right, though. If something is wrong, then who else will help them? Judging by the blackened houses on every side of me, I'm the only other person awake. Then again, if I make this call and I'm wrong, everyone won't avoid us because of the house we live in, but because of the crazy lady who lives inside. That's just what Jack needs.

She stops. *Thank goodness.*

Before I can take a breath, she punches the wall, an act so unexpected I almost drop my mug.

She glances down the hallway toward the couple, who haven't heard a thing, then punches the wall again, and again, and again, and again.

There's no way they don't hear this. She's only fifteen feet away.

THE NOISE

Maybe she's unstable and this behavior is usual for her. Maybe the couple normally blocks it out. Otherwise, I have no idea why the woman with the robe is sipping her coffee as the man grabs his coat and briefcase from a nearby chair, as if everything is normal.

The deranged woman punches the wall again, the echo reaching my porch.

They *have* to hear this.

Another punch, this time so loud it sends my favorite mug crashing to the ground, shattering into dozens of ceramic fragments.

"Oh no, no no no, no. Shit."

I'm not sure whether to focus on the couple, the strange woman, the fact that my mug is now destroyed, or the hot coffee splattered over my ankles, burning my skin. I scan from one to the next until something locks me in place—the woman across the street is staring at me.

I look away on instinct, afraid she'll run over here and do worse than punch my walls if she catches me.

But if I look away, then I won't be able to see her coming.

I peek back at the house. She's gone.

I glance at the street, expecting to see her dashing across it, hunched over, legs moving like a spider.

She isn't there either.

ALLISON A

I return my gaze to the broken mug at my feet, realizing the sharp pieces could be an easy weapon for her to use against me.

I drop to the ground, ignoring the rip in my lower back as I cup the bits in my hands. A shard slices my palm, but I ignore the pain. I can't look at what I'm doing and also monitor the street, and the more I try to do both, the faster my heart races, so fast that I feel lightheaded.

Feeling stupid for not seeing the easier solution right in front of me, I drop the ceramic pieces and race to the door, leaving behind drops of blood as I twist the lock. I move on to latch every window, checking each one again and again until I'm out of breath. Exhausted, I rest my face and hands against the glass panels of the porch door. I gulp down air as I watch, and wait.

She's here, somewhere. They're all here somewhere.

But all I see is my own reflection.

Look at yourself.

I release my hands from the glass and step back, mouth gaping at my appearance.

I look just like the deranged woman.

My posture is hunched, hair unbrushed, eyes sunken from lack of sleep. I've left behind a single bloody handprint, and as I stare at it, I realize what I must look like to anyone passing by. If someone were to spy spying on my own home right now, they'd have their hand wrapped around a phone, ready to call for help.

THE NOISE

I run a hand through my hair, smoothing the wild red strands as best I can, though it still looks untamed. My skin becomes hot from friction as I rub at the winkles in my cotton shirt to little avail. I straighten my shoulders and take another look. I can't do anything about my sunken eyes, and the wrinkled clothes are relentless, but I no longer see her. Not fully, at least.

I turn back to the house across the street, to the man tossing his briefcase onto the passenger seat before climbing in and starting his car. I don't see the distressed woman anywhere. But the other woman, the one with the brown hair and the robe, is sitting in an armchair, sipping coffee and reading a book, as if nothing has happened.

That should be me. Not the monster.

Possessed by a desire to correct this, I walk firmly to the bathroom and strip off my wrinkled clothing. Avoiding the mirror, I head for the shower and turn the knob to the coldest setting, to shock myself out of this, and step inside.

I don't want to be me anymore. I want to be normal. I want to walk Jack to the door and kiss him sweetly, seeing a look of love shining back at me, not worry. I want to enjoy coffee and read a book, not write about episodes that only prove how insane I've become.

I rinse the blood from my hand, feeling calmed by the sight of it turning pink as it circles the drain. I scrub my scalp raw with shampoo to correct the unkempt mess Jack saw this morning, and burnish my skin with the luffa until I'm sure I've welcomed the layer beneath. My flesh is so red and irritated that the cold water burns against it. *Good. Maybe this will teach me.*

***

I wrap my hair in a towel and head for the living room, where I'm greeted by the day's warm glow, as if the house is swathed in a ball of light. It feels new, and pure. Except for the red handprint marring the glass. A light scrub is all it takes to wipe it away, leaving the room looking as refreshed as I feel, and my confidence grows. *I can do this.*

When Jack returns, I will look confident and clean, I will act happy, and—no, I will *be* happy—and maybe I'll bake something so the house smells warm and inviting. He'd be ecstatic to walk in and see a plate of his favorite oatmeal chocolate chip cookies sitting on a clean white dish in the middle of our redone kitchen. It'll look just like a page out of Better Homes and Gardens, and he won't lose any sleep tonight.

After taking a stick of butter from the refrigerator to soften, I grab my book and head for the porch.

Before my new day has even begun, the book falls from my hand and slaps against the floor.

I hide behind the half-wall separating the porch from the living room and cautiously peek around the side of it, wondering whether my eyes are playing tricks on me again.

THE NOISE

A shadow approaches the door, followed by a knock on the glass, and I pull away to conceal myself.

Another knock, followed by a loud, "Hello!"

"Why are you hiding?"

"Why would I want to see her?"

"What would happen if you opened the door?" My dad asks.

"You know what would happen," I tell him. "We'd argue. Or worse, she'd give me a fake hug and act like we've reconnected just because I opened the door."

"You don't know that."

"I don't care to find out."

"I think you do care."

"Even if I did care, I shouldn't."

I dare to look in time to see her waving at someone as they pull into the driveway.

He shouldn't be home for a few more hours.

Jack sees my mother. I know he does, because his eyes are wide with alarm.

He runs so quickly that he reaches her before the door of his truck even slams shut, banging his leg against his front bumper in the process.

I watch them exchange words, though I have no way of knowing what they're talking about. Whatever he's saying, it works, because she walks back to her car, a crappy little black sedan with peeling paint and a crack in the windshield. A familiar wave of guilt rushes over me, guilt that she has to drive such a piece of shit while I'm living in a large house by the water. A run-down house, but large and by the water nonetheless.

Jack peers inside as he turns the key, stepping lightly as he enters.

"Hey," I say, startling him.

"Hey," is all he says. "I forgot some of my tools," he announces as he starts down the hallway with no mention of my mother whatsoever.

He reemerges, lugging his tool box under one arm, and kisses my forehead. "You smell nice."

"What did she say?"

He blinks the panic out of his eyes. "I wasn't sure if you saw. I didn't want to upset you."

"What was she doing here?"

"She came by to talk to me, actually. I don't know what about. I told her I was just on my way back out." He pauses in a way that lets me know I won't like whatever he's about to say next. "She asked if she could come by tomorrow. Said it's important."

"And?"

"I didn't know what to say. I blanked," he tells me, remorse flooding his voice.

"I *do not* want her here tomorrow. Or ever, for that matter."

THE NOISE

"I know, I'm really sorry. I swear I'd call her and tell her not to come, but I don't know her number. We always delete her messages."

"Then I don't want to be here when she comes," I say, hearing how childish the words sound the moment they exit my lips. "I'll stay in the den tomorrow," I press on anyway. "Just please tell her I'm not home?"

"Of course. I'm sorry, Angela."

"It's not your fault," I say, softening. It isn't his fault, after all. "She caught you off guard. She does that."

He wraps me in a warm hug, and I realize sawdust and metal aren't overpowering his usual scent of Endymion, like it almost always does when he comes home from the shop. Maybe he wasn't there long enough, I consider.

After Jack leaves for the second time this morning, I find myself staring at the door with disbelief that my mother was standing there not too long ago. That was the closest we've been in four months.

The door creaks open in my mind, allowing memories to slip out from the cracks. I try my hardest to slam it shut, but the weight from the other end is resilient.

We sat on her couch, to talk. We couldn't have been further away from each other, me on one end and her on the other, but the emotional distance between us was even greater.

Her house reeked of cigarettes. It was so strong that I only dared to breathe in small gasps, feeling like I was going to suffocate, and I already felt like I was suffocating. I noticed she'd taken down a picture, and there was a clean white square where it had once been, surrounded by yellow smoke stains. I couldn't figure out which picture she'd removed, but I assumed it was one of my dad.

"I want to talk about when dad passed," I began.

FOURTEEN

I've tried everything I can think of. I pruned the rose bushes, I wrote in my journal, I read, I even cleaned the toilet bowl. My spine fused from bending at the waist to scrub the porcelain, and it took just under ten minutes for me to fully straighten up, but even that wasn't enough to get my mind off of the incident.

I took a shower, hoping the pelting water would be louder than my memory, but it only forced me to remember the shower I'd taken four months ago. It reminded me of the hail, wind, rain, and my damp footprints leading up the stairs to the bathroom on the second floor.

Stop it.

I grab my journal once again and start for the porch. My wet hair slaps against the back of my shoulder blades with each fervent step, turning my pajama top into a soggy mess of fabric. It's only four-thirty in the afternoon and I'm already dressed for bed.

I never made Jack's oatmeal chocolate chip cookies, I realize as I plant myself down on the rocking chair, my hair drying almost instantly in the late afternoon sun. Maybe tomorrow.

I flip through my journal in search of a clean page with the intention of trying something new. Instead of writing about an episode, I'm going to write about something happy. I don't know what that will be yet, but I'm sure I can think of something. I'm sure I can.

My hopeful optimism is slashed with page after page of entries scribbled in the hand of an erratic person, each one further proof of how far gone I am. It's as if my journal is taunting me, reminding me that I've never written anything uplifting, only things that are dark and twisted. I'm struggling to hold on to any hope of feeling better today, and it shows in my posture as I slink down into myself.

Excitement jolts me upright as I come across a page that is legible, as if I was calm and composed when I wrote this. But my heart just as soon catches in my chest when I read the title: "homework."

The LPC assigned this to me at the end of my first visit. It's the same homework she didn't remember during my second, and last, visit. She told me to go home and write about the moment I started feeling different from other people. That was one of the things we spoke about. I told her I didn't feel normal

THE NOISE

compared to others, because everyone else seemed to have no problem waking up, day after day, going to work, doing their chores, eating right, or, alternatively, not caring about their health at all, having babies and baby showers and weddings and bridal showers, and whatever else. None of it felt right to me. Not anymore.

I trace my forefinger over the frayed center of my journal and think back on my attempts to find an answer for why I felt, why I *feel*, this way. I must have started the homework over a dozen times. Each attempt felt like I was lying to myself, like I was trying too hard to explain why I didn't feel normal, because the truth was that I just didn't know. I tried blaming it on being made fun of for my red hair when I was in middle school, or on my introverted personality, or on my relationship with my mother, or on my lack of sleep—though I didn't dare tell her about my episodes. All those things were true, but it wasn't until I wrote without thinking that I discovered the real reason I feel so different.

I sat down one morning, exhausted and empty, and decided to take the pressure off myself. I allowed myself to just think for a long while, as long as it took for my thoughts to go wherever they needed to. Once I felt calm and certain, I touched the pen to the page.

I trace my finger over the words and take in a long, deep breath.

ALLISON A

He was acting differently that morning. He and my mother had a fight the night before, so I was surprised to see him in such a good mood. Maybe good isn't the right word. More like...at peace. He seemed so oddly at peace.

He woke up early. It must have been before 4:00 because I was up at five and he was already dressed and had his coffee. He even filled all of our cars with gas. I know, because my tank was full when I drove to work a few hours later, and it was almost empty when I parked the night before.

When I came downstairs, dressed and ready to go, I saw he had a pot of sauce simmering on the stove. It was Mother's Day, and he was making spaghetti for dinner later.

He asked if I could call out of work and stay home, which surprised me. He knew how I felt about my mother, and I knew how he felt about her, too. It wasn't such an important day for either of us.

THE NOISE

On some level, I knew. I knew there was another reason he wanted me to stay home, but I pushed that feeling down, down down. I wish I hadn't.

I slam the journal closed, tears burning the edges of my eyes.

The LPC may have been a quack, but writing this entry actually helped me. I'd always wondered whether my feelings toward my mother were justified, or if I was just an angry teenager lashing out at a parent who I didn't prefer or understand fully. After I wrote this, I was reminded of how distraught I was when my dad passed. How I couldn't eat or sleep. How I wanted to die myself.

I remembered feeling as if my entire world had ended while life went on for everyone else. I remembered feeling like I no longer belonged. I remembered how I wasn't allowed to talk about him, and I remembered that I had, *have*, every right to be upset with my mother.

I tilt my head back and blink away the tears, then take a deep breath and open my journal once again. I skip through the pages, eager to erase the memory of my homework, until I land on an entry that shocks my muscles into stiffness. I know I shouldn't, especially because I've spent all morning trying to get away from it, but I can't seem to help myself.

I don't know what happened last night. I'm having a hard time remembering all of it. I remember sitting on her couch. I remember the oppressiveness of the cigarette smoke. I hated that stench when I used to live with her. I always stayed in my bedroom with the door closed and the windows open and the fan on, even in the dead of winter. I thought that if the smell got on me, then I would become just like her, and that was the last thing I wanted. But the smell clung to me last night. I couldn't escape it, and it made me so angry. Angrier than I knew how to control.

I rip the page from my journal, relishing in the distraction of tiny paper cuts which slash the inside of my palm as I ball it up in a tight fist.

My body knows what it's doing before my mind can catch up, and I go along with it, partly because I have very little will power remaining, but also because I'm hoping it knows something I don't, something that will help me forget. After tearing open the porch door, I follow myself into the side yard, toward the garbage, where I lift the lid and heave the entry into the bin.

I consider why I chose this garbage can when the one in the kitchen was much closer and the floor in the house isn't wet and muddy. I'm sure it was because I didn't want to chance

THE NOISE

Jack seeing the entry. If he did, then he'd know I was reminiscing, and he'd either want to discuss what happened or he'd start treating me like I'm fragile, even more so than he already does. He'd start doing that thing he did four months ago, where he'd ask me how I'm doing all day every day.

What is that?

Something in the bin catches my eye.

It looks at first to be a glossy square of white silk, or maybe ribbon.

It's an incomplete sheet of labels, I realize. The white velvet material beneath those which have been peeled glints off the passing sun, glowing like some kind of nefarious treasure. I ignore the stench of rotting garbage and reach in.

It's a sheet of barcode labels. I know, because I used the same brand of labels to catalog books when I worked at the library. But these labels weren't used for books. The two which haven't been peeled from the sheet look more like prescription labels, like the kind on my pill bottles.

They *are* the labels from my pill bottles.

The name Angela Blau stares me in the face, along with the dosage and instructions I always try to forget. The labels look almost perfect, except for two errors—an ink smudge over the letters "Bl" in my last name, and a misspelling of Sulfasalzine, spelled instead as Suldasalazine.

The only person who could have put these here is Jack. I certainly didn't do it. *Why would he do this?*

ALLISON A

Stop. Think rationally about this.

It could have been the pharmacy, I consider. Maybe they messed up on a few labels and accidentally put them in the bag along with my medicine. Maybe Jack saw this and threw them away, in the bin on the side of the house rather than in the kitchen, so I wouldn't be concerned.

That makes sense. Doesn't it?

He knows how I feel about my medications. I would understand if he didn't want to cause me even more stress by allowing this error to get in my head. If I'm being honest with myself, I might have wondered how good the pharmacy is at their job if they can't even spell the name of the medication correctly, and I very well might have used that as an excuse not to take it.

I don't have to look to recognize the sound of Jack's tires bounding over the pothole in the driveway.

I drop the labels back into the garbage, close the lid, and try my hardest to appear innocent, like I've been picking roses this whole time, in my pajamas, without any sheers.

"Hey," he calls over the slamming of his truck door. I look over in a way I hope says *oh, hey, I didn't see you pull up.*

He bends down, pizza box hoisted under one arm, and greets me with a kiss. I keep my eyes open, searching his expression for, well, I'm not sure what. For whether he's onto me, I suppose. For whether he knows something I don't. For whether

THE NOISE

my explanation of the labels is correct. For whether I can trust him, after all these years together.

For the brief moment his eyes are closed, he looks content. Happy, even. As soon as he opens them and takes notice of the state I'm in, however, concern takes over. He looks me up and down, noticing the mud stains circling the cuffs of my pants.

I swear I see his eyes flash to the bin for a fraction of a second before he looks to the handful of roses I carelessly yanked, stems split and stringy like celery, and then to me.

"I picked fresh ones this morning," he tells me, suspicion hovering in the air as I search for an acceptable excuse.

"I saw a few were dying on the bush, and…and I thought I should give them a proper send-off in the vase inside," I scramble, trying too hard to seem natural.

It seems to take forever, but he eventually softens and allows his smile to return, though I can't tell whether it's forced.

"Hungry?" he asks, and we head inside together.

***

After ringing the last bit of excess water from my hair, I head into the kitchen, wearing the fresh pair of pajamas Jack left beside the shower for me. Thanks to the muddy ground outside, it was my second shower of the day, and I have to admit it felt good. I haven't felt this clean in a long time, and it helps me think more clearly.

Jack is setting up plates and drinking glasses on the counter, my prescription bottles waiting idly nearby. By the smell of it, he got my favorite chicken Parmesan pizza from Attello's. I can practically taste the ricotta cheese from here.

"How did it go today?" I ask as I climb up onto the stool.

"What do you mean?"

"The shop?"

"Oh, right. It went well. Nothing major to report."

"You're home earlier than normal."

"I got sidetracked and decided to call it a day."

"Sidetracked?"

"Just one of those days."

He opens a cabinet above the microwave, and as he stretches to reach the napkins, the bottom of his flannel shirt pulls up just enough for me to notice a folded piece of paper in the back pocket of his jeans. I don't remember seeing that when he left this morning.

It's something so trivial, and I know I shouldn't focus too much on things like this or else my thoughts will get away from me, but he clearly didn't go to the shop today. At least, he wasn't there the entire time. Otherwise, he'd smell more strongly of sawdust.

Before I know it, my mind is speeding full steam ahead, scanning the paper, recalling the labels in the bin, and I feel the sudden need to test him.

"I think I'll call the Doctor tomorrow and schedule an appointment."

THE NOISE

He turns so abruptly that a few napkins evade his grasp, floating silently to the floor like snowflakes. "Why? Is something wrong?"

"No," I say, studying him as he snatches up the rogue white squares. "It's been five months since my last check-up, that's all."

"And you're *sure* nothing is wrong?"

"Nothing more than usual."

He rests his fists on the countertop, napkins crumpling within them, drops his head, and releases a long breath. I can't tell whether he's relieved or trying to calm his nerves. I need to test him more.

He raises his gaze and opens his mouth to say something, but the words die in his throat. He looks like a parent trying to figure out how to explain something to a child in a way that won't frighten them.

"The Doctor said you only need to come in every six months."

"Right, but I also wanted to talk to him about possibly switching medications," I say, hoping for a reaction, as if it would somehow prove something.

His jaw clenches, but he gives nothing else away.

"But the medications you're taking now have been working, haven't they?"

"I just want to see if there's something else out there," I explain. "Something I don't know about."

ALLISON A

He goes on setting up for dinner without saying another word, as if the conversation never happened. *He's nervous.*

No, he's worried.

Minutes pass in complete silence. He takes great care to arrange my plate, gives me the largest piece of pizza in the box, and sets out my favorite kind of soda. He even puts garlic powder in front of me, because he knows how much I like it.

He's guilty.

Or, I'm a terrible person. A terrible wife.

He may not know what I've silently accused him of, but that is of little consolation. I've been untrusting of the only person who loves me. I've been ungrateful for everything he's done, and continues to do, for me. Now I've made him worry I'm getting sicker, or that my medications aren't working, or that they *are* working, but I want to shop around for others, just for the fun of it.

I'm sure he remembers the adjustment period I went through when I started taking my current medication. I'm sure he remembers the nausea, dizziness, stomach pains, and insomnia, and I'm sure he's wondering why I'd want to go through that again.

I think back to the first night I started Sulfasalazine, when I threw up all over the air mattress. He scrubbed it clean and washed the bedding without a single complaint. He was elbow deep in my puke while I took a nice, hot shower. I hate that I

THE NOISE

did that to him. That I'm *doing* this to him. *How could I be suspicious of someone who's only ever cared for me?*

It's just a white piece of paper. It could be anything.

It could be anything.

This is the same man who wakes up in the middle of the night to cover my feet with the blanket. The same man who rubs my head just to calm me down and help me sleep when those same hands are exhausted from working hard all day.

Without my consent, my mind runs back to the labels in the garbage can. I'm certain they're the same ones I used at the library, the ones I brought home after I left my job and stored in the basement, along with everything else from my old desk. The pharmacy could use the same labels too, I suppose. Or Jack could have taken them from downstairs.

What is he hiding from me?

"Do you need help?" I ask him.

"No, I can take care of everything."

"Are you sure?"

ALLISON A

FIFTEEN

I haven't heard the noise all day, I realize, as Jack collects my empty mug and plate of crumbs from the cookies he put out earlier.

"It's almost seven," he announces, turning for the bathroom.

"I'll get them," I say, stopping him. "I have to go anyway," I lie, remorse creeping in as I watch him fluff the pillows on the couch for when I return.

I close and lock the bathroom door behind me, then snatch the pill bottles from the medicine cabinet. Under the fluorescent light, I carefully inspect the labels, searching for any sign of foul play. They look perfectly fine, as far as I can tell. I've never paid much attention to what they usually look like, so I wouldn't know how accurate they are, but I don't see any obvious mistakes.

Of course they're fine. It's Jack.

THE NOISE

I dump an array of medication into my hand and lift the pills to my mouth, but I can't bring myself to go through with it.

Jack is loving, dependable, and honest, so why can't I take these stupid pills he refilled for me?

I try again, and fail.

I quietly dump the pills back into their respective bottles and run the faucet for as long as it would have taken me to guzzle eight ounces of water, just in case Jack is within earshot.

I peek around the corner of the bathroom door to check whether he has been listening, and I see an old man standing in our kitchen.

I do a double-take. *Am I seeing things?*

He isn't the kind of specter I'm used to. He looks like a real person.

I take a few steps down the hall, allowing the man to come into full view.

He is *a real person.*

He's talking with Jack, who looks at me from the corner of his eye.

He's not a tall man, but he was probably a bit taller earlier in life, before his spine curved enough to shrink him a few inches. I assume he's in his eighties, judging by his loose skin and glassy eyes. To his credit, he's kept almost a full head of curly white hair which orbits a shiny bald spot. He's dressed simply—blue jeans and a dark blue pullover, the collar of a green plaid button-down emerging from the top.

ALLISON A

I can't tell where I know him from, but he looks familiar. If he lives in town, then it's possible I've seen him around, even though I never go anywhere. He could have been a gawker who walked past our house one day, I suppose.

"We bought this house eight months ago, back in February,"

Jack says, gesturing in my direction as if to casually introduce me so I don't scare the man with my sudden appearance. He doesn't seem startled, though. He looks briefly in my direction, smiles, then returns his gaze to Jack.

I notice a bouquet of white roses laid out on the counter, but before I have the chance to ask where they came from, the phone rings, causing Jack to jump as if it's a noise he's never heard before.

He looks afraid to answer the call, like he doesn't want to take his eyes off the man. *Should I be afraid of this person? Are we in danger?*

"Do you need to get that?" the man asks.

Jack hesitates, then turns to grab the phone before just as quickly turning back around to face the two of us.

"Hey," he says to whoever is on the other line. Rob, I'm sure. "Yeah, sure, okay, hold on." He turns halfway to retrieve a pen from the junk drawer and scribbles something on an old Attello's menu.

Unsure if I should properly introduce myself to this potentially dangerous stranger, I decide a nod and a brief smile is sufficient for now. Just as the man returns a nod, Jack hangs up and pivots back to us.

"Everything alright?" the man asks.

I can't tell if Jack is looking at me or the man, or at the space between us, when he answers, "Just the animal shelter. They don't need me to volunteer tomorrow. They gave me a different day instead."

"Oh, you volunteer?" The man asks, impressed.

"When I have some free time."

"I used to volunteer myself."

"Oh yeah? Where?"

"Well, I was an ER doctor for some time. After I retired, I couldn't seem to stay away." He tries to laugh, but a wheeze comes out instead. After a short coughing fit, he composes himself and continues. "So, I went back to volunteer. I mainly provided comfort to patients who were on the verge, though I found they didn't need it as much."

"I'm not following."

"Most dying patients get more attention than they ever have in their lives. Last time they ever will. It's the dead who need it more." He laughs again, this time with more success, and adds, "I'm sorry, I haven't had much interaction with others in a while. My wife and I divorced, and it's just me now."

"I'm sorry to hear that."

"I'm sorry too," I say.

"Which hospital did you work for?" Jack asks.

"A hospital up north."

"Century Medical Center?" Jack asks, likely remembering that time six years ago when he rushed me there for stomach pain that turned out to be appendicitis. I was in surgery less than an hour later. I'll never forget waking up in the hospital bed to find it was dark outside and that Jack hadn't left my side the entire night.

That's *the man you're suspicious of.*

"Something like that."

A few moments of awkward silence later, Jack says, "Well, thanks again for stopping by, Arlo. The flowers are beautiful."

Arlo.

"I'm sorry I haven't come by sooner. I wanted to welcome you to the neighborhood months ago, but there's been a lot going on," Arlo explains. I assume he's referring to his divorce, and I'm sure Jack assumes the same, and neither of us pushes the issue. "Anyway, I hope you enjoy the roses."

"Come by again any time," Jack says, handing Arlo his hat.

Jack clearly wants the man to leave, but I'm not sure why. He seems nice. We never even offered him something to drink.

"Where did you say you lived again?" Jack asks.

"A few houses down," Arlo answers, lazily pointing to the left. "Well, I should get going."

Both Jack and I walk Arlo to the door, saying "goodnight" at the same time.

THE NOISE

Jack holds the door open as Arlo walks through, then watches over him as he ambles down the steps and onto steady ground.

"Nice to meet you," Arlo says, offering a wave before heading into the dark.

"I didn't even hear him knock," I tell Jack as he closes and locks the door.

"He didn't," he tells me. "I was heading for the porch to turn off the light, and he was just standing there."

"And you invited him in?"

"It scared me at first, but he said he was just about to knock. He was holding those," he nods to the roses.

"Who visits their neighbors this late at night?"

"I don't know. That's why I was weary of leaving you alone with him," he tells me, and I nod, understanding now. "But after talking to him, I think he might just be lonely, and out of practice with social interaction," Jack says as he adds Arlo's roses to a clean vase and fills it with water.

While Jack looks for a suitable location for the vase, my eyes wander to the porch windows, half expecting to see Arlo standing where Jack found him earlier. Instead, I see him walking down the street, off to the right, in the opposite direction of where he said he lived.

SIXTEEN

I don't remember getting out of bed, but as I stand here, staring down at Jack while he sleeps, I realize I must have. He looks passive, and peaceful. I wonder if this is how he would always look if he'd never met me.

"The gunman entered the first classroom, where he shot and killed fourteen children, as well as two adults." A woman's voice breaks through the stillness. "He then entered the second classroom," the voice continues, though I have no idea where it's coming from. Whoever she is, she sounds professional and restrained. Her only goal is to state facts. "In the second classroom, he murdered two more adults, and," she pauses, finally choking on the emotion she's been holding back, "six more children."

A burst of white light fills the living room, blinding me.

THE NOISE

I shield my eyes from the intense glare, then split two fingers to peer through, searching for the source.

There's a television mounted above the fireplace mantel. It's a small, silver flat screen from the early 2000s, with netted speakers on either side. A middle-aged blonde woman sobs into a napkin as she struggles to find the composure she held moments ago.

We don't own a television.

I look back down at Jack, surprised this hasn't woken him. Only Jack is nowhere to be seen. I search the room for any sign of him, but it's not only him that's missing—everything we own has been replaced.

The kitchen backsplash is no longer the white subway tile I love. It's now blue striped wallpaper. The cabinets aren't green, but a rich chestnut. The floor in the hallway is still hardwood, but it lacks the shine from when Jack refinished it. It's dull and scratched, and it practically melts into the burnt umber walls climbing from floor to ceiling.

Something soft twists between my bare toes. I'm standing on a plush red rug. I trace the rug back to the fireplace, where the air mattress has been replaced by two brown corduroy armchairs, each one revealing the tops of two strangers' heads.

Stone blue light floods in from the window and washes over the room, eating away at the darkness. As I turn to look at the changing scenery outside, I find it's snowing. Seconds later, the fireplace roars to life, encouraging sparks to dance against the grate. Despite the orange flames, I don't feel anything, neither cold nor heat. It's as if I'm not even here.

"The gunman took his own life, ending the rampage in less than eleven minutes," the voice continues, drawing my attention back to the television.

I remember this.

Jack and I were in New York City, on our way to Madison Square Garden to see The Killers perform live, when we noticed people stopped in the street, still as statues, staring up at the Mega Screen. We joined them, gaping in horror as news reports flooded in, detailing a horrific school shooting at Sandy Hook Elementary.

This can't be right. That was 2012. That was ten years ago.

It sounds like firecrackers at first, coming from the back den. It isn't until the person sitting in the chair on the right drops their wine, the fragile glass exploding against the hardwood, that I realize what's happening.

A window has shattered.

Frozen with fear, neither person moves as footsteps bound down the hallway, rattling the red wine as it oozes through the cracks in the floor.

I squirm beneath the icy sheets, sheets that are usually soft cotton but are now more like cool silk from the frigid temperature in the house. I can't get comfortable. I look at the clock on the stove and realize it's two in the morning, and that the cold air has aggravated my joints and woken me up.

THE NOISE

It feels as if someone is pulling on each of my limbs, trying to rip them from their sockets, and my heart flutters like a butterfly struggling to escape the captivity of my rib cage. Skipping my medications was a mistake.

Pounding commences from somewhere unseen, and I shoot up, beads of sweat encumbering my head as it swivels around the room, searching my surroundings. I tune in for the thundering footsteps I suddenly recall hearing mere moments ago, and release my breath only when I'm comforted by the realization that it's raining. I glance to the kitchen, finding solace in the white tile backsplash and green cabinets. Everything is back to how it should be.

It was only a dream.

I ease back onto my elbows and take in a deep breath to calm the palpitations hammering at my chest wall. I try the bear down technique my doctor taught me, the one where you push like you're going to the bathroom. It's supposed to reset your heart rate back to its normal rhythm. It works for all of five seconds before the fluttering sensation takes hold again.

I stretch and crack each fused joint one by one, starting with my neck and continuing on to my chest, shoulders, elbows, wrists, fingers, back, hips, knees, ankles, and toes. To my dismay, I hardly feel any relief. It will take hours to fully recover from this stiffness.

Careful not to wake Jack, I army-crawl to the bathroom door, my pajamas ruffling and catching periodically on the nails in the hardwood. Though I can't see much in the dark, I'm certain they're now ripped and will have to be tossed in the garbage, but that's the least of my concerns. I need to stop these palpitations, and the only other technique I know of is a hot shower.

Once I reach the bathroom, I clutch the toilet seat and use it to push myself to a kneeling position. A searing pain prevents me from straightening my spine all the way, and I choke back tears as I realize I will have to continue on my knees.

I stagger into the shower, silently suffering through each hard knock of my kneecaps against the tile floor. At least I can barely feel the left one.

I turn the knob as far left as it will go, then offer my poor bones a reprieve by curling up like a pill bug beneath the hot steam.

Minutes go by with my skin roasting under the scalding water, but the pounding in my chest persists. I try to bear down again, but there is no relief from this.

Each palpitation feels like my heart will either jump from my chest or stop altogether, and I can't help but wonder if this is what my dad felt just before it happened. *Did he feel a jump and then nothing, or did his heart stop before he had the chance to feel anything at all?* I hope it was the last one, because this would be a terrible thing to feel during your last moments here on Earth.

THE NOISE

My mind spins with the fear that my last moment could happen any second now, and what would I have to show for my life? I've done absolutely nothing to impact the world in any way. I can barely impact my own home. The only thing I've impacted is Jack, and I've done so in the worst way possible. I've turned a thirty-three-year-old man into a caretaker. Worse, I can't even take my goddamn medications without him reminding me. Or at all, apparently. Who knows what I've done to my body that he will now have to deal with, all because of a fucking piece of paper.

Maybe I should give in to the palpitations. Maybe I should let them take me.

I stretch my arms out, reaching for something, anything, but there's nothing except the cold portion of the shower floor the steam hasn't yet warmed. The chill of it shocks and instantly exhausts me, as if I've expended all my remaining energy just by being surprised. My eyes close, and I allow it. I allow pang after pang in my chest, and I sink into nothingness.

***

I wake to the sound of the faucet squeaking off, followed less than a second later by the sensation of being wrapped in a dry towel.

"Angela," a panicked voice drifts in. "Hey, wake up."

My eyes slowly open, but fatigue has blurred my vision. I can see enough to recognize his sharp jawline and stormy blue-gray eyes crawling out of the steam.

ALLISON A

"Are you okay?"

"I'm...I'm fine," I mumble.

"You could have drowned," he scolds me, the tone of his voice rising now that he knows I'm alive. "Your face was right under the shower head."

"I'm...sorry."

"Jesus Christ," he swears as he lifts me from the shower floor. I can hear the water from my wet body sloshing over the tile, then the hardwood, and finally the air mattress.

Before I can say anything, he wraps me with blankets, pulls me close to his warm, dry chest, and begins running his fingers through my hair straight away. His hand shakes with nerves as he wrestles through the tangles of my wet strands, and I'm awake enough now to wish the palpitations had won.

"I'm so sorry, Jack. I didn't mean to scare you. I just...had trouble sleeping is all, so I took a shower, and I guess I fell asleep. I'm sorry," I say, not daring to tell him the truth, which is that I don't trust him and therefore skipped my medications and ended up here.

"It's okay. You don't need to apologize."

Yes, I do.

"I didn't mean to scare you, I promise. I didn't mean to fall asleep."

A long sigh escapes him. He presses his lips to my forehead and grips me beneath the sheets, his hold unyielding, like he's afraid of what will happen if I slip away again.

THE NOISE

"It's okay, okay? You don't have to apologize, for anything."

"But I—"

"I'm sure, okay? I promise I'm still sure."

SEVENTEEN

I don't know how long I've been awake. Over three hours, I think. It was two hours ago when I watched the rising sun chase away the shadows of night on the ceiling. It was an hour ago when Jack woke up. It was sometime after that when he brought me my medications. I figure it must be past seven. How far past, I have no idea.

My heart and my body feel a little better now that the medicine is coursing through my veins once again. Things might be getting back to normal, whatever normal means, except my mind feels as heavy as my bones did hours ago. I don't want to see her today. Or ever, for that matter. I need time to rest and recover. So does Jack, I know.

"I'm sorry about last night." Jack says as he curls up beside me on the air mattress.

"You're not the one who should be apologizing."

THE NOISE

"I'm sorry you felt you couldn't wake me up," he tells me, the backs of his knuckles caressing my cheek. "I don't care about sleep. What I care about is not finding you like that again." He sucks in a breath. "I thought you'd drowned."

"I didn't mean to scare you. I couldn't sleep is all."

He presses his forehead against mine and closes his eyes. "I worry about you," he says, his voice nearly a whisper.

"I know. I wish I was better for you," I admit, my eyes growing damp. "I'm sorry."

"Hey," he says, brushing his thumb over a stray tear. "You're perfect for me."

"Yeah." A sarcastic laugh escapes me.

"*For me*," he says, his gaze imploring.

"I'll do better," I promise him, and I hope I mean it.

"I don't need you to do better. I just want you to wake me if you ever need me. All I care about is you."

"I feel like I'm draining the life from you."

"If something happened to you, *that* would drain the life from me."

"I *am* sorry, Jack," I say. "For last night, and for today."

"It'll be fine. Everything will be fine," he says, leaning back. "She probably just misses you."

"She's not coming here to speak with me," I remind him, trying hard to conceal my rising annoyance. After what I did last night, he has a get out of jail free card today.

"Do you truly believe she doesn't love you?" He asks, unknowingly testing my patience.

"I'm sure she thinks she does. Or, I'm sure she tries to convince herself she does, because it's better than admitting she's a terrible mother and never should have been one."

"Maybe she doesn't know how to show it," he suggests half-heartedly.

"If someone is loved, they know it."

"Listen, why don't I help you out of bed?" Jack asks, propping himself up on his elbows. "If you lay here too much longer, it'll be harder for you to get up, and after last night…" he trails off, but I know what he means, and he's right. Despite how badly I want to lie here all day with his fingers running through my hair and just rest, it would cause more pain than I'm already in, which would create more worry than he already has. Besides, she'll be here soon, and I want to be hidden in the den by then.

With his help, I sit up on the mattress, plant my feet on the floor, and allow myself to be pulled to a standing position.

"You should keep moving," he tells me. "At least for a little while."

I nod, my face crumpling at the pain surging through my body as he hands me my cane.

"How about you show me your plans for the bathroom?" I ask, remembering him saying he wants to tackle that room

THE NOISE

next. I figure it's a short and easy walk to begin working through the stiffness.

With one hand on my lower back and the other trailing along the wall for added support, he guides me to the bathroom doorway. He cradles his arm around my shoulders, allowing me to list into him, as we look out over the space. I would worry that bearing the weight of my entire body is too much for him if he didn't feel so sturdy. He doesn't even look like he's struggling to hold me up. His soft eyes scan me over, checking to see that I'm okay, before he details his plans.

"First will be the toilet and the shower," he says, keeping a watchful eye on me. "Hopefully, both on the same day, so we can keep using the bathroom while I finish the rest. The tile is good, so I won't have to rip that up."

"Why don't we work on the stairs next?" I interrupt him. "Then, we can fix the second-floor bathroom while we use the one down here, so we don't have to rush?" *We,* as if. But it's too hard to say *while you fix the one down here,* because then I'm a drill sergeant barking orders rather than a loving wife trying to figure out the best solution.

He hesitates, and I wonder if he's thrown off by my use of the word *we* or by my suggestion to fix the stairs.

"I'm not sure I can fix the stairs, to be honest," he admits. "I think I'll have to call in an expert. I haven't found one yet."

He can fix anything, but he can't fix stairs?

How hard is it to find a stair expert?

ALLISON A

Do those even exist?

The urge to ask him about the paper I saw in his pocket parts my lips, but then the memory of him finding me on the shower floor floods in and they promptly seal themselves shut.

There's a knock on the door.

I don't have to look to know it's her.

"Hello! Anyone there?" My mother calls. "Jack? Door!"

I remember going to the home improvement store with her a few years ago. She was looking for copper nails to hammer into the roots of a tree in her yard after reading that doing so would kill it. She didn't want to pay someone to take the tree down, and she thought this DIY hack would be a cheaper alternative. It didn't work, from what I remember.

"Hey! Screws this way?" She called to a cashier, who was about fifty yards away and very confused. He didn't have a chance to answer before she kept walking in that direction anyway, chest puffed out, arms swinging from side to side. I wondered what the point of yelling to him was if she already knew where she was going, but I guessed it was just an excuse to be loud. She has always seemed to like being loud, which confused me as a child because my dad was the complete opposite. As I got older, I realized the same thing he did, which is that being loud makes her feel heard, because she's never known how to express herself otherwise. Unfortunately for me, the louder people are, the quieter I become, and the less I myself feel heard.

THE NOISE

Jack's face melts into a look of remorse, and I know it isn't only from inviting her here. He just helped me up, and now he has to hide me away, at my stubborn request, and worry about me turning into a fused woman while he entertains my mother.

"It's okay," I tell him. "I'm feeling a lot better."

He doesn't believe me, but before I can attempt to convince him, he's already carrying a blanket into the back den and spreading it over the sawdust-covered ground. He lifts the air mattress as if it weighs nothing and lugs it down the hallway, placing it atop the blanket. He sets up a book, for company, and lays down another blanket, in case I get cold, and I want to slap myself for how suspicious and ungrateful I've been.

"Hello!" my mother calls again, growing impatient as Jack eases me onto the air mattress.

Her daughter—who also lives here, by the way—has AS. Doesn't she stop to think for even a second that maybe that's what's taking so long?

"I love you," Jack says as he places a kiss on my lips. "If you need me, knock, okay? I'll make something up so she won't know you're here. Just, let me know if you need anything, anything at all—"

"I'll knock," I tell him.

He forces a smile, but it's only half convincing. He's not happy at all to leave me here, I know, but I can't go out there. I can't see her.

"Jack!"

"Knock." He tells me once more, and I nod.

My mother's voice is suddenly louder, letting me know Jack has invited her inside.

"Beautiful house," I hear her say. "I don't know what you've done to it, since this is the first time I've been inside," she comments, breaking her own personal record for the amount of time it takes for her passive aggressiveness to rear its ugly head. "From what I can see, it looks great."

"It's just these few rooms that are done for now," Jack explains. I can tell they're in the kitchen because one of them has stepped on the creaking floorboard by the refrigerator.

"What about upstairs?"

"I haven't touched that yet."

"Right," she says. "Would it be okay if I took a peek anyway?"

"I'm sorry, no."

"No?"

"I'd prefer it if we stayed on the first floor," he tells her.

I might wonder why he's being so elusive about the rot if I didn't already know the answer. My mother has a tendency to act on impulse, and I wouldn't be surprised if she tested the stairs by running up and down them before Jack could utter a single warning against it.

"Gotcha."

"Do you want coffee?"

THE NOISE

"What about the back rooms?" She asks, her footsteps already approaching. "I haven't seen those."

"Nothing to see." Jack's voice is desperate, and I'm as relieved as I'm sure he is when her footsteps stop. "Just sawdust and work tools at the moment."

They recede back into the kitchen.

"Black."

"What?"

"I take it black," she clarifies, referring to the coffee Jack offered her.

My mother's horrid coffee breath made me despise the beverage all the way through my mid-twenties. She would drink it first thing every morning, with a side of diet coke, and wash it all down with a cigarette. I remember having a migraine once, the kind not even four Excedrin could fix, and I was so desperate for the pain to stop that I sipped a cup of her black coffee, hoping the caffeine would help. It barely touched it, and I was so disappointed with the stench of my own breath that I swore off ever being in the same room as coffee again.

Years later, when Jack and I were visiting his parents, another migraine took hold. I'd forgotten the promise I made to myself, and I tried it again. That time, though, Jack poured me a mug of cinnamon-flavored coffee and added French vanilla creamer, and I was hooked instantly. Turns out, I don't hate coffee. I just hate anything that reminds me of her.

A stool scuffs against the kitchen floor.

ALLISON A

"So," my mother begins, matter-of-factly, as if she's preparing to catch him in a lie. "How have you been doing?"

"Not too bad. Everything's going okay over here," he answers. He and I both know that not everything has been okay, but I appreciate him keeping her out of the loop.

"That's great to hear. I'm glad you seem to be doing well."

I wait for her to ask Jack how I've been doing, seeing as though she's been harassing me with voicemails for months, but she doesn't. Knowing my mother, she's waiting for him to offer up that information, so she doesn't seem too desperate. After all, why would you want to show too much concern for your child?

After twenty minutes, but what seems like hours, of them making painful small talk over his shop and her going for her Nurse's license, Jack finally asks what brought her by.

"Well," she starts, and I can hear the excitement in her voice from here. "I have some news, and I wanted to tell you in person rather than over the phone, seeing as this is likely the last…well, hopefully not the last, but maybe the last time we see each other."

"I'm not following."

"I sold my house," she says, pausing for dramatic effect. I know her so well that I can imagine her face in this moment—like a child's all lit up with glee, penciled eyebrows raised, false eyelashes fluttering, the tips of her fingers gingerly covering her thin lips. "I'm moving to Tennessee!"

THE NOISE

"What? Why?" Jack asks, sounding as shocked as I feel.

Tennessee? Why there? Why now? Why so far?

"There's nothing here anymore, Jack," she tells him, her voice hardening. She was expecting him to be happy for her, no questions asked.

"Your daughter is here."

"No, she's not. Not anymore," she tells him, the words spilling out without a single shred of difficulty. "Look, I know this must be hard for you to hear, but I need to do this, for me. Quite honestly, you should think about doing the same."

"What are you talking about?"

She takes in a breath, as if what she's going to say next will be difficult, though I'm sure it won't be that hard. "You're consumed by Angela. I know you can't see it, but I see it. Take it from me—it won't lead anywhere good. I promise you that. Look, I love my daughter more than anything in the world, but this is not healthy for you."

"I—" he begins, but she stops him.

In the gentlest voice I've ever heard her use, she says, "I've always thought of you like a son, and I don't want to see my son get hurt."

Their conversation continues, but I can't make out what they're saying through my muffled cries. I feel the same way now as I did when my dad passed, like I have to keep my pain silent so she doesn't hear it. Back then, I had to be quiet so she wouldn't get angry that I was upset, because that would have taken the attention away from her and her quest for happiness. I would sit in my room and cry as quietly as I could until my eyes were sore and my head pounded and I couldn't breathe. I would cry for so long that I wouldn't realize I was hungry until my stomach gnawed at me, but I was too afraid to get something to eat for fear she would see the red blotches on my face. Now, I'm quiet so she doesn't know I'm here. I might as well not be here at all.

"It's alright," my dad tells me as he pulls me close to his chest.

He used to hug me this way when I was a little girl. He would pull me in so tight that I couldn't even move a finger. I was so amused by it, and I'd laugh wildly as I tried to wiggle free, though I didn't actually want to get away. He'd tell me he was never letting go, and I would smirk and ask him how I would eat, or sleep, or go to school, believing I was outsmarting him. He'd always say the same thing—

"You'll figure it out."

As hard as I pulled away, he'd only hold on tighter.

In all the years I've pulled away from my mother, she's only ever let me go.

EIGHTEEN

He was acting differently that morning. He and my mother had a fight the night before, so I was surprised to see him in such a good mood. Maybe good isn't the right word. More like...at peace. He seemed so oddly at peace.

He woke up early. It must have been before 4:00 because I was up at five and he was already dressed and had his coffee. He even filled all of our cars with gas. I know, because my tank was full when I drove to work a few hours later, and it was almost empty when I parked the night before.

ALLISON A

When I came downstairs, dressed and ready to go, I saw he had a pot of sauce simmering on the stove. It was Mother's Day, and he was making spaghetti for dinner later.

He asked if I could call out of work and stay home, which surprised me. He knew how I felt about my mother, and I knew how he felt about her, too. It wasn't such an important day for either of us.

On some level, I knew. I knew there was another reason he wanted me to stay home, but I pushed that feeling down, down down. I wish I hadn't.

After packing my lunch, I realized I'd forgotten to grab my ID badge, so I went upstairs to get it. I had to pass my mother's sewing room on the way, and it was there I saw my dad sitting cross-legged on the floor a few feet from her as she worked on a toddler's shirt. The warm yellow sun was intent as it encased him, like it had risen for that moment only. I'll never forget that image of him, sheathed in light and practically glowing, or how odd it was that he was in that room to begin with. And smiling, nonetheless.

THE NOISE

Like I said, my parents fought the night before, and to see him so at peace was confusing, almost unnerving. On top of that, he had COPD, which prevented him from trekking up the stairs whenever he could avoid it. Yet, he made the trip that morning.

Both he and I went back downstairs, he to tend to his pot of sauce and me to slip into my sneakers. The last thing I said to him before I left the house was, "I'll see you later. I love you."

I worked in a theme park at the time, drawing henna tattoos on guests. I was in the middle of tattooing a cowboy hat on a middle-aged woman's breast when my phone rang. I didn't answer it, but I knew. I don't know how I knew, but I did, and I didn't want to face it.

My phone went to voicemail. Then it started ringing again, and then it went to voicemail again, and then it rang, and rang, and rang. It kept ringing until, finally, I stopped what I was doing and handed the henna pen to my boss. I walked a few feet behind the cart, answered the call, and my life changed forever.

ALLISON A

"Hello?"

"Angie, you have to come home," the voice on the other end said. It was my neighbor, Carmine.

"What's going on?"

"You just have to come home."

"Tell me."

"Just...just come home, okay?"

"Say it," I demanded, but all he did was weep into the phone. "Say it!"

"Your dad is dead."

I don't remember if I hung up, or if the phone slipped from my hand, or if Carmine hung up and I put the phone in my pocket. I just remember crying, and then screaming. I didn't know sounds like that could come out of me before that day. I didn't know a human being was capable of making those sounds. My supervisor tried to hug me—because what else could she do?—while I continued to scream, "My dad is dead! My dad is dead!" I remember looking up and meeting the gaze of the woman with the

THE NOISE

cowboy hat tattoo, her eyes wide with horror as the brim turned to sludge between her breasts in the hot sun.

The ambulance brought my dad to a local hospital, which made sense. But, whenever he was sick in the past, he would always go to the hospital my mother worked at, the one that was forty-five minutes away. The logical part of my brain hadn't yet processed what was happening, and I assumed that's where he was, so that's where I went. I thought he would smile at me as I walked through the doorway of his room, like he always did. I thought he would tell me to sit on the bed beside him. I thought we'd look through the hospital menu together and pretend to consider the options, all while knowing we were going to order a pizza and sneak it past the nurses. I thought that because I wanted that. I wanted that more than anything.

As soon as I parked, my mother called to ask when I would arrive, and it was then I realized I was in the wrong place. Not only did I let him die alone on the kitchen floor, but it took me over an hour to get to him.

ALLISON A

When I arrived at the right hospital, I sprinted from my car, through the doors, and charged down the hallway, only to come to an abrupt stop in the doorway of a room I will never forget. My dad wasn't sitting there smiling at me. His bed was lifted to prop him up. He was still, and quiet. He looked like he was sleeping, and I convinced myself that maybe he was, that maybe I misheard my neighbor's words.

My mother stood beside his bed, sniffling, but there were no tears. My neighbor, who'd found him when he stopped by to drop something off, was sitting on the floor inside the doorway. He was good friends with my dad, and his eyes and face were red, like he'd cried everything he had inside of him. My aunt and uncle, on my mother's side, stood with their backs against the far wall. Their faces were blank.

Everyone seemed to stop breathing when they saw me standing there, like this was the moment they'd all been waiting for. I took a step toward him, and there was an unspoken understanding in that room that he and I were

THE NOISE

the closest any parent and child could be, and that this moment would monumentally shape the rest of my life.

When I reached his bed, it was easy to convince myself that he was in fact sleeping, that everyone had gotten it wrong. His skin wasn't pale at all. It was still tanned from when we worked in the yard the weekend before. His closed eyes looked restful, like he was dreaming of something he loves, like fishing, or cooking, or me.

"Do you want to hold his hand?" My mother asked.

Without thinking, I turned my palm upright, and she gently lifted his hand and placed it in mine. His skin felt only slightly warm, I remember, like he had saved this last bit of life for me to hold, and as I felt it finally slip away, I knew. I knew it was real, and I lost it.

"Do you want to get a soda?" My uncle asked my aunt as I cried over my dad's body.

I went numb for a while after that. I would cry here and there, but I'd always swiftly reign it back in, partly because I didn't feel like I was allowed to mourn him, but also because I didn't know how. I saw myself as an orphan who no longer had parents. I had no guidance. My dad had passed, and my mother was, well, my mother. She was as absent then as she is now. I had no one.

Even at his funeral, I kept my emotions at bay. At one point, I found myself talking to an old friend from school and smiling as I thanked her for complimenting my dress. I was on autopilot. I reacted to a compliment the same way you're supposed to in every other situation. But this was not every other situation. The dress she was admiring was the same dress I frantically searched for in Macy's a few days prior. I'd never bought a funeral dress before, and I was so angry that I even had to. Every black dress I found either didn't fit or was out of my price range, and I hated the store for not knowing I needed something perfect. I finally grabbed one without even looking, paid, and stormed out in a huff. It fit, but it was short, and I was thankful that I at least had the mind to buy black tights.

I'd never seen so many people attend a funeral before. There were so many that a line extended out into the parking lot, and the funeral home had to open a second

THE NOISE

room to accommodate everyone. This surprised me, because I'd heard from my mother my whole life what a loser my dad is, and while I never thought she was right, I didn't expect to see so many others who agreed with me. It gave me an unexpected sense of comfort.

I had scribbled a few thoughts on a note card a couple of days before, but when the time came for me to give his eulogy, I could barely see the words through my tears. It shocked me, because I hadn't properly cried since the day he passed, and I suddenly couldn't stop. As I stood there, looking out over the sea of mourners, it hit me—anything I wanted them to know about him before their memories were solidified forever, I had to say then and there. So, I spoke from the heart, and even though I hadn't rehearsed it, I still remember every word.

"My dad is the greatest person I know," was all I could say before catching the eye rolls coming from my mother's side of the family. I took a deep breath, composed myself, steadied my shaking fists, and continued. "My dad has always been misjudged by others, but to me, he is the greatest man in the world. If you didn't get to know him the way I have, then it is truly your greatest loss." A loud whimper escaped my cousin, and my aunt pulled him into her shoulder to shush him.

"He is a genuine and caring person," I continued, ignoring the wide eyes popping at my use of "is." I'm sure they all thought I was having a mental break, that I couldn't accept his passing. They weren't totally wrong, but they weren't totally right either. It's true I couldn't accept it, but I more so couldn't stand to be anything like my mother, a woman who moved on so effortlessly that her online dating profiles practically created themselves. "A person who would go without to give to others. He is a deep thinker, a romantic, a joker, a man who would ruin his own life to make sure his loved ones have what he thinks we deserve."

"He is the greatest father anyone could ask for, the kind who waits up after midnight just to make sure I get home safely, and then sits and talks with me about my day, even though he's desperate for sleep." I laughed to myself as I

THE NOISE

remembered the night I came home from work to find him and my mother playing pool in the basement. He was drunk and acting silly, and I got such a kick out of it that I sat on the basement steps and watched him lose as I ate the dinner he'd left warming in the oven for me. "Before each of his turns, he would rub my head, like it was some kind of genie's lamp, and say I was his good luck charm. He didn't realize that any good luck I had...it came from him being my father."

Maybe, if I stayed home that day, I could have given him all the luck I had to offer.

I told those two rooms full of people that I'd never been prouder to be so similar to another person, and that I inherited all my best qualities from him. I asked them not to think of him as being gone, because he isn't, because I will carry him with me, and I will never let go of his memory. I might have asked them to do the same, if I thought they were capable. I ended by saying that, while there will always be an empty seat at every table, my heart will forever be full.

ALLISON A

After a funeral, they do that thing where the loved ones of the deceased stand beside the casket and everyone in attendance forms a line. One by one, mourners shake hands with the grieving family and tell them how sorry they are, what a great person they were, how kind they were. It seemed to go on forever. I so badly wanted it to end, because any sense of peace I'd achieved through his eulogy was slashed with each faint-hearted grip. None of them cared. Not really. They'd all go home and thank God they and their loved ones were alive. They'd forget about their sorrow for me when they woke up the next morning, and they'd forget about him, too.

There was one person, though, who gave me hope. He was a middle-aged man with dark hair who I'd never seen before. He didn't just shake my hand—he encased it tightly within his leathery fingers, as if to impress upon me the significance of what he wanted to say. His eyes were full of intent as he told me he hoped that, one day, when he passes, his children talk about him the same way I spoke about my dad. He said, "That's all anyone can ask for after

THE NOISE

death." Then he left, and I never saw him again. I stood there in awe as dozens of dead handshakes followed, and I hoped my dad was as proud of me as that stranger was.

There weren't casseroles piled up in the kitchen, like you see in the movies. No one brought us anything, really, except for flowers. I realized even then that bringing food was too personal—you have to knock on the door of the grieving family, face them, see their eyes fill with tears, and hand them the food while saying how sorry you are. People have a thing about death, you know? Flowers are at least delivered by a third-party, that way you never have to face another's loss and be reminded that you will be in that same situation one day.

White roses were everywhere. I never knew they were mourning flowers until a sea of white took over every square inch of our house. There were so many roses that it was hard to move around, let alone breathe without their perfume clogging my throat. I could never tell if I wasn't hungry because of grief, or because, whenever I opened my mouth, I would choke on the stench.

ALLISON A

I was happy when the delivery person stopped ringing the bell. More than happy—I was relieved. I was so incredibly relieved. And then I wasn't, because then I had to watch all the flowers in the house wilt and die. They died because time had passed, and as time passed, others' memories of my dad died along with the floral arrangements. The smell dissipated, the phone stopped ringing, and the house fell silent.

My mother moved on almost immediately, dating a slew of men she'd met online. She and I fought every time I refused to greet them at the door and offer them a drink while she finished getting ready. I had no one, not even my friends. None of them had lost a parent and they couldn't understand what I was going through. They had no patience for me. They just wanted me to move on and be happy again so I didn't bring this dark cloud of reality into their lives. I was alone. Completely and utterly alone.

I thought I saw him once, the week after his funeral. I was driving down a winding road while blasting the radio and not paying nearly as much attention as I should have been. When I came around the last bend, a stop sign emerged out of thin air and I slammed down hard on the breaks, forcing my old Pontiac to screech to an agonizing halt. In the same instant my tires dug into the pavement, I felt five distinct fingers grab my leg, like a hand had seized me out of fear. As I sat staring out of my windshield, at the gray smoke filling the road, I felt the hand release. I turned, and there he was in the passenger seat, for just a second, maybe even less, and then he was gone. I sat there and cried for longer than I can remember.

Seeing him made everything worse. I missed him so much, and it felt like a tease, like a trick to remind me of what I'd lost. I didn't know what to do, so I ignored the promise I made during his eulogy and I did what I saw others doing—I moved on.

I blocked him out. I refused to think about him at all. I ignored his life, his memory, his laugh, his jokes, our late-night talks, all of it. I kept it all inside, where I thought it could never hurt me. Everyone else does that, I thought, and they seem happy enough.

ALLISON A

I soon came to learn that I'm like everyone else, though, as much as I wanted to be. I couldn't keep it up. I couldn't ignore his memory. The more I tried, the emptier I felt. I was a shell of who I once was, someone going through the motions, trying to find peace and happiness while unknowingly moving away from both of those things.

I was sitting in the backyard under a tree one warm autumn day, six months after he passed, reading Endymion by John Keats, when a gust of wind blew the book right out of my hands. It blew into a gathering of tiger lilies—my dad's favorite flower—and landed upside down, like a tent. Was it a coincidence that the book landed in that very spot? Was it a coincidence that the lifted binding protected the prospering stem beneath that was in fact not a tiger lily at all? I didn't think so. There was no bud yet on the flower, but I recognized it right away, because I'd seen it all over the house six months prior.

I felt compelled to bring it inside. I knew I was playing with fire, that I was risking bringing back all the emotions I'd been trying so hard to push down. I knew I was setting

THE NOISE

myself up to be heartbroken all over again, but I did it anyway. I can't explain it, but maybe grief isn't meant to be explained.

I put the rose in a small pot of soil by the window. I watered it, and I watched it bloom, and then I watched it die, and my heart did break.

My mental state was deteriorating faster than I could keep up with. I was in survival mode for my sanity, and so I rushed to hang the dead flower upside down, hoping it would dry out and petrify forever so I wouldn't have to throw it in the trash, like I watched my mother do to so many others. I hoped it would make me feel better. I hoped it would stop the crushing weight of the emotions flooding in.

To my surprise, it worked. The rose dried beautifully, and I felt better than I had in months. I bought a white rose bush after that and planted it in the far corner of the yard, by the tiger lilies. As the flowers grew and bloomed, and died, and dried, and more grew, and more bloomed, I started feeling…right. I felt happy.

ALLISON A

And then I saw him, and then I never stopped seeing him.

And then the episodes began.

NINETEEN

Jack sets a warm mug of decaf down beside me, and I close my journal. It's a nice gesture, but I can't bring myself to drink it. I feel sick to my stomach with the memory of my mother's words. I thought that by reading this entry, I would be reminded of how horrible she can be. I thought it would somehow prove that what she said isn't true, that *she's* the problem. Not me. But I only feel worse.

"I'm sorry for what your mother said," Jack apologizes, his voice tense as he eases onto the air mattress. "I told her to leave."

I cringe thinking about her biting words.

Won't lead anywhere good.

Will bring you down.

Not healthy.

Don't want to see you get hurt.

"Maybe she's right."

The mattress loses air from how quickly he gets up. Before I know it, he's kneeling in front of me, cradling my hands in his as tension pulls at his brow.

"You need to listen to me, okay? You mean *everything* to me. Don't you dare, even for a second, believe any of the shit your mother said." He's convincing, but my shame is overpowering, and I pull my hands from his.

He pulls my hands right back, holding them even tighter now. A bit too tight, actually. "If anything, you've made me a better person. You've built me up. You've taught me how to love someone, *truly* love someone." His glazed eyes focus on mine. "Angela, the only reason I'm able to love you the way you deserve is because *you* showed me how."

I want to believe him, but I can't banish this sinking feeling that he's wrong. Before I know it, despair crumples my face as tears moisten my cheeks. I've hurt everyone I've ever loved, and maybe he doesn't realize yet that I will, that I *have*, hurt him too.

"What was it you always said when you were a librarian?" He asks, his voice panicked and desperate, as though he's worried what will happen if he doesn't pull me back from the edge.

"I don't remember—"

"Check your sources, right?"

I nod.

THE NOISE

"Remember the person who said those words in the kitchen this morning. Do you remember her?"

I nod.

"Good. Do you remember all the terrible things she's done to you?"

I'm trying to, but all I see are my own mistakes.

"Do you remember when she pulled your hair because you wouldn't wear it the way she wanted you to?"

I was ten-years-old, and we were getting ready to go to our neighbor's fiftieth anniversary party. She called me a princess and yanked my hair because I wouldn't wear it in a half-up-half-down ponytail. I ran for my room and locked the door, crying as I pressed my feet against the wood for added safety as she pounded away, trying to get in. Once she calmed down, she made our neighbors drive me to the venue because she couldn't stand to be in the same car as me.

"But—" I begin, wanting to tell him I was young, that maybe I don't fully remember what happened, that maybe it was my fault.

"It wasn't your fault," he says, as if reading my thoughts. "You were just a kid. And it isn't your fault now, either." I take a deep breath to steady myself. "Now," he says, "remember who *I* am. Remember the person who loves you. I have always loved you, Angela, and I always will. That's all that matters," he tells me now. He opens his mouth to say something else, but he doesn't have the chance before my lips press firmly to his.

ALLISON A

It's the worst timing, I know, but all I can think about in this moment is how badly I want to be close to him, as close as I possibly can be. Being near him makes me feel sane. It makes me feel safe and loved. It's addicting, and I need more of it.

The baseless suspicions I've been harboring don't matter anymore. They never mattered, because they were never real. I'm certain Jack would never do anything to hurt me. I trust him with my heart, and I want to show him.

I run my hands along the sides of his torso, lifting his shirt and tossing it out of sight. He cradles my lower back as he lays me down against the floor, then moves his hand up to my face, his thumb brushing the sides of my mouth as he kisses me. I move from his lips to his neck as he unbuttons my pants and pulls them halfway down, allowing me to kick them off the rest of the way while he strips his own pants. He steals my lips from his skin long enough to lift my shirt over my head, and I hear it float to the floor, crumpling into a soft pile of cotton, as our warm bodies tangle beside the thriving fire.

TWENTY

Jack walks on the outside of the sidewalk, ushering me close to the grass. He's done this during every walk we've taken over the last thirteen years. He says it's meant to protect me, because a car would hit him before it hits me. No matter how much I protest at the idea of anything bad happening to him, he refuses to budge. Knowing I'm safe puts him at ease, and I'm at ease when he's at ease.

Leaves and acorn shells crunch beneath our feet as we take the path around the river. I've always loved the fall, especially the light breezes which blow crinkling foliage across the roads and carry with them the scent of pumpkin. I breathe it in, feeling rejuvenated by the ambiance, and by our renewed intimacy.

It had been a while since we last had sex. It hasn't been because of lack of desire, or because the house has been keeping Jack busy, or because I've been keeping him too exhausted, but rather because my body can't handle it like it used to. My bones are fragile, and inflammation runs rampant with the slightest opportunity. Whenever we have sex, my joints hurt worse the next day and my heart palpates non-stop. But that's tomorrow's problem. Right now, I'm content.

As the sun sinks beneath the horizon, the evening light welcomes the moon and a few stars to twinkle through. It reminds me of my first date with Jack, when we laid beneath the night sky, only it wasn't nearly as beautiful then. I slip my hand into his, just as I did all those years ago, and blush as I remember how forcefully this same hand grabbed my hips earlier. I breathe in the smell of pumpkin once more and bask in a kind of optimism I haven't felt in a while.

"Am I walking too fast?" He asks.

"Not at all."

Just after my diagnosis, Jack and I took a trip to New York City with some friends. It was one of the worst days of my life, because it was the first time it sunk in that I was no longer like everyone else. Our friends walked fifty yards ahead of us the entire time, remembering here and there that we weren't with them and stopping to let us catch up. I felt like a ghost trailing behind, forgotten, like I was holding them back, while they were laughing and joking and enjoying their day.

Jack stayed by my side, and he never even looked upset about it. I kept searching his face for any hint of remorse that

THE NOISE

he was stuck with me when he could have been with them, but all I saw was a serene love shining from behind his eyes. He tried so hard to make me laugh, to get my mind off of everything, and while I refused to allow even a sliver of a smile at first, he eventually broke me down. I soon found myself laughing as we strolled through the city streets, and I stopped caring that our friends had left us behind because I was with the only person who mattered.

He told me something that day, something I'd forgotten about until now, but it couldn't have come back into my mind at a better time. He said that if someone leaves you behind, then they aren't worth trying to catch up with.

Once I was content with the growing distance between us and our friends, I could take it all in, and I noticed things I wouldn't have otherwise. I noticed the sounds of the city, the smells from passing restaurants, the beauty of the older buildings, the rooftop flower gardens. I don't think I would notice the sky right now, the stars, the crunch beneath my feet, or the faint smell of pumpkin, if it wasn't for him. If it wasn't for him, I'd be stuck fifty yards behind, limping like some ghoul as I stagger to keep pace with life, growing angrier and less like myself as the world gets further and further away.

"Is that Arlo?" Jack asks, looking at a man who's seated on a park bench. He's facing the opposite direction, but his familiar curly white hair is enough to confirm it's him.

"Should we say hi?"

"I don't know. He looks deep in thought," Jack says, and I see what he means. Arlo isn't facing the expansive river, like most people would be. He's focused on a house across the way.

"It would be rude to walk past and not say something," I suggest. There's no opportunity for Jack to disagree because Arlo turns at the sound of our footsteps.

"Ah! Hello!" Arlo exclaims, his voice practically singing, as if he'd been expecting us.

Jack takes the lead with the conversation, rattling off about the white roses and how nice they look in our kitchen, which I find odd considering he wanted to sneak past without saying a word.

"I'd love to stop by and see how they're holding up," Arlo says. "When would be a good time?"

The thought of Arlo visiting again drops a heavy weight into the pit of my stomach. He seems nice, but he's also lonely. Anyone can tell that just by talking with him once. I worry he'll become too attached, leaving Jack and me with barely any time to ourselves.

"Stop by whenever you're free," Jack tells him, though I can hear it in his voice that he's as hesitant as I am.

Jack's face twists as he notices the house Arlo was staring at. Curious, I follow his gaze, landing on a small woman sporting a buzz cut as she walks across the lawn to her mailbox. The glare from her large purple glasses is blinding even from here.

"I live over there," Arlo explains.

THE NOISE

"Oh, which house is yours?" Jack asks.

Arlo points across the way, his finger shaking as it hovers in the air. I look in the direction he's indicating, but it seems to be a space between two houses. I don't know enough about the neighbors to determine which one is his, and I'm not sure how to ask him to clarify without sounding like I'm interrogating him.

"How are the renovations going?" Arlo asks.

There's a pause as Jack adjusts to Arlo's change of subject, and I might have finally been able to answer before him, if not for the woman digging up dirt with her bare hands who steals my attention.

I look around for anyone else who might also see her, but I seem to be the only one. The young mother pushing her toddler on the swing is oblivious, as is the man at the water fountain, and the teenagers playing basketball less than a hundred feet away either don't see her or can't be bothered. *Is it normal, what she's doing?*

Out of habit, I wonder whether *I'm* the insane one here, because if her behavior wasn't normal, then everyone else would notice.

But what could be normal about what she's doing? Has she lost something valuable that she's desperate to find? Is she planting something, and feels more comfortable digging with her hands than a shovel?

ALLISON A

For half a second, I consider pointing the woman out to Jack and Arlo, but I hesitate when that little voice creeps in to remind me that maybe she isn't there at all.

Maybe this is what my mother meant.

A deep growl emanates from somewhere nearby, and I look for the vicious dog I assume is the cause. There is no dog, though, only the creaking wooden bench that screams as Arlo adjusts his weight.

I look back at the woman, who's now staring at me. The sound of the bench must have attracted her attention. She stands perfectly still, her frizzy light brown hair blowing in the wind and nearly blending into the low hung leaves of the tree above her. Her eyes are wide, as if she's desperately hungry.

My head snaps to Jack, then to Arlo, then back to Jack, and then to the woman, who is now a step closer. Her filthy hands are clenched in fists at her sides, as if she's harboring anger she can barely control. All I can do is stare as she takes another step, slow at first, then another, before progressing to a determined stride.

I want to say something to Jack and Arlo. I want to ring their alarm bells and warn them of the danger staggering toward us, but I can't bring myself to say anything because I'm terrified this isn't real.

Faster now. She's getting close. Too close.

This has to be real.

THE NOISE

"There's a—" I begin, but before I can get the words out, Arlo abruptly stands and waves his hand in front of my face. I think he might be trying to hit me until I realize he's swatting away a bee.

The woman stops moving, but her focus hasn't left me. She's close enough now for me to see the dried blood over a gaping wound on her forehead. The rest of her face is still in shadow, but I can tell her eyes are unnaturally dark, without even the smallest bit of white glinting in the sun. She looks less like a person and more like a monster, and I can't fathom why no one else is alarmed by this.

She moves toward me again, slower this time, as if she's unsure.

From the corner of my eye, I see Arlo swatting his hand left to right and back again, but I keep my eyes on her, preparing to scream if she gets any closer.

Arlo's hands are picking up speed as they sail through the air, so much so that Jack feels it necessary to ask him if he's okay.

"Oh, I'm fine," Arlo responds. "Just a damn bee," he says as he goes on slapping the air. "Hey!" Arlo yells, to the bee, I assume, but it startles me enough that I take my eyes off of the woman and pull them toward him instead.

He sets his sights firmly on me as his head pivots so inconspicuously from side to side that I wouldn't have noticed it if my gaze wasn't glued to his. He says nothing, but I somehow understand what he means—I shouldn't look at the woman. I keep my eyes on him instead, all while Jack goes on talking about his plans for the bathroom, unaware of our secret conversation.

My heart is pounding so hard in my chest that I can hear it in my ears, and as much as Arlo is warning me not to, I'm desperate to look at her. I worry that, the longer I keep my eyes off of her, the more opportunity she will have to strike.

Arlo narrows in on me, as if cautioning me to remain steadfast, and I do.

"You know what I mean?" Jack asks, and Arlo's face softens, a smile spreading across his lips.

"Yes," Arlo responds. I don't know what he's responding to, and I doubt he does either.

Without turning my head, I peek at the woman. She's back at her hole, digging through the dirt as weeds and grass and mulch fly through the air.

The same way I understood Arlo's unspoken words, I have a dreadful understanding that she still knows I can see her.

TWENTY-ONE

I don't have to look at the clock to know it's the middle of the night. It's pitch-black outside. The kind of black that swallows everything, save for the intermittent silhouette of trees swaying in the moonlight. Wind wafts through an open window, filling the living room with a biting autumn chill, and I'm surprised Jack is sleeping through it. I know he likes the cold, but this is *too cold*.

In my fatigued state, I wonder whether I can will the window to close on its own. I focus on it for half a second, believing I could slam it shut using only my mind, but as the fog of sleep drifts away, I realize how ridiculous I'm being. The only way to close it is to get up and do it myself, but the excruciating pain in my back and joints makes that an unfavorable option—I knew being intimate with Jack would catch up to me.

ALLISON A

I pull the covers up to my chin, but it brings only mild relief. I try closing my eyes and forcing myself back to sleep, but sleep stands no chance against the frosty air. Out of options, I lay frozen stiff on the air mattress, vulnerable to the wind humming through the curtains.

It's as if the house smells more in the cold, or maybe I'm only now noticing certain smells because I'm looking for anything to get my mind off of the whistling wind and frigid air. Whatever the reason, I'm practically choking on sawdust and stainless-steel cleaner. I always thought our house smelled like roses, but the roses are struggling to break through.

There's no chance I'll be able to sleep like this. Closing the window is my only option if I don't want to be a complete zombie tomorrow.

I bite the inside of my cheek in order to stay quiet as I slither out of bed and flop onto the floor. After a quick look at Jack to make sure I haven't woken him, I release a sigh of pain, long and measured. I breathe in deep as I ease to a standing position. Or, as close to standing as I can get right now. With my back bent nearly in half, I creep toward the window, where I'm surprised to find the temperature is warmer than it was by our bed.

I close the window gently, making as little noise as possible. I would cheer for my accomplishment if my heart didn't sink at the sight of the curtain fluttering between the glass and the screen like a caught fish. I consider leaving it until morning,

THE NOISE

but I'm certain the constant whooshing would wake me as soon as I lay back down. My shoulders drop as I resign myself to starting over so that I can free the fabric, but it's wedged into the—

There's someone standing in the kitchen behind me.

At least, it looks like a person.

As I peer closer at the window reflection, I consider it could be a shadow cast from a tree outside, one that looks a lot like the figure of a person. *That makes sense, doesn't it?*

Good. That's good.

Proud of myself for talking my mind off of the ledge, I return to freeing the curtain, just as the unmistakable smell of mud fills my nose. It smells like moss and weeds, and if *wet* had a smell, then it smells like that. It smells wet and thick, and I have to cover my nose with my shirt or else I think I'll suffocate from the stench.

In my pursuit of the curtain, I carelessly glance back to the window. It's closer. It must be. It was by the kitchen island before, I remember, but now it's well past that. *Has the moonlight shifted and caused the shadow to move?*

I squint through the darkness to examine the figure as it moves one step closer, then another, and another, and I avert my eyes straight away because I realize it isn't a shadow at all.

With my head down, I dare to lift my gaze just enough to confirm my hunch as the white veneer of moonlight sets upon her frizzy hair.

It's the woman from the park.

There's something in her hands.

It looks like weeds that died and wilted long ago, their poor necks slackened over their own stems. *Is that what she was digging up earlier?*

She takes another step and I avert my eyes, feeling my heart turn into a raging engine ready for flight.

What is she doing here? How did she get in here?

Another step, and as I hear the floorboard creak beneath her feet, the engine in my chest takes off, booming so loud I worry she'll hear it.

I look at Jack, nose whistling and breath sighing in a deep state of sleep.

Another step, this one more certain.

I know it's the worst idea, but fear propels me, against my better judgment, to whisper to him, to try to wake him.

She tilts her head to one side; her face entering the strip of light ribboning into the room. She looks dead. Worse than dead. She looks decayed, like she's been walking around in the world rotting for years. I can see the gash on her forehead clearer now, and I realize the star-shaped wound must have been caused by blunt force trauma. I remember my mother explaining once that, when patients come into the hospital with a wound like that, they almost always were in some kind of accident.

THE NOISE

Her eyes appear even more lifeless than her greenish-yellow skin, like two little white bulbs glowing in the dark. Whatever kind of accident she was in, it must have injured her mouth too, because half of her lips have been ripped off, revealing an unintentional smile on the left side, while a tight grimace holds fast on the right.

My gut tells me to look away, but I'm terrified of what she might do if I take my eyes off her. The image of her sprinting toward me and clawing at my face with her sharp fingernails consumes my imagination, or choking me to death while Jack sleeps, unaware of my guttural cries. More than anything, I don't want her to come closer. I don't want to see her nightmarish face in any more detail because, if I do, I think it would mean I'm about to die.

She takes another step, followed by three more.

The floor creaks in rapid succession, and all I can do is close my eyes and brace for her assault.

The creaking stops.

My secret conversation with Arlo in the park comes rushing back, and I remember she stopped walking toward me once I looked away. That must be why she stopped now, too—because I closed my eyes.

It takes all the courage I can muster, but I keep them closed.

After an excruciating minute of complete and utter silence, I hear a creak, followed by another, and another.

ALLISON A

The creaks don't sound like they're approaching. Instead, they sound like they're coming from the kitchen, like she's stepping back away from me.

My breathing is heavy, and there's no doubt she hears it, and there's also no doubt she sees me, but the longer I keep my eyes closed, the more the creaks fade and the smell of mud dissipates.

I don't dare lift my head, but I crack my eyelids just enough to peer at the woman.

I'm relieved to see her shadow is back where I first saw it, but I know I'm not out of the woods yet, so I don't linger for more than a second. Instead, I set my attention on the curtain and I resume my efforts to free it. If I keep looking away, if I pretend that I don't even know she's there, then maybe she will leave.

I have no choice but to allow the click of unlocking the window so I can wrestle with the fabric. I suffer through every tug and pull, each bead of sweat which falls from my forehead and catches in my brows, unsure if my hunch is even correct, or if she will attack at any moment.

The curtain is nearly free, except for the bottom corner, which has somehow embedded itself between the sill and the screen. If this was a newer window, then I could lift the screen to release the curtain, but this one is from the 1950s and requires a latch, one I can't seem to get it to budge.

THE NOISE

I start to tug. Lightly at first. Then, once I'm sure I'm not making too much noise, I tug harder, and harder, until I'm knocked back by the force of the curtain releasing. The wind from outside blows the material straight into my face, suffocating me and shrouding my senses. I wrestle it off my eyes, my heart seizing in my throat as my attention races to the reflection.

She's gone.

It isn't until I gasp for air that I realize I'd been holding my breath, and now that I'm aware, it feels harder than ever to breathe, like I've forgotten how. Even when I manage the smallest inhale, my shaking body struggles to suck it down.

Jack stirs, and another wave of fear hits me. The last thing I want is to explain to him why I'm awake, what I'd seen, and why I can't breathe or get a hold of myself. I don't want to see that look of worry on his face any more than I want that woman to return, and before I know it, this fear propels me to steady myself. I start to take in air. Small gulps at first, then larger ones.

I slink back into bed and curl my body against Jack's back, burrowing my face in his shirt as I continue my breathing exercises. *If I can't see it, it's not there. If I can't see it, it's not there.*

***

ALLISON A

I'm awake again in an instant, though it must have been longer because the orange glow of the rising sun is poking into the room.

I'm lying on my back, and I realize I must have changed positions at some point. I try to turn back over into Jack, but I can't. I can't move anything, not even a finger, and dread weighs heavily on my chest.

The only movement I can manage is the shaking of my body from the cold. It's *so* cold in here, and I realize why—the window is open again. All the windows are open.

The room is empty. I may not see her, but I know she's here. I know it, and my chest heaves with what I know as small whimpers escape my frozen lips.

I smell the stench of wet, thick mud. It's overwhelming, more so than it was before, and in the same moment as I realize why this is, I feel a slight breeze on the top of my head.

My tears turn to icicles in the cold fog of her breath. The more I cry, the more that same rancid breath wafts over me, and I know I need to stop, but I can't.

I remember how I got her to disappear before, and I pull on any remaining courage I have to move the only thing I'm able to—my eyelids. I squeeze out a few tears as I seal my eyes shut, knowing full well that I'm leaving myself completely vulnerable, and I focus on taking in small, quiet gasps.

THE NOISE

Her breathing continues to waft through my hair and over my forehead, trickling down my nose where I can smell the putrid rot steaming from her decomposing body.

I keep as still as possible, but it seems as if her presence will never cease, not until Jack wakes hours from now. I can't wait that long. I'm so desperate. Cries rise up my throat, begging to escape.

Don't do it. Don't give in.

A gurgled sob seeps out, and I press my eyes closed harder, the taut skin painfully wrinkling the corners of my eyes. A heavy huff skims over my head, like she's a predator investigating whether her kill is really dead.

It will be okay, as long as I don't look. Don't look.

At last, her breath gets smaller and smaller, and the stench dissipates enough so that I no longer feel nauseous.

I want to look and make sure she's gone. More than that, I want to turn over into Jack. Instead, I lay still, and quiet, and I keep my eyes closed.

TWENTY-TWO

"Tell me something I would have no way of knowing. Something you've never told me before."

"Why?"

I don't answer, but then I don't have to. My dad knows me and he knows what I'm thinking. He may not know what happened last night, but he can tell I'm questioning myself and my sanity. I'm desperate to know whether it's all real. Whether *he* is real.

"Don't misinterpret the things your mother said," he warns me. "There's a lot you don't know."

"What's there to misinterpret?" I ask. "She thinks I'm unstable and a danger to those around me, and I'm starting to think she's right. I've already brought myself down, and you can't say I'm not dragging Jack down with me."

"Why are you saying this?"

THE NOISE

I almost tell him about the muddy woman, but the thought of seeing that look of worry on yet another person's face is too much to bear, and I stop myself. Instead, I again ask him to tell me something I don't know, something that proves he really is here talking to me. If he is real, then maybe everything else is real too, and maybe I'm not crazy, and maybe I won't ruin Jack's life.

He releases a disapproving sigh, but he gives in. "North Railroad Avenue."

"What does that mean?"

"You'll understand soon. That's what you wanted, isn't it?"

I nod.

"Why do you think these things about yourself, Angela? Is it because of what your mother said?"

"Dad…I'm seeing you. I'm *talking* to you."

"Why is that crazy?"

"Why can't anyone else see you?"

He moves to sit beside me on the porch, his voice softening as he answers, "You can see me the same way you can see Jack, or your mother, or anyone else. There's no difference."

"That doesn't make sense."

"It does."

"No, it doesn't," I demand, growing agitated.

"Angela—"

"I've barely slept, dad, and I've made it so that Jack has barely slept, and in the midst of it all, he's working and volunteering and renovating and, somehow, he still finds the energy to take care of me, because he *has* to take care of me, because I'm broken," The words tumble from my lips faster than I can keep up with. "When he left for the shop this morning, he looked dead tired, and that's *my* fault. I'm *broken*. Every part of my body is broken and even my mind is broken and I can't fix any of it." I stop to take a breath, but my shaking body allows only rattles of air to get through.

"There's nothing wrong with you," he tells me, wrapping his arms tightly around my shoulders, like he did when I was little. "There never has been," he adds, but tears pour down my cheeks anyway, because I know he's wrong.

"Is this about the woman?"

Panic booms through me.

He can't mean the woman from last night, can he?

"Yes, I know about her. I know about all of them."

I pull away and cover my face with my hands.

"None of them have ever gotten that close, have they?" He says, more a statement than a question.

"Please stop," I beg him, wanting to block out the memory.

"You're not crazy. Angela, look at me," he says, and I do. "Don't you trust me?" Of course I trust him. Other than Jack, my dad is the only person I've ever been able to trust fully. "You're not crazy," he repeats.

"Then they're real?" I dare to ask.

"They're real to you."

THE NOISE

"Can they really hurt me?"

His brow furrows as his eyes set seriously upon me. "Not if you don't look at them." I start to speak, but my shock allows barely a mumble before he follows up with an even more disturbing surprise. "Have you heard the noise lately?"

My gaping jaw slaps shut.

I've never mentioned the noise to my dad. Not once. My first instinct is to ask him how he knows, but then a wave of realization washes over me. There's no way he could know.

I see him. I've *been* seeing him. But I've never seen him when the noise has happened. I've never even seen him during my episodes. Yet, he somehow knows about all of it. *If I can see him, then why would he be hidden when those things happen?*

It's because he isn't hidden. It's because he isn't here at all.

He's in my head, like the rest of them, and he knows because I know.

"No," I answer, feeling the life drain out of me because I now know I've been talking to myself for the last fourteen years. "Not for a few days."

"Pay close attention when you hear it next."

"It'll come back?" I ask, as if his answer could ever be real.

"There's only one person who can stop it from returning, and that person isn't you."

"What are you talking about?" What am *I* talking about?

There's a knock on the door.

ALLISON A

TWENTY-THREE

"Do you want something to drink?" I offer Arlo as he lays his coat over a stool in the kitchen.

"Coffee would be wonderful," he says, and I'm grateful I brewed extra this morning so we don't have to make awkward small talk while the pot whistles. "They look beautiful."

"I'm sorry?"

"The roses."

I turn, cradling his hot mug of coffee, in time to see him pointing to the vase.

"Oh, those are from our garden," I say, sliding the mug across the counter to him. "We always keep a vase of white roses in the house."

His eyebrows lift from behind the ceramic rim as he takes a sip. I can't tell whether he's curious or scoffing. "They're for my dad," I explain. "They remind me of him."

THE NOISE

"I'm sorry," he says, a gentle click coming from his mug as he sets it down on the counter.

"He passed fourteen years ago. It never gets easier, but the roses help."

He nods.

"I'm sorry to say yours wilted, but I've taken care of them." I say, removing a bag of potpourri from the drawer.

"You don't let anything go to waste."

"No, I don't," I admit. "I'll have to figure out what to do if this bag gets any bigger, though," I manage a small laugh. "I wasn't planning to put any out until the house is finished. I don't want sawdust to stifle their scent."

"It'll be a nice finishing touch once this place is complete," he agrees. "It's impressive, you know, what your husband has done with it." I offer a faint-hearted smile to hide my embarrassment. Arlo has only met us three times, but he can already tell I'm dead weight. "By the way, where is Jack today?"

"He's volunteering."

"He volunteers a lot?"

"I suppose."

"Do you ever go with him?"

"I used to. Not so much anymore," I say, glancing at my cane resting against the wall. "It's hard for me to keep up."

"Understood."

ALLISON A

As I'm about to change the subject, a creak echoes from above. It doesn't sound like the noise. In fact, I'm positive this creak *is* actually the house settling, but the absence of the noise somehow makes this sound, and the whole house, for that matter, seem louder. I've been on edge, waiting for the noise to start up again, and I'm only now realizing how unnervingly silent it has been, a silence that pounds on my eardrums, taunting me.

"Everything alright?" Arlo asks, following my gaze toward the ceiling.

"Just an old house settling."

"These old houses do that, don't they?" He asks, and I nod. "Does this house settle a lot?"

"Up until recently, it seemed to be settling every day."

"Are you sure it isn't an animal?"

"You sound like my husband," I say with more bitterness than I intended. I reset my tone and try again. "Jack seems to think so, but we haven't found any."

"You've checked?"

"Just once. He borrowed a ladder from a neighbor," I explain. Then, realizing how odd that sounds, I add, "because the stairs can't be used. They have rot."

"Do you mind?" Arlo asks, easing himself up from the stool.

"Uh…sure," I say, not knowing what he's about to do, but not exactly feeling like I can tell him to sit back down either. I offer him a hand, but he either doesn't notice, or he has too much pride to accept my help.

He carefully inspects the stairs with a small flashlight he keeps in his back pocket. I watch his expression, intent and laser focused, and it reminds of the look he wore when he silently warned me about the woman in the park. The urge to ask him questions about her rises to the surface, but I push it back down. I don't know that bringing it up would be a good idea, because I'm not entirely sure our secret conversation even happened.

"How do you know the stairs have rot?"

"Jack's pretty handy. He inspected them himself."

"Is anything else rotted?"

"Not that I know of."

He huffs and straightens his back as he returns the flashlight to his pocket. "I'm no expert, but I don't see any rot. These haven't been sitting here abandoned long enough for that to happen. And, well, has there been any water damage, or termites?" I shake my head. "I would get a second opinion. That's just my opinion."

Suspicion creeps up inside me, and I allow myself to indulge in it because, deep down, I've been desperate for someone else to question Jack. If someone else has doubts, then that would mean I'm not being paranoid about the labels, or all of his trips to the shop and the shelter, or the folded white paper in his back pocket.

ALLISON A

No matter how badly I want to give in and prod Arlo further, my protectiveness over my husband is second nature, and I set out to defend him against this stranger. As I open my mouth to speak, however, I catch sight of myself in the hallway mirror and my lips slap shut in horror at my reflection.

I look unkempt. That's a nice way of putting it. I forgot to brush my hair this morning, let alone my teeth. Suddenly, the stench of coffee is unbearable even to me, and I'm embarrassed that I've been spewing it at Arlo this entire time. Deep circles cling to my eyes, emphasized by my paler than usual complexion. If I saw myself, I would question *my* credibility, not Jack's, and it occurs to me that maybe I'm the one Arlo is skeptical of.

I open my mouth again, this time to apologize for my appearance, but Arlo cuts in before I have the chance, commenting on how much we've renovated, and how different the place looks from what he remembers.

"You've been here before?" I ask, disbelief superseding my previous train of thought.

"I have," he confirms, looking the house over floor to ceiling. "I was close with the people who once lived here."

"I thought you said you only recently moved to Hidden Heights?"

"I had friends and family who lived in town," he explains.

"Are they what brought you back here?"

THE NOISE

"No, they're all gone now," he says, his voice full of sadness, and I finally understand why he's been coming around so much. He has a connection to the house Jack and I now own, the house we've been, *Jack's* been, tearing apart and rebuilding anew. He has memories here.

"Do you and Jack have friends and family in Hidden Heights?"

"Not really."

"No friends?"

After a beat, I answer, "No, no friends."

"What about family?"

"My mother recently moved down south," I answer, feeling like I'm being interrogated all of a sudden.

"Down south?"

I nod. "She needed to get away, I guess."

"Mm. And your dad, you're close with him?"

"Well, he passed," I say again, wondering if Arlo remembers our conversation from earlier.

"Right, of course. My apologies. I didn't mean to upset you."

Arlo's lips crumple into a sympathetic smile, the same smile I often saw when my dad passed. It's one that says *I'm very uncomfortable, so I'm just going to smile and try to make things normal, even though nothing about this is normal.* I say the same thing now as I did back then, "Let's talk about something else."

"It's alright," Arlo tells me. "It's alright to not be alright. In fact, you *shouldn't* be alright."

"I'm sorry?"

"Death is supposed to affect us, change us, make us see things differently. Don't let anyone make you believe you need to ignore that."

My mouth falls open and my eyebrows crinkle into a sort of puzzled appreciation that I hope he picks up on, because I know no other way of thanking him for these simple words. A few seconds ago, I was ready to show him the door, but now I'm glad he's here. I'm so used to hiding how I feel about death because it makes others uncomfortable. I'm not sure I ever thought about how I would act in a situation where I didn't have to pretend.

Maybe Arlo isn't like other people, I consider. Maybe I don't have to follow the usual social norms with him. Maybe I can talk to him openly and honestly. Before I can stop myself, I decide to test this theory.

"Can I ask you about the people who used to live in this house?"

His face falls grimly serious, prompting an apology to bubble at my lips. But before I can deliver my regret, he begins talking about her, about the woman who used to live in this house.

"She was beautiful," he begins, "and her husband was lucky to have her. He'd been with a few other women before, but none of them even compared. It wasn't just her beauty, but her personality, you know? She was attractive in a quirky kind of way," he says with a laugh. "She was odd, no getting around that, but it made him love her even more. If only that was enough."

"What happened to them?"

"They drifted apart, like so many couples do," he says, eyeing me. "She lives a few houses down from here."

"The woman with the short gray hair, right?" I ask. "I'm sorry. I don't know her name."

His eyebrows perk up in surprise, and I realize it's been a while since they've seen each other.

"She used to have long blonde hair," he says, smiling fondly. "You've met her," he adds matter-of-factly.

"She visited recently. She wanted to see the house she used to live in. She's the woman who Jack borrowed the ladder from so he could check the second floor." I know I should stop talking, judging by the glare forming in his eyes, but my nervousness propels me forward despite my better judgment. "She told us her husband passed, and that's why she moved. But you said they drifted apart?"

"They drifted apart long before he died. He just didn't know it."

"Please stop me if I'm bringing up any bad memories. It's just that we don't know much about this house, and I thought…"

"I understand," he says, waving a hand at me. "You did nothing wrong. *She's* a coward." he continues, his voice changing, hardening. "If she really wanted to escape the memory of this house, then she would have moved further than down the street. To a different town, at least. People do that, you know? They convince themselves, and others, that they're in *just enough pain*. Like people who limp unnecessarily and then peek at you from the corner of their eye to see whether you've noticed. They love the attention. She moved close enough so people will still pity her, but far enough that she won't have to remember him or this house."

I've only met Arlo less than a handful of times, but I've never seen him this angry before. It's more than anger—it's a seething hatred concealed only by the innocent glint of his icy blue eyes. Those same eyes set on mine for what feels like a lifetime, and I recall how familiar he looked when I first saw him standing in the kitchen, talking to Jack. I must know him from somewhere. I'm certain I do.

He seems to sense my uneasiness and pulls away long enough to sip his coffee, which is now lukewarm at best.

"Do you want me to reheat that for you?" I ask.

"No, that's okay, thank you," he answers. "Though I could use some milk and sugar."

"Oh, I'm so sorry," I apologize, realizing I never asked him how he takes his coffee. It's been so long since I've entertained—too long, obviously. I can't remember the last

THE NOISE

person who stepped over this threshold before Arlo, other than my mother, of course, and Charlie's wife. Charlie's wife's visit didn't call for entertaining, though, as she barely spoke to me.

I open the refrigerator to retrieve the milk while muttering under my breath about how inconsiderate I've been, then place it on the counter, along with a spoon, before heading to the cabinet for sugar. I prefer powdered creamer in my coffee because it doesn't cool down as fast as milk and sugar, and I do little baking anymore, so we keep the granulated sugar on the top shelf, along with the other misfit ingredients, like cardamom and sprinkles. It's almost out of reach, and as I struggle to get to it, I wish I baked more just so this single task was easier.

"Do you need help?" Arlo asks, watching me attempt to draw the canister forward with just the tip of my middle finger.

"No, thank you, I got it," I answer as the tendons in my heels stretch and snap. I hide my wincing face in the cabinet as I pray for the pain to subside, all while I continue to stretch toward the sugar, making the pain even worse.

Eager to end the searing sensation in my ankles, I suck in a breath and give myself one more decent push upwards, finally grasping the canister. The relief I feel as I come back down onto the soles of my feet lasts only a second before the pit in my stomach opens wide at the sight of a folded white piece of paper, which was hidden just behind the sugar.

ALLISON A

Before, it was just a piece of paper. Before, it was easy to convince myself I was letting my mind wander. Now, I can't deny that, whatever this is, he hid it here, out of my reach.

"Everything alright?" Arlo asks.

"Sure, of course," I say as I hand him the sugar.

The clink of his metal spoon rounding the inside of the ceramic mug is muffled by the echo of his story from earlier, about the couple who lived in this house before us. I wonder if their love was once as passionate as mine and Jack's, before they drifted apart. I wonder what came between them. I don't want to end up like Charlie's wife, but I'm starting to fear that another happy couple is in danger inside of this house.

THE NOISE

TWENTY-FOUR

The first thought that crosses my mind as my eyes drift open is how bad the pain is going to be. Whenever I sleep, or even just lay down for a period of time, stiffness takes the opportunity to attack all the bones in my body. It felt like only a minute ago that I climbed onto the air mattress to take a nap, but judging by the dark skies outside, it's been much longer.

Despite how long I must have been lying here, I don't feel pain anywhere in my body. I test my limbs one by one, starting with my toes and ending with my neck. Not only does nothing hurt, but I can move more freely than I've been able to in a long time.

Maybe I'm more rested from the nap than I thought, I consider. After all, I slept through the entire day, it would seem. If that's true, then Jack must have come in without waking me. I'm usually such a light sleeper that he would have had to tip-toe. Maybe he knew I needed the rest.

I look beside me, expecting to see him there, eyes closed, nose whistling, but his side of the mattress is empty.

I look to the kitchen, then to the hallway, and then to the porch, searching for any sign of him—any light coming from a room, any sound—but it's dark and quiet, and I'm alone.

I get out of bed with surprising ease, then rotate my ankles one by one to check for soreness. There is none. My back straightens itself like a pin with no effort, and I bask in a luxury most others take for granted. I don't think I've ever felt this tall before.

I take a hesitant step, expecting it to set off the pain that's gone dormant in my body, but I feel nothing. Another step, then another, and before I know it, I'm standing at the refrigerator door, filling a glass with water.

I raise the glass to my lips and gulp more than I intended, enjoying the coolness as it drips down my dry throat and into the pit of my stomach. I must be dehydrated after sleeping all day.

I place the empty glass in the sink, then glance at the clock on the stove. It's eleven at night. *Where could Jack be at this hour?*

Panic sets in, catapulting me back to the day my dad passed. That day traumatized me. It made me realize how fragile life is,

THE NOISE

and how, at any moment, you can lose someone you love, as if they mean nothing to the universe.

I'm unable to predict or control the thoughts that come flooding in—*was he in a car accident? Is he hurt, or worse? Is he lying in a hospital morgue somewhere because no one can contact me because they don't know our home phone number? Do I need to rush to the hospital? Which hospital is the closest one? Will I go to the wrong one, again?*

I race to the porch, where I can view the driveway from the windows. His truck isn't there. *Something is wrong.*

I run for the phone in the kitchen, planning to call every hospital in the area, but it's missing.

It was just here, less than a second ago. My eyes wash over the counter in search of where the phone is hiding, and I realize my glass is no longer in the sink.

I don't remember putting it away.

I open the cabinet, expecting to find a sopping wet glass staining the new wood, but instead I find rows upon rows of food. Lipton tea packets. Del Monte fruit cocktail. Too many boxes of Jell-o to count. Spam. Assorted Betty Crocker cake mixes. *None of this is ours.*

I close the cabinet, only now realizing it is not the green veneer I love, but a rich chestnut. Beyond the cabinets, a blue stripped wallpaper has taken over our subway tile.

I'm dreaming.

ALLISON A

I'm back in the same kitchen as before. The same house as before. Our house, but it's not our house.

My head snaps to the hallway, remembering the intruder who came rushing through moments before I woke up.

There's no one there.

There's no one here at all.

The television is quiet. The brown corduroy armchairs are empty.

A sound from above draws my chin parallel to the ceiling, and

I'm surprised by the anger bubbling in my gut at the fact that the noise is haunting me, even in my dreams.

I edge nearer to the stairs, the tips of my bare toes lining up with the barrier I promised Jack I wouldn't breach.

I'm dreaming, I realize once again. *The stairs can't hurt me if I'm dreaming.*

I lift my foot onto the first step, amazed by how real the hardwood feels. I can detect every dent, every knot, every splinter.

I take a second step up. Then a third.

I'm almost at the top of the stairs, close enough to the second floor to see that the soft yellow wallpaper I love is intact. It wasn't even this perfect when we toured the house.

A guttural scream resonates from somewhere nearby, freezing me in place.

THE NOISE

"Please," a male voice begs, sounding like his mouth is full of rocks.

The scream turns mechanical, grinding and drumming.

The drumming follows me, stalking me, as I edge back into reality. It takes me a second to separate from the nightmare, and when I do, I bolt upright, sweat sticking hair to the sides of my face. All the lights are on, and I blink repeatedly as I struggle to adjust.

My panting slows as I edge further into waking life, but it soon returns with a vengeance when I realize the scream has followed me. It's coming from down the hallway, from the bathroom.

TWENTY-FIVE

My palm roves over my lumbar spine, nursing a pain that reminds me just how awake I am. In my lucid state, the vibration coming through the floor beneath the air mattress is unmistakable, a vibration so intense it jars each of my vertebra. The scream I thought I heard was Jack's power tools, and I'm surprised I was able to sleep through it. I'm guessing it's because I've been so exhausted.

I remember seeing Arlo to the door. I was so tired from his visit, from entertaining and talking to another person besides Jack. It had been a while since I've done either of those things, and it took more out of me than I expected. I carried my book with me and laid down, hoping I would drift off into a nap. I expected to sleep for only a little while, if at all, but my dream was right about one thing—the skies outside are dark.

THE NOISE

The veil of night makes it harder for me to accept the nightmare didn't happen. On the one hand, I know I must be awake because everything is the way it should be. There are no corduroy chairs. No wallpaper backsplash. No carpet. Everything feels tangible and real, and yet I can't shake the notion that I really did climb those stairs, or that someone really was screaming, just moments ago.

My hair is damp with sweat, and I tuck it behind my ears in an attempt to tame it, then rub my eyes to help them adjust to reality. Still, the nightmare clings to me. It's the second nightmare I've had like this, and I don't understand where it's coming from. I would blame it on having watched a dark movie that's still stuck in my head, but I can't remember the last time I even watched TV. It can't be the book I'm reading either, because *Voices in the Snow* has nothing to do with a home invasion, unless you count the inhuman hollows, and this intruder was most certainly a flesh and blood man.

I can still picture him from the first dream I had, where he ran down the hallway from the den, dark eyes piercing his black ski mask, ice cold and full of rage. He was larger than I would expect any man could be, though I understand that was likely my mind playing tricks in a dream state. Perhaps I thought he was so large because he was unequivocally in control. I didn't get a good look at the people occupying the chairs, but I knew they didn't stand a chance. Judging by the screams I heard tonight, I was right.

ALLISON A

The most unnerving part about the nightmare, though, was that Jack was missing. I remember fear washing over me at the thought of him being hurt, or worse, and I remember being consumed by panic. It felt so real. But as the fog of sleep drifts away, that worry grows less and less, replaced now by curiosity. *Was there another reason he wasn't there?*

Back when I first learned about sleep paralysis, I read a theory that dreams are just unfinished thoughts, that whatever you think about during the day, your brain then makes sense of while you're asleep. I only had a few moments to consider the white piece of paper I found in the cabinet earlier today, because Arlo was here. Maybe, after I fell asleep, my brain continued to ruminate on it and came up with an answer—Jack was missing, in every sense. My deepest fear is that the man I fell in love with will disappear, either physically or metaphorically.

I need to know what he's hiding.

The power tools haven't taken a break. They're going strong, drumming away at the porcelain and metal, giving me the perfect opportunity. My only opportunity. I could wait until he leaves the house, but there's a chance he could move the paper before then. If I'm going to do it, then I need to do it now.

The only problem is that my dream had vastly underestimated the amount of pain I'm in. Even though I slept splayed out on a cushy mattress, it feels like I've been kneeling on gravel for hours. My knees are taking the brunt of the pain, but my shins aren't in the clear. The fragile bone feels like it may snap if I put too much pressure on it. My hips are just as stiff and painful, to the point that I fear my femur will pop out of its socket if I'm not smart with my movements.

I ease my right thigh up to my chest, slowly rock it side to side to loosen the joint, then switch to the left. It helps enough for me to swing my legs over the side of the mattress, but when it comes time to push myself up, a sharp pain stabs at my lungs, prompting an audible gasp to rush past my lips.

I press my hand over my mouth as I ease back down onto the blankets, taking in short, steady breaths.

Before I was diagnosed with Ankylosing Spondylitis, before I knew what was wrong with me, I would occasionally suffer from a sudden stabbing pain in what felt like my rib cage. One minute, I was fine, but then I'd take a breath and, out of nowhere, it seemed, I couldn't. I couldn't breathe. When I tried to inhale, it felt like my rib cage wouldn't expand with my breaths, forcing my lungs to push only as far as my chest wall would allow. Now I know, of course, that inflammation is to blame. It doesn't happen often, but it happens enough for me to have learned how to deal with it, which is by taking shallow breaths to ease my chest wall open.

Once I'm able to take in a full breath, I push myself up a second time, biting through the resuming stiffness in my hips. I would take a moment to stretch them again, but I worry I'm already running out of time—Jack's drill has slowed.

ALLISON A

If I wasn't so certain I'm awake, the weight of my feet might convince me otherwise. Sleep has affected them as well, fastening unseen weights to each foot, weights which push down whenever I attempt to take a step. The kitchen cabinets grow closer one agonizing inch at a time, slowly, painfully, until I can reach out and touch the handle.

I forgot how high the top shelf is, and my heart sinks as I realize I'll have to force at least six more steps—three steps to the stool, three steps back, and then somehow drag it toward the cabinet without making a sound. There's no other option. There's no way I'll be able to stretch myself and reach up the same way I did earlier, when Arlo was here. I wasn't in nearly as much pain then.

Three steps there, and the weight has just barely left my feet. I pause, listening for the drill, which is still going strong, before setting my sights on the stool. It's a heavy metal chair with a thick leather seat. If I had to guess, it weighs close to thirty pounds. Dragging it would make too much noise. Lifting and carrying it is out of the question. I decide on walking it.

I step with my right foot, at the same time pivoting the legs on the right side of the stool an inch forward. I alternate, stepping with my left foot while pivoting the stool forward again, like some kind of daddy daughter dance. The drill is still going when I reach the cabinets, but I don't have relief yet, as my arms seem to have taken the brunt. As much as the adrenaline inside my chest is screaming for me to climb up and

THE NOISE

snatch the paper before it's too late, my arms yell back in protest. They feel limp and useless from steering the stool, and if I'm not careful, I won't have enough strength to move it back, and then he'll know what I did and all of this will have been for nothing.

I breathe in and out, unintentionally matching the drill as if revs, then quiets, then revs again. Deep breaths, accompanied by resting my tired arms on the countertop for three racking minutes, does the trick. I suck in another breath and begin climbing the stool.

Relying on my tired knees to hold my body weight, I open the cabinet slowly, testing its creaks. I've never paid attention to whether the cabinets make noise. I've never had to. I'm relieved to find the creak it makes when opened is small enough that it won't be detected over the power tools, so I rip it all the way open.

There it is, in the same spot where I saw it earlier. I haven't admitted it to myself until this very moment, but there was a part of me that feared I didn't actually see it, that I imagined the whole thing. But I did see it. The paper is real, and it is in my hands.

The drill stops.

TWENTY-SIX

The drill resumes.

I unfold the paper, harboring the irrational fear that he might hear the crumpling over the drumming, and find that it isn't one paper, but five papers folded inside each other. They look like photocopies, the first of which I immediately recognize as a deed to our house. But it isn't *our* deed.

The drill stops again.

Panic sets in, and I wonder if I have time to refold the papers and return them to the top shelf before he catches me.

Footsteps approach.

Instead, I open one of the lower cabinets, the one where we keep the pots and pans, and toss the papers inside. I grab a sponge from the sink and try to act casual, like I was just about to do the dishes, even though there are no dirty dishes in sight.

THE NOISE

I snatch a mug from the drying rack and prepare to give it a second scrubbing, but just as I soap up the sponge, his boots recede back into the bathroom, and the drill picks up again.

False alarm.

I'm sure he moved to stand in the bathroom doorway and admire his work, like I've seen him do so many times before. Still, I wait a few seconds before daring to try again.

Once I'm sure it's safe, I grab the papers so quickly that I accidentally knock over a stainless-steel pot, suffering through its crash and rattle as it dances into stillness across the brick. I draw back, this time certain he's heard. Inner alarm bells ring as I wait for him to come bounding into the kitchen to see what's happened.

Moments go by, but the drill doesn't stop. It's just me, alone in the kitchen.

You're safe, this time. Be more careful.

I kneel down, testing my knees as I ease the pot back into its spot, inadvertently finding that the open cabinet is the perfect shield. Concealed behind this little door, I once more peel open the papers.

The deed is from 1955, listing the owner as one Charles Diggory. I'm sure Charlie's wife lived here with him at the time, though her name isn't listed. I assume the mortgage was taken out under his name alone, likely because he was the main source of income. I remember Charlie's wife's self-proclaimed position as a proud housewife, and it would seem she was telling the truth.

Behind the deed is a brief document describing the land on which this house was built. From a quick scan, I learn the house was constructed in 1955, making Charlie and his wife the very first owners. Before that, in the 1930s, Farragut owned the property, and it was used for recreational activities.

I look up to the window, beyond which I can faintly see the yard under the cover of night, and I wonder what fond memories took place here, all those years ago. I imagine men playing football during their time off from the academy, or perhaps they had bonfires here. I don't know what it was like back then, but there aren't many trees on the property now, making it a perfect space for something like that. Or they could have practiced shooting here. Jack and I did find an old bullet in the dirt when we cleared space for the rose bushes.

Maybe I was wrong. Maybe Jack wasn't hiding this from me. After all, these are pretty mundane facts to keep from someone.

But then why did he put them in the cabinet, out of my reach?

The drill stops again. In its place, hammering vibrates through the walls, and I turn to the next page.

It's a news article. Before I have the chance to read and understand it fully, my eyes ping-pong from "Charles Diggory" to "905 Prospect Drive" to "unidentified suspect."

THE NOISE

The hammering stops in the same moment panic possesses me, because I understand now why he did in fact hide these from me. Something awful happened in this house, and he doesn't think my mind can handle knowing about it.

But I can *handle it. I can.*

I'll prove it.

HOME INVASION LEAVES VICTIM WITH SERIOUS INJURIES
December 20th, 2012

Hidden Heights police detailed a home invasion that occurred yesterday evening at 905 Prospect Drive. The victims, 83-year-old Charles Diggory and his wife, were spending the night at home watching television when an unidentified suspect broke in through a window in the back den. Both Diggory and his wife were tied up in a bedroom on the second floor and beaten. The suspect ransacked the house and stole $107.00 in cash and Diggory's wife's jewelry.

Vomit surges up the back of my throat, acid burning my tongue as I choke on the memory of my nightmare. My hands tremble so violently that I almost tear the paper in half. *It was real. It really happened.*

I look back at the news article in my hands, to the words I already know because I watched this tragedy happen. Not all of it, but enough. Enough to know my mind doesn't make everything up.

I gag on the realization that other things may also be real, like the woman from the park. I fight the urge to run and wash my hair to rid the memory of her breath wafting over the top of my scalp. If she was real, then her putrid, rotting breath was also real, and it's on me.

You said you could handle this.

I breathe in and squeeze my eyes closed to ward off forming tears. *Focus.*

Diggory and his wife were found an hour after the suspect left, by a concerned neighbor who noticed the window in the den had been smashed. Both Diggory and his wife were hospitalized for their injuries. Diggory's wife, whose injuries were less severe, was released this morning, but Diggory himself remains in critical condition.

I force my hands to turn to the next article, desperate for a positive resolution for Charlie.

HOME INVASION VICTIM RELEASED FROM THE HOSPITAL
January 30th, 2013

Home invasion victim, Charles Diggory, was released from Century Medical Center yesterday afternoon. Diggory spent over a month in the ICU recovering from injuries he sustained during an attack in his home on December 19th, 2012. Diggory's wife, who was also a victim, was released from the hospital the day after the incident occurred. Charles' wife, as well as friends and family, say they're excited to have him home.

My relief doesn't last long, as the following paper, an obituary, sends a nauseous quiver up my spine.

IN LOVING MEMORY OF CHARLES DIGGORY, 83
June 2nd, 1930-April 12th, 2013

Hidden Heights – Charles Diggory, 83, of Hidden Heights, passed away peacefully at Century Medical Center on April 12th, 2013. His passing was due to complications from injuries he sustained during a home invasion, which occurred in December 2012.

Charles was born in Hidden Heights on June 2nd, 1930, to Sylvia and Edward Diggory. He lived in his town of birth until the time of his passing. Charles attended Admiral Farragut Academy from 1948 to 1952, where he met his future wife, who was working in the admissions office at the time. The two married in 1954, and built their home in 1955. Charles served in the Navy during the Vietnam War from 1961 to 1965, and earned a purple heart.

ALLISON A

Charles was predeceased by his brother, Alberto, who died while serving as a marine in the Vietnam war. Charles is survived by his wife, as well as extended family and friends.

A viewing will be held on April 16th, 2013, from 2 P.M. to 4 P.M., and again from 6 P.M. to 8 P.M. at the Foster and Baker Funeral Home, located at 11 Main Street in Hidden Heights. A cremation will be held privately the following day.

This must be why Charlie's wife was so averse to the second floor, I realize, because of what happened up there. I can't say I blame her. If something like that happened to me, I'd never step foot in this house again. I understand now why she had to force herself to knock on the door when she first arrived, because what she really wanted to do was run far away.

What Charlie and his wife experienced here must be why the people in this town seem to despise our house, and why it sat abandoned for so long before we got such a great deal on it. It isn't us, and it isn't because our eyesore casts a shadow on this Pleasantville—it's because of what happened inside these walls. I'm sure the townspeople are all wondering why we chose to live in this murder house. I'd be wondering the same thing if I were them.

Anger creeps up toward our Realtor, Sal, who was just clever enough to elude two out-of-towners. Technically, Charlie passed peacefully in his sleep four months after the attack, as the obituary details. By law, Sal didn't have to tell us about the violence that occurred here, because the death did not occur here. Not unless we asked, which we didn't. We sunk all our savings into this house, and Sal and his fancy Realtor outfits got to walk away scot-free with a modest commission.

Something still doesn't make sense, which is why Jack suddenly started digging into this house's past. I was right when I thought he lied to me by saying he was going to the shop. I knew he didn't smell strongly enough of varnish and wood. He might have been there for a short while, but I'm certain he spent most of his time researching all this. *But why?*

Did he see something?

I realize only now, in this moment, how silent the house is. Except for the medicine bottles rattling in his shaking hands.

I dare to look up. I've known him for thirteen years. I know every expression his face makes, but I don't know this one. His face is dark, unreadable.

"Where did you find them?"

"Where did *you* find them?" I power through a shaky voice, finding my nerve. "And why were you hiding them from me?"

I seem to have earned myself a glare, his stormy eyes glinting in the light as they narrow in on me.

"You think my mind is too fragile to handle this," I press on, raising my voice as much as I dare to. "And that if I read these, I'll lose it, more than I already have."

He reaches to help me as I struggle to stand and face him, but I refuse his hand, instead using the counter to pull myself up.

Once I'm steady on my feet, I waste no time picking up where I left off. "Because if I knew something horrible happened in our house, then I would think everything I've been seeing is real, right?" *Isn't it?*

"I don't think that..." he struggles to explain, his voice softening as remorse sweeps his face, which only confuses me more. "I can't explain. I mean, I don't know how..."

"Admit it."

Jack sets my medications down on the counter and tries to take my hand, but I pull away. He always does this. He always takes my hand to calm me down, to show me he's not trying to fight with me, that he loves me, and it always works, but I won't let it work this time.

"You really are Doubting Thomas."

"What?" He asks, eyebrows raised high.

"Why do you have such little faith in me?"

"It's not that. Of course I have faith in you. But, Angela, you've been under so much stress ever since the—"

"Don't you *dare*," I whisper in warning to him.

He takes a breath, then proceeds with caution. "It's not that I didn't think you could handle it. I just didn't want to burden you with it. I wanted to carry this, for both of us."

THE NOISE

"Why did you even look into this? Did you know about this when we bought the house?"

"Of course not." His voice is tense, but firm. "I was curious after Charlie's wife came by. *That's all.*"

I study his face, his eyes, for any trace of something I can believe, but I'm unsure of everything in this moment. His explanations bounce around in my brain, and the more I try to make sense of it all, the more I wonder what *could* have made sense had I known all of this. Instead of burdening me, this information could have given me peace of mind that I'm not losing it, that something *is* happening in this house, that everything I've seen and experienced is real. *Right?*

"If I'd known about this, it could have proven—"

"What?" He interrupts. He knows what I'm about to say, and he's tired, I can tell. "What could it have proven?"

"Something horrible happened in our house, Jack," I go on anyway. "And sometimes, horrible things like this," I add, shaking the papers in my hands, "they leave imprints."

I feel nauseous by the familiar look of worry directed back at me. It's worse than his usual worry. Much worse. He looks like he may cry, but I don't understand why. *Is it rage? Is it pity? Does he want to cry because he thinks his wife is crazy?* I retrace everything I've said, and I know it sounds crazy, but it also sounds plausible. *I* have *been seeing things, and I* have *been having nightmares about something that* really *happened.*

ALLISON A

He steps toward me and takes my hand in his, and I allow it this time because I can't think fast enough to make sense of whether I'm in the wrong.

"I don't want anything bad to happen to you," he pleads in a choked voice. "I love you so much, Angela."

"Tell me the truth."

"You have to trust me," he asks as the tears he was fighting back begin trickling down his cheeks. "I don't want anything to happen to you," he repeats.

"What is going to happen to me?"

"I know you don't understand. I don't know how to make you understand without bringing it up—you just have to trust me, please," he begs.

"How can I—" I began, but then I stop, because I do understand.

I look at his crumpled face, and I get it. I read three articles about a home invasion and became convinced that what I've been seeing, what I've been dreaming, is real. The truth is that there are a lot of blank spots in my memory. I know, because, ever since the incident, I've worked hard to put them there. I've blocked things out for so long now that I don't even remember what I'm blocking out anymore. I'm the only one to blame for what doesn't make sense.

It's possible, I realize now, that I heard about what happened in this house from a passerby during the many times I've sat on our porch, drinking coffee. I can hear everyone's conversations

THE NOISE

as they walk by, and it makes sense someone would talk about it. Of course they would talk about it. And of course I would block it out, like I've done with so many other things.

I have to wonder what I would think if Jack were the one acting this way. *What would I do if he woke up screaming at night and swore he saw things in our house, swore he heard things, things I've never seen or heard myself?* I don't know what I'd do. I would be terrified. I would hide things from him, to protect him.

I try to imagine a scenario where I would look at him the way he's looking at me, where all I could do is squeeze his hand and beg him to stop, to come back down to earth. It would take something terrifying, a fear of losing him, and I understand now why he did it. I understand why he hid this from me.

ALLISON A

TWENTY-SEVEN

It was difficult for Jack to leave for the shop—I could tell by how long he lingered in the doorway after kissing me. I had hoped he felt better, more secure, after our long talk last night, but worry still possessed him this morning, no matter how hard he tried to hide it.

We stayed up until one o'clock discussing the articles and whether we're comfortable continuing to live here after knowing the history of this house. We both agreed that too much work has gone into it to quit now, and that, no matter what happened, it's in the past.

Jack explained he went to the library the day after Charlie's wife visited. With the help of an old colleague of mine, he found these documents through searching the very same microfilm I used to work with almost daily. It was an odd thing to hear, because I'd almost forgotten about that machine. It

THE NOISE

hasn't been that long since I stopped working, but it somehow feels like a lifetime ago.

He didn't have time to read the papers while he was there, so he made copies and brought them home, then hid them where he thought I wouldn't find them. He admitted he hid them because he was worried about how they might affect me, which hurt me to hear, but I understood. I asked if he was ever going to show them to me, and he told me he planned on doing it when the time was right. I'm still not sure I believe that, though it doesn't matter now, I guess.

It felt good to discuss everything openly. For the first time in a long time, I felt like his partner as opposed to his fragile other half. I hoped we could talk more today, about everything, openly, but then Rob called. Apparently, the customer requesting the bench wanted to meet with Jack in person today, and since our income depends on the success of his shop, he had to go.

He placed the papers on the counter by the mail before he left, to prove he's done hiding things, I assume. I appreciated the gesture, but all it did was remind me he hid them in the first place. Again, I understand now why he did it, but it's awful to think the person who loves me the most also doesn't trust me, and for good reason.

I carry my mug of coffee and my journal to the porch, then ease myself into my usual chair. It's almost ten o'clock, but it's still dark outside from the storm that hasn't yet passed.

ALLISON A

Through the dreary light, I can see the tips of the white roses blowing back and forth below the windows, and I hope they won't get too drenched with all this rain. In a funny way, it almost seems like they're saying hello, and I realize it's been a while since I've clipped any for the vase. I poke my head around the doorway to check the state of the roses on the counter. They're fresh. Jack must have picked new ones.

I sip my coffee as I stare at my journal, wondering whether I should write about the muddy woman, or the nightmares. That was my intention when I came out here, mainly because it's routine, but as my fingers tap on the cover, it's starting to seem like a foolish idea. If I write about these things, if I acknowledge them, then any progress I've made will be wiped away with the stroke of a pen.

I push the journal aside and sit back in the chair, sipping my coffee and listening to the wind and bustling leaves in the yard.

The more I think about it, the more I realize these entries have never actually helped me. The only thing these entries have done is create a record of everything I've ever *thought* I've seen.

I remember when I used to deal with records like this, back when I was a reference librarian. I wouldn't create the records, of course, but I would gather them. I searched for and gathered records for the purpose of proving, or disproving, a reference question—if there was enough credible evidence to corroborate a theory, then I was comfortable delivering my findings to the patron as the most accurate and credible truth.

Is there enough evidence here, in this journal? Sure, it's all primary sources, but they're *my* primary sources, with no one else to confirm them. If I found something like this in the archives, I'd think it was interesting, but nothing more than that, and I certainly wouldn't supply this journal alone as proof of a truth.

Back then, searching for and finding the most accurate and credible truth was my specialty, and I always knew where to look, and how to search, and how to evaluate my findings. I was an expert, but I've never applied that same know-how to my own life. I never had to, because I've never been able to admit, really admit, that I could be crazy. Seeing that look on Jack's face, seeing him cry, it almost broke me. I never want that to happen again, and I never want to make him feel like that again. I want to trust myself so he can trust me, so he can leave papers out in the open like it's no big deal.

It's time to find the truth, I decide, and I open my journal.

The first episode happened 14 years ago, around the time I began seeing my dad.

This seems like a good place to start, as it is an accurate and credible truth.

ALLISON A

If the episodes are real, and if I'm truly seeing my dad, then what was the catalyst for this sudden ability?

I can't think of one.

Have I ever heard of someone else possessing this same ability?

No, I have not.

If I fabricated both the episodes and the visions of my dad, then something must have happened 14 years ago, something that made my mind snap.

Did something traumatic happen?

My dad passed, of course, but that happened six months prior to when the episodes began.

The passing of a loved one, especially a parent, would make anyone's mind fragile, but if that's what indeed weakened me, then wouldn't these episodes have started closer to when it actually happened? Why six months later?

Next question.

Did anything else happen, anything besides my dad's passing, that would qualify as a legitimate stressor?

I was living with my mother when the first episode occurred, and God knows that qualifies as a stressor.

But the episodes continued long after I moved out of my mother's house. They happened when I lived with Jack and his parents, the year before we finally got our own apartment together. That was stressful also, because his parents didn't like me. They think I'm not enough for him. I mostly hid in Jack's bedroom during that period of time.

Once we moved into our own apartment, everything got better. Living alone with Jack helped me see that it's okay to exist, quite literally to exist. With Jack's support and the freedom of our own place, my mental health improved. Yet, the episodes continued. I can't think of any stressors during that time in our lives, beyond rude neighbors.

Discouraged, I move on to when we purchased this house, feeling less energized toward my theory now.

My diagnosis, I suddenly recall.

ALLISON A

While I hadn't been properly diagnosed until we moved into this house, I was suffering daily from persistent pain and immobility when we lived in our apartment. I may not have had a name for it yet, but feeling sick is undoubtedly a stressor.

Then we moved here, and my stress continued because I now had a name for it—Ankylosing Spondylitis. Learning I might end up in a wheelchair one day, or have to risk spinal surgery, or perhaps die before I make it to either of those two nightmares, is enough to send anyone over the edge.

And then the incident happened, which was probably the cherry on top of it all. In fact, the episodes, which only happened occasionally over the last fourteen years, ramped up full force after the incident. Before, I experienced them ten times a year, at most. Now, they happen almost nightly.

I realize I haven't written any of this down, so I scribble a few sentences to recap:

Stressed while living with my mother. Stress continued after moving in with Jack's parents. Feeling sick. AS. Incident. And, of course, renovations and feeling useless to do anything to help.

I look down at everything I've written, and it makes sense. I've been stressed for longer than I realized. Maybe

THE NOISE

I *have* snapped. Maybe I've imagined everything. Maybe this is the most accurate and credible truth.

I lean back in my chair, feeling like I've just run a marathon. If it was possible for a person's brain to be out of breath, then mine certainly would be. But just like how a runner feels energized after their struggle, I feel good, too. I feel healthy. I feel right. As I look at the dark gray windows, I'm immune to the weight of the foreboding weather lurking just outside. The gloom of it all should be enough to bring me down, but I feel uplifted, and sturdier than I've felt in a long time.

I've been imagining everything because of stress, and now that I've realized this, I can get better. I can make it all stop, and I can rescue Jack from the sleepless fog he's been in, and then we can finally be happy.

I say all of this to myself while looking right at it, at the dark shadow silhouetted against the porch door.

… TWENTY-EIGHT

I know it isn't a living person. I've known that for the past three minutes I've spent staring at it, because we don't know anyone who would venture to visit us in a rainstorm, let alone stand outside for this long without knocking. I know it isn't real, whatever it is, because nothing has been real. Yet, as much as I repeat this to myself, the figure remains. It stands there, head tilted to one side, staring. *It isn't real. It isn't real. It isn't real.*

How many times do I have to say it isn't real until it disappears?

Maybe I should open the door and prove to myself there's nothing there.

On the heels of the epiphanies I've uncovered through my journal entry, I feel more emboldened than I have in a long time. I pull from this newly gained insight and muster the courage to push myself up from my chair, ready to rip open the door and face these delusions head-on.

Just as my hand touches the knob, a knock breaks through the silence.

My nerve evaporates, and I'm not sure why. If it's not real, then the knock isn't real. I'm seeing *and* hearing things. *That's all.*

Another knock, and my hands start to shake.

A third knock, harder and more insistent. It won't stop until I prove this is all in my head.

I wrap my fingers around the cool metal, take in a breath, and retch the door open.

In place of an empty doorstep, I find Arlo, soaked and shivering, without so much as an umbrella.

"Oh my God, Arlo, come in," I usher him. "Is everything okay?"

"Of course," he answers happily, as if he isn't on the verge of pneumonia. "I just thought I'd stop by."

After helping him to a stool at the counter, I hobble to the bathroom and return with a fresh towel, doting perhaps a bit too much as I help him dry off. The last thing I need is for an elderly man to die of hypothermia from standing on my porch.

I pour a mug full of hot coffee and pass it to him, with milk this time, and head for the sugar, which Jack moved to the counter. "Drink this. It'll warm you up."

"Very kind of you." His blue fingers rattle against the ceramic as he fixes his coffee.

"How long were you out there?" I ask, but what I really want to know is why he didn't knock sooner.

"Not too long. I hope I didn't frighten you." His glassy eyes peer up at me as he takes a sip.

"Not at all. I didn't even see you until you knocked," I lie. It's unsettling to think about how long he was standing outside, head tilted, staring, in the pouring rain, but I'm trying to get a hold of my suspicions and remain steadfast in my pursuit of sanity. I'm sure it wasn't what it looked like.

"Just thought I'd go for a walk. Beautiful day, isn't it?" Even though he's smiling, I can't tell whether he's joking. "Jack off volunteering again?"

"No, he's at the shop."

"Ah," he says through a gulp of coffee. "New project?"

"How did you guess?"

"He's talented," he acknowledges, glancing around the house at what he guesses are Jack's creations—the cedar end table, the hickory clock. "I'm sure he gets new projects all the time."

"He's good at what he does," I agree, sipping my own coffee that is now barely warm.

"When did he get into that sort of thing?"

"Not until later in life," I tell him, resting my palms on the countertop to support my weak hip. I expected to leave my answer at that, but Arlo's extended stare prompts me to explain further. "He grew up in a house that didn't care much for creative expression. It took years of me pushing him to follow his dream before he dared to."

"So you're to thank for all these beautiful pieces of furniture, then?"

I can't help but laugh. "Not at all. I may have pushed him, but the results are his and his alone."

"And what do *you* like to do?"

It's a simple question, but it catches me off guard. I never told Arlo I don't work, or that I'm disabled. I'm sure he thinks I'm a normal, everyday neighbor with a job and ambition, and I'm hesitant to shatter that visage. I'd rather not reveal how pathetic I am to at least one person, if I can help it.

I choose my words carefully. "In my spare time," I start, insinuating I'm busy otherwise, "I like to read."

"Never had the patience for it," he says, teeth chattering as he sips more coffee.

"We have blankets?" I offer, already walking toward the red flannel blanket on the couch.

"No, no," he stops me. "Didn't come here to impose."

"It's no imposition," I say, snatching up the throw.

"Really," he says, his voice serious. "It makes me feel alive."

I allow the blanket to slip from my fingers and slink back onto the couch, questioning whether I should insist. I don't want to be responsible if anything *else* were to happen in this house. I can't force him to take the blanket if he doesn't want it, but I will keep a close watch.

"If you're not here to impose," I say lightly, a smile brushing my lips, "then what brings you by?"

"I'll be honest with you," he says, his hands and lips slowing their chattering, and I'm grateful for it. "It's lonely, couped up in a house all by yourself."

"I'm sure it is," I say. If only he knew how much I understand.

"A person can only eat so many TV dinners." He chuckles.

"If you're hungry, I can make—"

"What are those?" Arlo asks, cutting me off, his face falling grimly serious.

The tips of my fingers rush to cover my lips, as if they are responsible, when my own carelessness is the real culprit. I left the articles face up by the mail on the counter, their headlines large enough for an old man to see from three feet away. The moisture forming in his eyes batters my chest as shame flashes inside of me. I should have been more careful when I first brought him inside. I should have realized. I should have moved them, or in the least not have sat him so close by.

I rush to turn them over, but I know it's too late. The damage is done. He came here to visit a neighbor, and instead I've reminded him of the event that caused him to lose a friend.

"May I?" he asks, easing himself down from the stool and ambling toward the articles, hand stretched out in front of himself. His fingers are still damp, causing the headline to bleed where his thumb brushes over it.

"I'm sorry—" I begin, but he holds up a finger, halting my apology.

As he looks over the articles, I try to decipher any hint of a reaction, but I can't. His expression is blank, as if he has no connection to the story whatsoever, though I know that can't be true.

When he's finished reading, he sets the papers down neatly, taking care to line up their edges. I wait for him to say something, to react to the memory he's just rehashed, but he gives nothing away.

"I'm sorry. I shouldn't have left them out like that," I say, reaching for the papers and wishing I could make them disappear.

"Leave them," he says, placing a hand on top of the stack. "You don't need to feel bad. You're curious about the house you live in. I understand that. I would be too. Besides, I came over unannounced." He sighs and drops his shoulders, then licks his lips before speaking again. "It's been a long time. There are many things I don't remember. Time forgets you and you forget time, I suppose." I nod. "What do you want to know?" he asks, looking up at me with his blue eyes, and I wonder what they looked like when he was younger, when they weren't shrouded in wrinkles, back before he was an old man with no friends and no family, standing alone in the rain on the doorstep of a neighbor he only just met.

"You don't have to talk about it, Arlo. Really. I never meant for you to see this."

"But I did," he offers a smile. "I wouldn't know how to go back to ordinary conversation now."

"I don't know. It doesn't feel right."

He clutches the articles in his hands, then makes his way back to the stool and climbs up. I can't help but notice how much heavier his breathing has become from the minimal exertion he's putting his body through, and I worry that the cold did more harm than he's letting on. He is elderly, after all, and he should never have been standing outside in this weather, let alone for as long as he was. I'm ashamed it's taken me until now to consider the possibility that he stood there for so long because he forgot where he was, or why he was here. If I had more control over my mind, then I would have opened the door sooner, instead of letting him freeze out there.

"You'd be doing me a kindness. I won't be able to rest tonight with all these thoughts swarming my mind."

I sigh and give in, if only because I'm consumed by the remorse of my actions so far today, and I don't think I can handle any more guilt. If this is what he wants, then I will talk with him about what happened here. "If it would make you feel better to talk about it..."

THE NOISE

He drops his head, collecting his breath and his thoughts. "I think his wife stopped loving him after this. Or, at least, she realized she hadn't loved him for a while. That's the saddest part of it all."

"Why do you think that?"

"You can tell by the way two people look at each other, you know? You can tell by how they speak, how they fight, how they make up. On the outside, they looked sturdy, and they thought they were. They thought they were like every other happy couple who occasionally struggled. They learned the truth the hard way."

"What truth?"

"No patience."

He cocks his head at my raised brow.

"You don't know?"

"Know what?"

Whatever it is, he shakes his head, as if it's too terrible to put into words. "The articles don't say what happened after he passed." Is all he says. "I can tell from one conversation with you and Jack that you two love each other. It's nice. There's love inside these walls after all these years."

I want to press him to explain further, but I fight back the urge. This is his story, and he can choose which details he feels comfortable sharing. I keep my response simple. "They must have been in love once."

"They were, in the same way most people think they're in love. It isn't until tragedy hits that the opportunity to prove your love presents itself." He nods to my faltering hip. "It seems your love has been tested, and Jack's still here. Charlie couldn't say the same."

He knows, I realize, and redness plumes over my face at how obvious my disability is. I wonder how long he's known, and what he's thought about me because of it. I wonder if most people can tell just by looking at me.

Embarrassment floods my insides, and while I don't normally like to talk about my AS, I feel the need to address it now. Of course, the one time I want to talk about it, I can't, because Arlo moves the conversation along, and I have no choice but to go with it.

"She thought this house was haunted," he says, chuckling only a little, as if it amuses but also saddens him. "After Charlie died, she swore he was haunting her."

The shock of his words jolts the thought of my AS aside, replacing my focus with the noise. *Did Charlie's wife hear it too?*

"Turns out, she was right."

"I'm sorry, you said she was right?"

"She was haunted by her failure," he explains, and my heart sinks. I was so close to getting confirmation of what I've been hearing, and the rejection of it stings.

You haven't been hearing anything, remember?

THE NOISE

"She failed him." He pulls in a breath and lowers his eyebrows, his lips sealing in a tight line that lets me know he's done explaining.

"Are you alright?"

He nods, wiping the corners of his eyes with his forefingers. "So, what is it called?"

"What is what called?"

He gestures to my hip a second time, and a pit forms in my stomach. I was ready to address my disability mere moments ago, but the desire has since been traded for more worrying thoughts, and I'm not sure what to say.

"I used to be a doctor; you remember? Lay it on me."

"I'm sure you've never heard of it," I say, using my shirt sleeve to wipe at a brown coffee ring on the countertop, hoping he'll just move on. Instead, he leans in, eyes laser-focused on me as he waits.

"It's called Ankylosing Spondylitis," I yield, and he nods as if he knows exactly what I'm talking about.

"I'm assuming you were diagnosed late, like most others with the disease?"

My eyebrows shoot up so fast I think they might actually lift off my head. AS is notorious for being misdiagnosed, or diagnosed too late, leaving those who suffer from it susceptible to complications. Only someone familiar with the disease would know this.

"By the time I found a decent rheumatologist who took me seriously, it was far along. It's been progressing since."

I first started experiencing symptoms when I was twenty-seven. I could hardly sleep because of the aching pain in my back and the burning in my hips. I would lie on one side until it felt like my hip was about to detach from the rest of my body, then turn over onto my other side until the same feeling set in. Back and forth, back and forth, all night. I couldn't even lay on my back or my chest to relieve the pain, because those positions, for whatever reason, instigated heart palpitations.

I started getting up for the day around three in the morning, because what was the point of tossing and turning for hours until the sun rose? Might as well make coffee and read a book, I figured. Only it would take me forever to get out of bed. Twenty minutes, in fact. Twenty minutes to walk ten steps to the bathroom. I didn't know it then, but my bones were fusing overnight, something I've since learned they do whenever I'm immobile for a period of time.

Before I found my current rheumatologist, no one took me seriously. I was a young girl, which meant I was just nervous, or perhaps I had my period, or maybe I was a hypochondriac obsessing over death because my dad passed unexpectedly. That's what they all said. One doctor even told me he didn't have time for "silly girl issues," and that I was taking him away from serious patients. I left his office in tears.

"By now, it's likely affecting some organs, am I right?"

THE NOISE

I try to answer, but the words die in my throat.

"Mhm. Tough disease. You're taking what? Biologics?"

"Meloxicam," I correct him. "And Sulfasalazine. The biologics didn't work for me."

"Sulfasalazine is an outdated drug. Even I know that." He glances back at my unsteady hip. "If you don't mind me asking, what's your dosage?"

I pause, trying to recall, but I'm not sure. I remember I started off at 500 milligrams once a day, then it was increased to 500 milligrams twice a day, and then it was increased again, but I can't remember what it is now. I try to picture the labels, but my mind is blank.

The labels.

"I don't mean to intrude," Arlo offers.

"No, it's fine. I don't know why, but I can't remember the dosage," I say in a distant voice as I float back to the labels in the garbage.

"Have to be careful with those medications. Too high a dose, and the risk of side effects increases dramatically."

"I've been tolerating it," I say. "The occasional headache, but nothing too bad."

"Be thankful for that."

"You've seen worse?"

"Once or twice," he answers. "I had a patient on such a large dose of Sulfasalazine that he suffered hallucinations." He catches sight of the fear behind my eyes and attempts to alleviate my worries. "He was accidentally taking too high a dose," he says matter-of-factly, as if he's charting for a patient. "Hallucinations resumed, which thankfully were caught early due to his attentive mother, who brought him in for treatment. These side effects are extremely rare. You will likely never experience them."

"I'm sure I'll be fine," I tell him, but I can't help thinking about the hallucinations I *have* been having. *Is that what they are? A simple side-effect that can easily be corrected with a lower dose?* Maybe it isn't stress after all. Or, maybe it isn't *only* stress.

Although, everything started before I went on these medications, I realize. *Was it started by stress and then made worse by too much Sulfasalazine?* It's possible. *But why would I be taking a higher dose than is necessary?*

The labels.

"I worry I've upset you."

"I just have a lot on my mind, if I'm being honest."

"Anything I can help with?" He asks, and as I connect with his gentle eyes, I get the feeling I can tell him anything.

"Whatever is bothering you," he says, "It'll eat you up if you try to contain it. It'll turn you into someone else," he goes on, "someone you don't recognize. Someone no one recognizes. You won't be able to look at yourself, and no one will be able to look at you." The color of his eyes grows intense, like a bright blue sky being overrun by storm clouds. "I've seen it too

THE NOISE

many times with too many people. Everyone blocks things out to get through the day, but you're not getting through anything, and it *will* catch up with you." He breaks away to sip his coffee, then looks back at me, only now his eyes have changed, softened. He looks like a different person when his eyes are soft.

ALLISON A

TWENTY-NINE

I told myself not to do it. I swear I did. I begged and pleaded with myself. But I'm stubborn. It's the same reason Jack rarely convinces me to use my cane when I'm struggling to walk. I know I should use it more often, just like I know I *shouldn't* do this. But it doesn't deter me. I can't stop. Jack will be home soon, and I won't have another opportunity.

My lumbar spine extends an uncomfortable, but necessary, amount as I bend at the waist, leaning head-first into the trash as rain pelts the back of my neck. The more I stretch to reach the bottom, the more I expect each of my vertebrae to snap one by one, which should discourage me, but all it does is convince me to dig faster. If I give up now, then I'll be soaked and shivering, not to mention I'll smell like garbage, for nothing.

"What are you doing?"

"You know what I'm doing," I snap at him.

THE NOISE

I dig past the discarded renovation materials, the food wrappers, the used napkins, and my finger slices on something sharp—old piping from the bathroom. I stop, panic taking hold as I imagine Jack noticing the blood on the trash can and realizing I was out here looking through it. I consider wiping it away, but the only thing I have to use is my shirt, and that won't do anything to hide the evidence.

As I waste time brainstorming a solution, the universe provides one for me. Rain washes the stain away, as if it was never even there. I pick up steam, arms and hands whirling like a windmill inside the bin.

"Stop," my dad insists, but I don't.

I haven't been able to stop thinking about the labels since my conversation with Arlo. *What if they weren't a mistake made by the pharmacy? What if they were manufactured right here in my own home?* I have to know, once and for all.

"You don't realize what you're doing. This won't end well. You have to stop."

I want to tell *him* to stop, that he has no clue what I'm looking for because, if he did, he would help me. *But what's the point?* He isn't real. He never has been. He's a figment of stress and medications. But these labels *are* real. I've seen them. I've held them.

"I think it's time we talk about what happened that night."

I wince at the word "incident" hovering in the air, and my digging becomes more feverish, as if reaching the bottom of the bin will stop him from continuing.

"You need to face what happened."

"I don't want to talk about it!" I yell, louder than I have ever yelled at my dad, as I emerge from the garbage.

My heart pangs with guilt as the look on his face burns itself into my memory, but I can't give in. He isn't real. I need to focus on what *is* real.

"Angela."

"I don't want to remember it!" Shaking, I scream so loud that an instant soreness forms in my throat, and he steps back from me. If he really was my dad, if he really was here, then this would hurt him, crush him, forever. But he isn't real, *he isn't real*, and I will never talk about that night, especially not with myself. "Just leave me alone."

I can't tell whether it's only the rain dripping over his face, or if he's crying. I mean, if he *was* here, if he *would be* crying.

I can't look at him. I can't let the illusion of him distract me. *He's not real. He's not real. He's not real. HE'S NOT REAL!*

The bottom of the bin glares up at me as if to say, "I told you so." It's empty. The labels aren't here.

But they *were* here, and the garbage truck hasn't come yet this week. *They were here.* Did they deteriorate in the rain? *They* were *here.*

THE NOISE

Weren't they?

I look down at my hands, at the streaks of garbage stains and blood disappearing from my flesh amid the downpour, and it hits me. It finally, truly hits me.

I need to choose a path forward.

No more back and forth.

I can stay here, in the trash, searching for labels that were never real, just like my dad isn't real, or I can wash it all away. I can wash away the hallucinations and the paranoia, and I can be happy, and I can make Jack happy.

I see the pain on my dad's face. It's the same pain I've seen on Jack's face, and I can't stand it. I avert my eyes, allowing them to fall on the window, where I catch sight of myself in its reflection. Or, where I catch sight of someone who I assume is me in its reflection.

She kind of looks familiar, but she's a distorted familiarity. She has my red hair, though it's dirty and disheveled. She shares my pale skin and my height, but she's whiter than she should be, and her posture is slouched. She looks back at me with eyes I thought I knew, eyes which, my whole life, people told me are the same color as my hair. But these eyes are dark, almost black, and they're scared.

"Everything will be okay," my dad promises me, but I know there's only one way for that to be true.

"I don't see you," I tell him, removing any trace of emotion from my voice. "You're not real, and I don't see you."

ALLISON A

His face contorts as the rain picks up, drenching his eyes to the point where he can barely open them. Only it isn't rain.

"I can't talk to you anymore," I press on, because I have to. "Stop visiting me."

"Don't turn into your mother."

I remember what led up to it—my whole life. My whole life being called a "princess" and being told I wasn't normal, or being told how to feel according to what makes my mother happy. It all exploded that night as I sat on her couch that smelled like cigarettes and listened to her bullshit. And then when she said, when she told me…

After what my mother said, I knew I needed to go or else I'd end up killing her. So I left. I fled into the night, into a rainstorm just like this one.

I walk past my dad without looking at him.

"Please don't do this," he begs, but I keep walking toward the house anyway.

I turn the knob. I step inside the porch. I close the door behind me. I leave my dad outside in the rain.

On my way to the shower to wash off the garbage and blood and hallucinations, I grab my journal and toss it in the trash. I won't need it anymore.

THE NOISE

THIRTY

I dry my hair with a fresh towel as I stare at my reflection in the bathroom mirror, at my pale skin and the dark circles lining my red eyes. Even after a hot shower, I can't seem to wash her away—the woman who looks like me, but isn't me. Can't be me. I'm so repulsed that I cinch my robe painfully tight, like some kind of punishment, as I glower at the impostor. *It will get better. If you stay on the path you've chosen, things will be different.*

"How did things go at the shop?" I ask Jack as I meet him in the kitchen, hiding my cut finger in the pocket of my robe. It's no longer bleeding, but I worry he'll notice the bandage. I've been so focused on moving forward that I haven't stopped to think of an excuse, so it's best to keep it hidden, at least for the time being.

He takes a break from chugging water to catch his breath. "It went well."

"And the bench?"

His eyes flicker to me for only a moment before dropping back to the glass in his hands, and I feel the monster welling up inside. *It's just a look. Nothing more.*

"I got everything fleshed out with it."

"Who is it for? And what *is* the project exactly? You never said," I ask, half out of curiosity and half because I can't seem to help myself.

"It's a memorial bench," he tells me with some hesitation, ignoring the first part of my question, though I can't tell whether that's intentional or because I asked too many questions all at once.

"That's an odd choice for a memorial," I can't help but comment. "Why a bench?"

"The woman who commissioned it said it's meant to symbolize a temporary place of rest, before moving on." He says the last part in a mocking tone, making me feel comfortable enough to tell him that's the most ridiculous idea for a memorial I've ever heard.

"I couldn't agree more. But she's paying well for it."

Whatever I was conjuring up in my mind couldn't be true, I realize, because this story is too detailed for him to have made it up on the spot. He could have said it's a simple park bench, or a bench for a bus station. Either one would have been

THE NOISE

acceptable to most people. A memorial bench is such an odd thing, though, and the reasoning behind this particular one is specific. It's not something that would come swiftly to most people searching for a lie. He must have been at the shop after all.

I made the right decision, I think, mentally patting myself on the back. *This is the right path.*

"I'm glad you're home," I tell him.

I can feel the muscles in his forearms tightening as he wraps his arms around my waist, the same muscles I like to imagine hammering away at furniture in the shop. If I stay on this path, then maybe we'll have more memories like this, and more moments like the one that took place on the floor of the living room the other day. If I stay strong, then life will be like it used to be. Maybe even better.

With his lips pressed against my forehead, and a hint of reservation in his voice, he asks, "What did you do today?"

"Nothing really," I say as nonchalantly as I can manage, trying to give him the impression that everything is fine. *Everything* is *fine.* "I read a little. Oh, and Arlo stopped by."

Jack pulls away from me, taking his arms with him, which bothers me more than the fact that something is clearly wrong with what I said.

"Arlo was here?" He asks, his face pale.

"He came by earlier. I made him coffee and we talked for a bit."

He swallows past a hard lump in his throat. "I don't want him coming here anymore," he orders.

"What?"

"We need to stay away from him."

"What are you talking about?"

"Do you trust me?"

"Yes, but I—"

"You shouldn't be alone with him."

"Jack, what's going on?" I ask.

He stumbles over an explanation, and it might seem like he's trying to come up with an excuse on the spot to someone who was suspicious, which I'm not. "I passed by Charlie's wife's house on my way home tonight and I saw Arlo on her front lawn. It was pouring rain, but he was just standing out there in it, staring at the house. She was inside. I could see her from the street, and he was watching. It wasn't right."

"Are you sure it was him? It could have been—"

"It was him, Ang."

"I'm sure there's a reasonable explanation. Maybe it wasn't what it looked like. Maybe you—"

"Didn't see what I thought I saw?"

"Fair enough," I concede, my hypocrisy showing in the shame that cloaks my face.

THE NOISE

"I'm sorry," he apologizes, his hand gently brushing my cheek. "Whatever he was doing, it wasn't right. I don't trust him, and I don't want anything to happen to you."

I'm hesitant to tell Jack about Arlo standing outside *our* door in the rain earlier. My intention in telling him this would be to suggest that Arlo didn't know where he was when he stood on Charlie's wife's lawn either, that he's a confused old man, but I fear Jack won't take it that way.

"You have to trust me."

"I do," I give in, and I mean it. I hope I mean it. "If that's what you think is right, I'll stay away from him.

"Promise?"

"Of course I promise."

He pulls me back into him, and I bask in the reward of his arms, enveloping me once again. I lean in, resting my head on his shoulder, and breathe in the scent of Endymion.

Whatever the reason for what Arlo was doing, I trust Jack, and I'll keep my promise.

***

It's seven o'clock. I know the routine, but this time I fill my own glass with water and rip a banana from the bundle on the counter, delighted with myself for eating half of it by the time Jack returns. He smiles proudly as he hands me my pills, which I down right away.

"I'm going to take a shower. Do you need anything before I go?"

ALLISON A

I start to tell him I'm fine and to enjoy his shower just as the shrill ring of the phone reverberates through the open kitchen. I pick up and hang up the receiver all at once to reject the call, if only to relieve my ears of its jarring noise.

It rings again. Again, I pick up and hang up. Ringing. Ringing. Ringing. I let it go on this time, waiting for it to go to voicemail, because it's the only way it will stop.

"Are you okay?" Jack asks as my mother's voice fills the room, but I'm too frozen to answer.

Why is she calling me? I thought she was done with me. Isn't that what she said?

"I landed safely in Tennessee and I'm calling you from my new house," she says, as if I could ever care. "It's much nicer than I expected. It's a one-story ranch, so I won't have to tackle stairs anymore, and it has a working fireplace, though it's way too hot here for me to use it." A doorbell rings in the background and she pauses to yell over it, telling the person to leave whatever it is on the matt. I start to wonder whether she ordered food, or perhaps got her first piece of mail in her new house, before I remind myself that I don't care.

"Anyway, I just wanted to let you know I'm here. Listen, Angie, I also want to say I'm sorry. I know it's long overdue, but this move has got me thinking, got me reflecting on everything that's led me here. I wasn't always good to you when you were growing up. I've been afraid to admit that, because I'm afraid that means I'm a bad mother." She pauses,

THE NOISE

her lips smacking as she puffs on a cigarette. "Your father and I didn't get along, I was struggling with the path I chose in life, and things were confusing. There was a lot going on inside of me. There was a lot of anger and resentment. I'm human, after all. I hope you can see me as someone who wanted to do so much better, someone who tried. Just know that I have always loved you. I still love you. So much. I just hope you believe that."

I've never heard my mother say she's sorry before. Not once in my entire life. I can't help the tears from spilling over my cheeks, but they aren't from relief. They're from anger. She finally tells me she's sorry, after everything she said about me to Jack mere days ago, and she does it through the answering machine no less. I'm enraged that *this* is how I get the apology I've been craving.

"Angela," Jack reaches for my hand, but I pull it away. I'm not upset with him, not at all. I just feel numb, and I want to go inside myself and hide. I don't want to be touched, and I don't want to be told it's okay, because it's not okay.

"Jack, if you're listening, I sent you a postcard from my new address. It looks like junk mail, but don't throw it away. It has a picture of Graceland on the front, and my new address on the back, in case you ever want to visit." *You*, not you *both*. "I've never sent a postcard before. It's not in an envelope, so if it's smudged or weathered by the time it gets to you, my new address is 62 North Railroad Avenue in Memphis."

ALLISON A

A jolt of lightning flashes through my chest and I feel my heart jump as if someone is trying to resuscitate me.

"I hope you'll visit, because I think this is the last message I'll be leaving. I can't do it anymore. It's time for me to start over. I hope you understand. Anyway, I wish the best for you, my son. Keep in touch, and remember what I said."

I don't know if there was any more to her message because Jack pulls the plug from the wall. I would have done it myself, but I can't seem to move.

He pulls me into his chest, and I allow it only because his grip is like steel and I'm not strong enough to fight back. The harder he hugs me, though, the more I want him to. He wraps his arms tighter and tighter around my back, pressing my face into his sweatshirt, which muffles my gurgling cries, and I bask in it. It's cutting off all feeling, and I need that right now. I need to not feel anything.

"It's okay," he tells me, but it isn't. "I'm sorry," he adds, but I'm the sorry one. I don't care that my mother apologized and in the same breath wants nothing to do with me. All I care about is what I did to my dad. *North Railroad Avenue.* That's what he said when I begged him to tell me something I have no way of knowing otherwise. He was real. This whole time, he was real.

How could I have known my mother's new address if I haven't been seeing my dad?

THE NOISE

It's possible my mother mentioned it in a previous voicemail, but I don't remember hearing it. I could have overheard it, if Jack listened to a message while I was in the other room, but then why would she give him her new address a second time? She wouldn't. The only explanation is that my dad told me.

If I really did hear it from my dad, then I really did leave him outside in the cold rain, where my mother left me four months ago. I did to him what she did to me. I'm a monster.

My thoughts snowball. I try hard to latch onto any bit of logic I can find, but I can't, because nothing is logical. Everything makes perfect sense, and at the same time, it's all impossible. If my dad is real, then everything is real. *Right?* Otherwise, why would I hallucinate some things and not others? Why would some things be caused by stress and others from reality?

If he's real, then it's all real. If he's real, then it's all real. It's all real. He's real. It's all real. I really *did that to him.*

My sobs become so guttural that Jack pulls away to look at me, to make sure I'm not choking to death on my own tears. He cups my face in his hands and tells me to look at him, to look in his eyes, and I do. "Remember who I am. I love you. *I love you.*"

But does he really?

If everything is real, then so are the labels.

Where are they?

"I'm okay," I tell him, forcing myself to take deep breaths and calm down. I will never learn the truth if I keep cracking like a thin piece of glass, ready to break at the slightest tap tap.

"You don't have to be okay," he says, and I can tell he means it.

"I am."

"Are you sure?" He asks, handing me the same glass of water I drank from to swallow my pills.

THE NOISE

THIRTY-ONE

I know I'm dreaming. I know, because I was here last time, in this very spot at the top of the stairs, bare feet pressed against the hardwood. The only difference is I understand what's happening now. A few more steps, a turn down the hallway, and there, in one of these bedrooms, are Charlie and his wife, tied up and desperate.

I don't decide to move toward the violence—I would never want to witness something that gruesome—but my feet draw me closer anyway. It's as if I'm floating. I glide past the bathroom, past the brand-new yellow wallpaper, past the first bedroom on the left, and I stop. The abrupt halt jerks my neck forward and then snaps it back, and while my first thought is to rub at it and soothe it, I find I don't need to. I feel nothing in this dream state.

"I know you have more," a thick, grisly voice resonates from inside the room, but I can't see anything. It's completely dark.

"We don't—" Another voice chimes in, but a swift whack chases away his words.

"Please!" a woman's voice echoes. She sucks in a breath, if only to be able to cry more as she begs. "Please, we have nothing else. Please stop hurting us."

"You think I give a shit that you're old?" The voice laughs. "There's no empathy here for you." His laughter mixes with the sound of a metal chain, and my stomach drops. "Last chance."

"We," an older man staggers, fighting to get the words past his shallow breathing, "don't have..." he fails to finish his sentence, his words replaced by gasping breaths.

The lights turn on in an instant, and my throat fills with vomit as my eyes struggle to take in the ghastly sight.

There are two chairs set up in the room. In the chair on the left sits Charlie's wife, frightened and weeping. Her hair is longer, but it's her. I'm sure of it. I could never mistake those glasses. On the right sits a man I can only assume is Charlie, because the intruder has mangled his face beyond recognition. Both of his eyes are swollen and black, with pus draining from the one on the right that seems to have taken the most hits. The cheekbone beneath his infected eye has been prey to so many punches that the skin has split open, revealing bright white bone beneath. His chin is dislocated, causing his mouth to hang open diagonally, and I understand now why it's so difficult for him to speak.

"I can do this all day, old man," the intruder says, eyes flashing from behind his mask.

"We don't have anything!" Charlie's wife is hysterical, desperate for this to end. She has taken nowhere near as close to the beating Charlie has. The only things marring her face are broken glasses and a split lip.

The intruder pulls the chain taught. I don't think Charlie's swollen eyes are able to cry, but even if they could, I'm sure he wouldn't. In fact, his face hardens, like he's back in the war, strong and resolute. He knows what's coming, and he braces himself for it.

The intruder walks up behind Charlie and wraps the chain around his neck without hesitation. He pulls it tight, prompting blood to bubble from Charlie's lips.

Charlie's wife cries and kicks her legs against the floor, trying desperately to free herself, to no avail. "Oh God, oh God," she cries, her head rolling back, away from the sight.

Charlie's head dips, revealing an intense wound on the back of his skull. I can't even imagine what could have caused something so vicious. Not a fist, certainly. I glance around the room, taking notice of a hammer lying on the floor beside Charlie's feet, and my stomach lurches, but I can't look away. The dream won't let me. I can only cover my mouth to force the vomit back inside as blood pours from the wound and matts his hair.

His breathing slows, becoming erratic. I can tell by the intermittent rise and fall of his chest that these breaths are close to being his last.

"You live in a nice house," the intruder says, his tone light and mocking, "by the water. Do you think I'm dumb?" He pulls tighter. Charlie chokes on the chain, his face turning blue and his eyes bulging.

Charlie's wife vomits on herself, then gags on the remaining bile she can't expel because she's tied too tightly to the chair.

"Fuck!" the intruder yells. He drops the chain, not because he feels remorse, but because red and blue lights are blazing through the windows.

Charlie's head drops. If I didn't know how the story ends, I would think he passed right then and there.

"Charlie, my darling, stay with me," his wife begs.

The intruder runs right through me, leaving a trail of Charlie's blood as he races to the last bedroom on the left, the one that faces the backyard.

That's how he got away.

"Charlie, please, please stay with me," his wife calls to him. "I love you. I love you so very much. All you have to do is keep breathing, okay?" She continues, her voice growing dull and muted as the room darkens once again. "If you stay with me, we'll take that trip you always wanted. The one to

THE NOISE

Yosemite. Okay? We'll do everything you've always wanted to do. It'll be okay, okay? I love you, Charlie. I love you."

My eyes burst open, wasting no time as they search the room for the intruder. I can only see in front of myself, though. I can't move my head to look anywhere else.

I know it must be the middle of the night because only a single strip of moonlight shimmers above me, spinning through the fan and turning the ceiling into a rippling ocean. It makes sense, because I feel like I can't breathe, like I'm drowning.

There's something moving at the foot of the air mattress.

I can't see it, but I can hear it shuffling back and forth. Even If I wanted to look, I couldn't because of the weight on my neck, pressing me back into the pillow. A headache forms from the strain on my muscles as they fight to free themselves, but a headache is the least of my concerns.

I want to tell it to get out, but all I can muster is a quiet "Ge…"

To my surprise, the shuffling stops. It's what I wanted, but it's more unsettling than I anticipated.

The shuffling resumes without warning, and I can't figure out if hearing it is worse. I just want it to stop. I want all of this to stop.

Despite my inner protest, the sound grows louder and louder, and I realize why—it's standing beside the mattress now.

Her head snaps down at me, and I can see she's a young girl, barely seventeen. Her long brown hair drips over a light blue sweater stained with blood, the sleeve of which is torn where her broken arm pierces through. Other than her sea-foam green eyes, her face is unrecognizable, as if it's been mutilated in some kind of accident. Her nose took the brunt of it—smashed flat, bones crunched against her cheeks. It's strange to say, but despite her appearance, she's the healthiest looking spirit I've ever seen. She doesn't look as gaunt and sickly as the rest of them. *Is it because she's so young?*

She resumes pacing up and down the side of the mattress. Back and forth, back and forth, back and forth. Her meaningless marching quickens and slows erratically, as does my breathing, and I try again. "Get...ou"

Her broken nose and sea-foam eyes materialize an inch from my face. Hair blows back from white skin as she screams like a banshee, and I scream back, my spine lurching just enough to make me realize I can move. Without hesitation, I make a run for it.

Only I can't run, because my body is fused stiff. I topple off the mattress, struggling to fight hands which reach out of the darkness.

"Get off!" I yell, but the hands only grasp me harder.

I can smell it—Endymion—but I can't let him hold me down. He doesn't know. He doesn't know what's inside the room with us.

I manage to break from his grip, then struggle to get up from the floor while yelling at him that we need to leave.

THE NOISE

"No, we don't, Angela. Please stop," he begs, but I don't fold. I grab my cane and begin searching for her. I open every door, every cabinet, and look under every chair. She's here, somewhere. They're always here somewhere.

Jack clutches my shoulders with such force that I feel a bruise forming this same instant. My crumpling face alerts him to his overuse of strength and he lets go, instead pulling my whole body into him.

"She's here," I tell him, but he only holds me harder. "I saw her."

"It's okay. I believe you," he says, running his fingers through my hair.

"No, you don't."

"I *believe* you. I promise you I do. I'm sorry I've made you doubt yourself. I never wanted this. I'm just scared. I'm so scared, Angela," his voice cracks, as if he's about to cry.

Maybe he finally saw something, I wonder. Maybe he's realized it's all real. Maybe this is it. It's all real. No more secrets.

He ushers me to the air mattress, where we sit side by side. "Tell me what you saw."

I'm confused. I thought he saw what I saw.

How can he believe me if he didn't even see her?

I consider he just wants to see if our stories match up, because I'm sure he's wondering whether he's crazy. I certainly did after I saw my first apparition.

ALLISON A

I tell him about the nightmare, about the girl and her pacing, but then I catch sight of that familiar look of worry on his face, and I stop. I realize he didn't see anything. He's not checking to see if our stories match up. He's not worried that he's crazy. He's worried I am. Still.

I remember when he used to look at me with so much love in his eyes, like he was grateful that, even though I'm sick, I was still here with him, that I was still looking back at him at all. Now he looks at me like this, like I'm sick in other ways and I just haven't realized it yet.

He looks so tired, so worn out. I look down at his hands covered in blisters and cuts from the shop and renovations, and yet still he uses them to sift his fingers through my hair, to calm me.

I don't want to be weak, but I can't help crying into his shoulder. I'm crying for everything that's happened, for everything I know is real and can't prove, for how much I don't trust him, for how much I want to, for how tired I am, and for how tired I know he is. I'm so very tired. I just want everything to stop, and at this point, I don't care how that happens.

I realize I'm dangerously close to how I felt four months ago.

"I think I need help," I tell him. "I think I need to speak to someone."

He wraps one arm under my legs, the other bracing against my back, and pulls me onto his lap. With my face burrowed in

THE NOISE

his neck, he runs his fingers through my hair, and my sobs only grow.

"I need to talk to someone about what happened," I admit. My dad was right. I need to face it.

"I know."

THIRTY-TWO

It's been quiet between Jack and me all morning. He retrieved my medications without saying much, and I took them without saying anything at all. He's been holed up in the bathroom ever since, but I haven't heard him working. I went to check on him a few minutes ago, and I found him just standing there, staring off into space. He paid no attention to me. He didn't even glance in my direction. I wasn't prepared for it to be so awkward, and I wasn't sure what to say to break the tension, so I pretended I needed to use the bathroom, and he left to give me some privacy.

As I come back out to meet him in the kitchen, I find him staring again, this time at the stairs. He's barely moving, barely breathing, but I know he's alive because his eyes are murderous, boring holes into the hardwood leading to the second floor.

THE NOISE

"Is everything okay?"

The sound of my voice snaps him out of it. "I'm fine. Just trying to figure out what to do with these damn stairs."

"I thought you were going to find an expert?" I remind him.

"I haven't found anyone," he answers, his voice dull and low.

"I'm sure we'll find someone," I offer halfheartedly.

I open the fridge, for something to do. I reach for the milk, but I find the carton is almost empty. I unscrew the cap and peak inside, finding about a tablespoon remaining. The shelves are barren. Jack usually does the food shopping on his way home from the shop or the shelter, but he forgot to go last time. He's had other things on his mind, like ghosts and Arlo, and labels.

I close the door and turn to Jack, but he's gone. He must be back in the bathroom, staring again.

I don't know what's real anymore, and I don't know what I'm supposed to do in this situation. Things don't feel normal between us. I don't even know if I can trust him. I don't know what to think.

I grab instant oatmeal and a small pot. Neither of us have eaten today, aside from the banana I took with my medication. Making oatmeal makes sense, and I need something that makes sense right now.

It isn't until I'm plating the oatmeal and arranging apple slices around the rim of the bowl that I remember Jack doesn't like oatmeal. He likes oatmeal *cookies*, but not oatmeal.

ALLISON A

I scrape the food into the sink, hoping he hasn't smelled it from the bathroom.

"Is something wrong with it?" He asks as he rounds the corner. I guess he smelled it after all.

"I didn't realize it was expired," I lie.

He smiles warmly, something I wasn't expecting, and wraps his arms around my waist. "I would have happily eaten the oatmeal," he says, his voice light and sweet, and I feel bad now for wasting it. "I know we don't have much. I'll get some things from Wallace's."

"We can manage."

"It's not a problem," he assures me.

"Are you sure?"

"I'm sure," he says, meeting my eyes for the first time this morning.

After walking him to the door and exchanging our usual "see you later," I watch his truck turn onto Hillside, guilt fluttering in my chest at the sight of him taking a break from doing something for us to do something else for us.

I'll clean, I decide. I'll clean, and it'll clear my head, and everything will make sense after.

I spend the next half hour wiping down the kitchen countertops, polishing the stainless-steel appliances, vacuuming the living room, picking fresh roses from the garden, and I even light a candle—Frasier fir, Jack's favorite, because it reminds him of Christmas.

THE NOISE

I step back to admire my work, refusing to pay any attention to my screaming spine. This was worth it. The space looks light and clean. No one can be crazy in a house like this.

As a finishing touch, I open the windows in the kitchen and the living room, allowing the cool air to shimmy through the curtains. I close my eyes, breathe it all in, and wait to feel sane.

There's a knock at the door. I don't have to look to know who it is. There's only one person who visits us, and as I open my eyes, I'm reaffirmed by the sight of his smiling face peeking through one of the porch windows.

I open the door just a crack, bracing my hand firmly against the wood. He's oblivious to my reservation and tries to step inside, forcing me to apply more pressure than I'm comfortable with.

He stops, confusion rushing his face, and I feel horrible. He's always been so pleasant, so kind and compassionate, and I've enjoyed talking to him. I don't know if I can trust Jack, but I need to keep my promise until I figure that out.

"I'm sorry, Arlo. I'm busy today."

"Oh, that's okay," he says, a hint of brightness returning. "Would later be better?"

I pause, trying to string together my words in a way that will let him down easy. "We'll be busy later, too."

Storm clouds roll over his blue eyes, just like they did yesterday. I know he understands, yet he forges on anyway.

"How about tomorrow?" He asks, his voice flat.

ALLISON A

"I'm sorry," I tell him. "I've enjoyed your company so much, Arlo, but we just have a lot going on at the moment."

Shadows of darkness swarm his face, highlighting his high cheekbones and deep-set eyes, and I feel myself shaking. I've never seen this look on anyone's face before, let alone his, and I start to wonder whether Jack was right after all.

With his eyes glued to mine, Arlo takes one small step back from the doorway.

"I'm sorry, Arlo."

"I bet you are."

"Excuse me?"

"I was wrong about you."

"What are you talking about?"

"You're no good."

"Please leave," I tell him, finding firmness in my voice now. His tone and his stare don't belong to the Arlo I thought I knew. But that's just it—I *don't* know him. I don't know Arlo. I know nothing about him. I still don't even know where he lives, or what his last name is.

"You're just like her," he tells me. "You're just like Charlie's wife."

His words send an icy shiver up my spine. They're cold and emotionless, as if someone else has possessed him, someone angry and dangerous. I force the door closed, feeling the wood push his body backwards, then shout through the window, telling him to leave or I'll call the police. I don't even realize

THE NOISE

I'm yelling at him, threatening him, until his eyes grow so dark only a glint of light shines through.

I want him to leave, right now. Jack *was* right about him. No sane person would ever act this way, not that I have any right to talk. At least I wouldn't come to someone's home and threaten them.

I feel the need to watch him as he leaves our property, to make sure he won't try to break in and hurt me for rejecting him. Yesterday, I never would have thought that about Arlo, but after today, after his words and seeing that look on his face, I don't trust him at all. Even as he steps up onto the sidewalk and ambles down the street, my unease persists.

I check and recheck the door to make sure it's locked. I consider closing all the windows, but then I realize how silly that is. He's over eighty years old—there's no way he'll be crawling through a window.

I head to the counter and toy with the white roses in the vase, more for a distraction than because they actually need fixing, while I wait for Jack to return. Only I can't stop shaking. My hands quiver so much that I cause a few petals to loosen and drop to the smooth wood counter. I pull away before I do anymore damage, inadvertently knocking the vase off the counter.

My breath catches in my throat and I lurch for the glass, full of momentum, as it sails to the floor. I catch it just before it collides with the brick, but it nearly slips again from my sweaty

ALLISON A

palms. I cradle it in both hands as I set it back down in its spot, finally allowing myself to breathe. I may have saved the vase, but most of the roses have fallen out, save for one.

I kneel down to scoop up the flowers, but I instead clutch at the shooting pain in my chest.

All the Doctors who believed nothing was wrong with me would have been all too happy to witness this overreaction to a fallen vase. They'd tell me I'm too anxious, and that I need to practice yoga or something, and it kills me to know they would be right. *It's just a fallen vase*, I tell myself. *They're only flowers. Arlo is gone. Everything is okay.*

I stand up and place the roses back in the vase, and the pain in my chest vanishes, like it was never there at all. *I just need to calm down.*

I place my sticky palms on the counter, close my eyes, and take in deep breaths, letting them out slow and steady, one by one. When I open my eyes, I feel calmer, until I notice my reflection in the stainless-steel refrigerator door. I put so much work into cleaning the house and keeping myself calm, but I put no effort into myself. If I want to be sane, I have to act sane.

After brushing my hair and my teeth, washing my face, and changing my clothes, I drop some sliced lemons into the pitcher of iced tea just as Jack's truck gurgles into the driveway.

"Did you hurt yourself?" He throws the groceries to the ground before rushing to check me for any sign of pain or injury.

"I'm fine," I assure him. "I took it easy. I promise."

His dark eyes fill with worry as they scan my face, trying to determine whether I'm telling the truth.

"I'm okay, see?" I bend at the waist, hoping it serves as proof enough for him to relax. I'm thankful that I mustered the energy to brush my hair, because it cascades over the twinge of pain my face would otherwise display.

His worry deepens regardless, and I realize he isn't only worried—he's angry.

"I didn't mean to upset you."

He holds my hand tight, his other hand cupping my cheek as his eyes focus in on me. "I'm not angry with you. I'm angry with myself. Do you understand?" I shake my head. "I need you to know something. I need you to hear this, okay? I don't need or want you to do anything that might hurt you or cause you pain. I know you feel helpless, but I don't see you that way. I promise you I don't. In fact, I think you're the strongest person I've ever known," he says, filling my eyes with unexpected tears. I'm not sure if I'm crying because I didn't know how badly I needed to hear these words, or because I'm stunned by his overreaction. He is definitely overreacting. "You don't need to prove anything. You have nothing to prove, and I'm angry with myself for not making you believe that."

"I just wanted to feel normal," I tell him.

He pulls me in close, his arms tangling behind my neck. "You are."

I would nod if I could, but I don't think he realizes how strong his hold is.

"I love you," he says.

His grip loosens. He kisses my forehead, his lips firm but tender, before bending down to pick up the bags he'd dropped. "I picked up the ingredients for your favorite dish. How does Swedish meatballs sound for dinner?"

I wipe the back of my hand across my eyes. I want to tell him Swedish meatballs sound great. I want to thank him for thinking of me, but I can't seem to form words. I feel like I'm dreaming.

He lays out the items he bought at the store as if they're prized possessions he won in battle. Among them is lingonberry jam, my favorite addition to this particular meal. He remembered. "And maybe cheesecake for dessert?" he adds, setting a small plastic container on the counter, and I feel myself returning to normal.

I never clean like I did today. He was taken aback, and it worried him. It's understandable.

As I help him unload the rest of the groceries, my stomach growls at the sight of this feast in the makings. Aside from tonight's surprise dinner, he bought all of my favorite snacks, even plantain chips and guacamole.

THE NOISE

"They haven't had these in stock for months," I tell him, holding up the bag of chips.

"They had a lot of things this time," he answers. "I don't know if that's why the store was packed, or because everyone wanted today's newspaper."

"What's so special about today's paper?"

He reaches into one of the bags and retrieves a rolled up Hidden Heights Tribune. "There was a car accident in town last night. A girl in her late teens, I think—she actually lives a few houses down—she was killed."

"Oh my God, that's horrible."

"She apparently got her license two days ago," he says, scanning the article. He shudders as he folds the newspaper and tosses it on the counter, as if that would somehow make the story disappear. "I didn't want to buy one, but everyone else was. I didn't want us to look like the newcomers who don't care, you know?"

"I'm sure no one would have thought that," I suggest, knowing I couldn't be more wrong.

"She was well known in town. Homecoming queen, top of her class, all that. Everyone in Wallace's was mourning over her like she was their own child."

Morbid curiosity strikes, and I pull the paper toward me. I want to see this young, popular girl who had the whole world at her fingertips. I want to see the kind of face that would make

ALLISON A

an entire town mourn. As Jack restocks our refrigerator, I turn to the front page, where I assume the article is.

BRIGHT FUTURE SLASHED FOR HIDDEN HEIGHTS TEEN

My eyes float below the headline and fall on her yearbook picture. I imagine this photo stings for the girl's family, who have to see her smiling beneath her cap and gown as if she's about to embark on the rest of her life. She looks like she would have succeeded, if you can even tell that from a picture. Even in black and white, she looks more put together than I have ever been. There's no blush evident in the monotone photograph, beyond a slightly darker shade of gray, but I can tell her cheeks are rosy, and not like she used make-up, but like she's just that healthy. Or *was* that healthy. She did everything right, and it still wasn't enough. It's never enough.

I keep going back to her hair—long and brown. It's such a normal shade, but there's something about it, something familiar. I look closer at her eyes, which look to be a light color, one that would be more apparent if the photograph wasn't in gray-scale. Perhaps even a color like sea-foam green.

THIRTY-THREE

It's been hours, and I still can't let it go. It's too much of a coincidence that a young girl with long brown hair and light eyes was in our house the same night a young girl with long brown hair and light eyes—who lived nearby—passed in a car accident. And the girl I saw *looked* like she'd been in a horrible accident.

As I lay here on Jack's chest, the warmth from the fireplace licking at my cheeks, I feel as if I'm containing an explosion. I can smell his cologne, and I feel his strong fingers brushing through my hair, but neither does anything to calm me. All I can focus on is how sure I am that she was the one pacing beside our bed. She's no longer alive, but she was here. Just like my dad has been here.

My dad, who I left outside in the rain as if he meant nothing to me. I can't even stomach what he must have thought as I closed the door in his face. He's never done that to me, nor would he ever, but I did it to him, twice. Deep down, I admit, there's a part of me that wanted him to be fake. I've been jealous of others for so long because, while I talk to my deceased father, they all lead lives they can share with others. No one thinks *they're* crazy. They don't curl up in a ball on the shower floor and cry until their head pounds because, fourteen years later, they still miss their dad terribly. They move on, and I always thought I wanted to be able to do that too. But I don't like this feeling. I don't feel good. I feel empty. *How do they not feel empty all the time?*

I remember riding in the passenger seat of my dad's truck when I was a teenager. We were on our way to the home improvement store to buy flowers for the garden, and he was playing country music. He put on a favorite song of his and told me to listen carefully to the lyrics. The song was about a man who held on to his love for a woman for years, a woman who had disappeared from his life, because he believed she would come back eventually. When the song ended, my dad told me that, to truly love someone, you have to put all your faith into what you aren't sure of.

"Do you have faith in mom?" I asked, and his eyes widened.

"I don't know."

"Why don't you know?"

He turned the volume down, then sighed as his shoulders dropped. "We aren't soulmates, Angie."

THE NOISE

Panic struck, and I worried he was about to tell me they were getting a divorce. I tried to find the words to ask him outright, but they died in my throat. He smiled calmly and assured me that they were staying together. He always knew, *knows*, what I'm thinking.

"For now, at least," he added.

"For now?"

"You're sixteen. You're old enough for me to tell you this," he said, and I braced myself. "When I pass, your mother will remarry. I'm sure of it. We're together now, but we won't be together forever. We aren't meant to be."

"Why not?"

"Because she will move on, and you don't move on from someone you love."

"What if she's lonely without you?" I asked, not yet understanding. "It wouldn't mean she doesn't love you, but she still has a life to live and she should be happy."

"Loneliness," he scoffed. "It's an excuse to cheat. If the person you're with, the person you love, passes, and you date or marry someone else, it's cheating. Plain and simple. Do you know why?" I shook my head. "Because they never died at all," he whispered, as if it was a secret he was sharing only with me. "They're still here, because dead doesn't mean gone. And *because* they're still there, they have to watch you move on from them, and replace them. That isn't love. Love isn't cruel like that."

"What if, before the person dies, they tell you they want you to move on?"

"First of all, never say *die*. No one dies, okay?" I shook my head up and down. "Second, when they make that seemingly selfless request, they have no idea what awaits them on the other side."

"How do you know what's on the other side?"

"Because I've been there."

I practically jumped out of my seat as I turned to face him.

"You never knew this, but I was in a motorcycle accident when you were about four. A truck swerved into my lane. It hit me head on and knocked me clean off my bike. Next thing I knew, I woke up in the hospital. Everyone was fussing over me because they said I died out there on the road. They swore it wasn't possible for me to be alive and talking to them, but I was. I didn't tell anyone what I saw, because I knew they wouldn't believe me. I never even told your mother. But I saw it, Ang. I was there. I was on the other side."

"How could you keep that in for so many years?"

"Because people don't like to talk about death, or what comes after. It makes them uncomfortable. No one would have listened to me. They would have made something up about my brain creating some kind of alternate reality to compensate for what was happening to my body. My brain was dead, plain and simple. But people can't be convinced if they aren't open."

"I'm listening," I told him. "What was it like there?"

He eyed me, contemplating whether I was mature enough. Apparently, he thought I was.

"Well, there's no euphoric afterlife where everyone suddenly knows everything and is happy and content all the time, I can tell you that. That's what people like to think, but it isn't true. It's just like this," he said, nodding at the passing road. "The world is the same. You're still you, still confused, still learning and growing, still experiencing fear and loss. All those people who tell their partners to move on and remarry after they die, they'll change their minds once they get to the other side. They'll realize nothing is different, that they're in the same room as the person they love, a person who can no longer see them, a person who no longer wants to even think about them because it's too painful. And they will have to watch everything."

"Some of my friends have parents who remarried, and they seem happy, and they all say they still love the person who di—who passed."

"I'm sure they do love them, but they were never soulmates, and *that's* the difference. The love you have for your soulmate is beyond words, and the only people who understand this love are the ones who have found theirs. You understand?"

"I'm trying to."

"If someone is your soulmate, your true soulmate, then you wouldn't *want* to be with anyone else after they pass. The thought of even holding someone else's hand would twist your gut. It would be more painful to touch someone else than it would be to miss them every day for the rest of your life. Instead, you'll hold on to their memory, and you'll be patient, so that when the time comes for you to join them, you can pick up right where you left off." He went on. "Tell me, if your mother remarries, who will she be with on the other side? Will she think I'll understand and run to her with open arms while she kicks my replacement to the curb? Will she decide she loves my replacement more than me? Whatever would happen here is what will happen there. Nothing is temporary."

It was at that moment I understood what my dad was trying to tell me. I remember looking at him while he drove with one hand on the wheel, the other resting on the window ledge, and I wondered what I would do if he passed. I knew I couldn't get another dad. I knew I would have to, as he said, be comforted by his memory until I saw him again.

I wondered—If you can't replace a parent, then why do people think they can replace a husband or a wife? We have the strength inside of us to live with open wounds. We do it every time a family member passes. Yet we convince ourselves we need a bandage when it comes to our partners.

Why did *I* convince myself I needed a bandage? Why couldn't *I* be patient? If I had been patient, then I would have heard the address on the answering machine, and I would have realized my dad is real. Instead, I couldn't live with the uncertainty, and I hurt him. I hurt him so badly.

THE NOISE

Jack turns to me, the tip of his nose touching the tip of mine.

"I had fun with you today, making dinner," he says. "You were a good sous-chef."

"I had fun too," I answer, trying to ignore the newspaper and the noise and the labels and the nightmares and the episodes and what I did to my dad.

"I have off tomorrow. Maybe we can go for a walk, and make another meal together?"

The noise thumps above our heads, and Jack's eyes flicker to the ceiling. I grow excited when he opens his mouth to speak, hoping he's about to say he hears it for the first time. Instead, he says, "I have a recipe for homemade pasta. We can break out the KitchenAid with the pasta attachment."

I can't imagine how he doesn't hear it, but maybe it sounds louder to me because I haven't heard it in so long.

When was *the last time I heard it?*

He yawns, and I reflexively yawn too, but I'm not tired. He lays his head on my shoulder and closes his eyes, rambling on about pasta dough with egg versus pasta dough without egg, while the noise taunts me from above.

***

Jack lies sprawled across the air mattress, his naked legs glowing in the moonlight. I know he's asleep by the way his chest shudders as it rises with his breath, as if he's in the middle of a REM cycle.

ALLISON A

I don't know when the noise stopped. All I remember is drifting off to sleep, then bursting awake, then watching Jack's eyelashes flutter over the course of a few hours. I tried to make myself tired, but each time I closed my eyes, they fought to spring back open. Maybe it's the pain in my back from cleaning earlier that's keeping me awake, though I know it's more likely the newspaper and the noise and the labels and the nightmares and the episodes and what I did to my dad.

I meant what I said to Jack the other night. I need to talk about it, about the incident. Maybe that's the only way all of this will stop. I've kept it inside for so long, though, that I don't even know where to begin.

Desperate for the advice I took for granted when he was here, I sneak out of bed and creep down the hallway, toward the den, where I hope to find my dad sitting in the moonlight under the window. But the room is only filled with everything I've put there—nothing.

THIRTY-FOUR

It's been there for months, the word DEN written in thick black marker, taunting me, reminding me of what I've lost.

As I listen to the pelting water of Jack's shower coming from down the hall, I wonder if it's time to unpack it, to touch the silky metal and put my talents to good use.

I can only pretend to be okay for so long before the dam breaks. I know it will, because it has before. To fix the dam before that happens again, I need answers, and this would be one way of getting them.

I'm not even sure it still works. It's been sitting in there for so long, through the heat and the cold. If I dared to dig it out, and if Jack saw, he'd be upset that I broke our agreement. If it didn't even work on top of that, then it would have been for nothing.

ALLISON A

Even so, opening that box would be easier than opening my journal. But I'm done doing things the easy way. It hasn't gotten me anywhere.

I pull my knees up to my chest, as if they will protect me from the memories I'm about to allow in.

My dad wasn't there last night in the den, because of me. But I remember what he told me before I banished him. He said this won't stop until I acknowledge it, until I remember what happened.

It's time to be brave.

"I never want to talk about your father again," my mother said that day as I sat on her couch that smelled like cigarettes.

I pause, testing the waters of my mind to see whether I'm able to continue, whether I can handle this. Reliving the memory is crushing, like someone is sitting on my chest, suffocating me. At the same time, purging it makes me feel like I can finally breathe, if only in small gasps. I can't explain it, but I know I need to keep going.

"I need to talk about him. He's my dad—"

"Was your dad," she corrected me.

THE NOISE

"Is." I stood my ground, watching her eyes grow in surprise at my insolence.

"Why can't you talk about him with someone else?"

"You're supposed to be my mother. You're supposed to be there for me when I'm in pain, but you can't put your own feelings aside long enough to do that."

"Because I have feelings too, Angela."

"I never said you didn't."

"But your feelings matter more?"

"You're my mother!" I yelled. I'd promised myself I wouldn't lose my temper, but I couldn't help it. It was such a simple statement, one any parent should be able to understand, but she just didn't. All she did was adjust her posture and lift her chin, as if my outburst didn't deserve a response.

I knew I needed to speak in a calmer voice. If I yelled, it would only prove to her that I'm emotional and therefore illogical. I closed my eyes tight, took in a breath, and started again. "I am your child. No matter what your feelings are toward my father, I am your child and I was in pain and you ignored me. Worse, you made me ignore my own pain, so that you could move on and be happy. Your feelings were all that mattered. Why can't you understand what I'm saying?"

"Why do you need to dig up the past?"

"Because we're still in the past," I told her. "You're still treating me that way, even now. I'm sitting here—your daughter is sitting here—begging you to show me you care about me, that you love me even."

"How is this conversation going to accomplish that?"

"You could show me how much you care by talking to me and listening to me. You never listen to me."

"Angie," she says, her voice exasperated. "I never listen to you? Really? Come on."

"You're not even listening to me right now."

"Because I'm tired of this. You're so sensitive about everything. I'm tired of always having to sit down and talk whenever your feelings are hurt."

"Sensitive?"

THE NOISE

"Yes. You get it from your father, not from me." Clearly, I thought. "Look, I know what you want from me. I'm not stupid. I hear you. But I can't give it to you."

"Can't or won't?"

"It's not who I am."

"Didn't you ever care that I cried alone in my bedroom over him? Didn't you care that my teachers were sending me to the guidance counselor every other day because they were afraid I was going to kill myself?"

"Of course I cared you were sad, but—"

"But not enough. Not enough to console me, because you just needed to move on, and my sadness was a constant reminder of him."

"Yes! Okay? Yes."

"That's selfish."

"I don't know what you want from me, Angela!" She yelled. Her eyes were smoldering and her jaw clenched hard. It was a look I saw often when I was younger, and I knew it well enough to know she was past the point of listening.

ALLISON A

"I want to feel the way dad made me feel, like I have a parent who loves me."

"Then go live with him!" She yelled. As soon as the words left her lips, a quivering hand raised up to cover them. Even she knew she had crossed a line.

I could tell she was sorry, that she regretted it, but it was too late.

I stood up from the soiled couch and towered over her, my fist raised like I was about to hit her, my own mother. I wanted to do a lot worse.

"I'm done with you. Forever," I told her, then bolted outside into the pouring rain.

I sat in my car for longer than I should have. A minute, maybe two. I thought she would come after me. I really did. I thought she'd run outside, hug me, tell me she was sorry. But she didn't. I sat there, nursing a crushing pain and unbearable feelings of worthlessness until I couldn't stand it any longer.

I sped toward the parkway. My foot pressed down harder and harder on the gas pedal, like it had a mind

THE NOISE

of its own. It took me two or three times of catching myself driving over ninety miles per hour to realize my body knew how desperate I was for the pain to stop, and it was trying to help me. It wanted me to end it. It wanted me to go live with my father.

I started hyperventilating. I wanted to cry, but I couldn't get enough air into my lungs to even breathe properly. I felt hopeless and unloved, alone and afraid, and the more my body tried to kill me, the more I thought I didn't deserve to be here at all.

I didn't realize it when I finally started crying. My vision blurred to the point that I could hardly see, but I just thought my windshield wipers weren't doing a good enough job. It wasn't until cars started beeping at me that I understood I was in danger, and it was then I saw the telephone pole straight ahead.

I got out of the way in time, which somehow made me feel worse, and I started hitting myself in the head. I punched and scolded myself for poking the nest. If I had just left things alone, if I had just accepted who my *mother is, then I never would have heard those words. I never would have realized how unloved I am by her. I never would have walked inside, sopping wet, and I never would have climbed the stairs to the bathroom on the second floor, where I never would have done what I did.*

I thought this would help, but I feel worse. So much worse. I feel empty inside as I rock back and forth to console myself, but it's going to take much more to push this memory back down where it belongs. As tears spill down my cheeks, I raise my fist and slam it into the side of my head. Again, and again, and again, each time allowing only a whisper of a moan to escape my lips.

I can't let Jack hear me. I don't want him to see me. I want to be in this moment, face crumpled, eyes stinging, chest heavy, by myself.

I don't know what I thought would happen if I let it back in, but I assumed it would bring nothing but pain, and I was right. It didn't give me answers. None at all. It only made everything worse. My dad was wrong.

There's nowhere left to turn, except for the box.

THIRTY-FIVE

"See you later," I tell Jack as he crunches over fallen leaves on his way to his truck. It won't be too much later, though. He wasn't supposed to go in at all today, but Rob needed his opinion on something. He said it won't take more than a few hours.

Jack apologized incessantly when he got the call, because he had promised we'd cook and spend the day together, like we did yesterday. I tried my best to seem upset, but the truth is that I want time alone.

The red blotches on my face eased up by the time he got out of the shower, but the emotional scars remain, putting pressure on the dam. I think this will help relieve some of that pressure, but I need to move fast.

My sense of urgency grows as the noise vibrates overhead, and before I know it, I'm tearing at the box like a rabid animal.

But the ravaged cardboard container holds only a mouse pad, post-its, pens, and a tangle of wires.

It's not here.

I spot another box, one also marked "DEN", and I pull it toward me, knowing as I claw it open that it isn't in here either. If it was, then I wouldn't have been able to move the box so freely. It might not be that heavy for someone without AS, but it would have been a substantial task for me. Even if I could manage to move something of that weight, my arms would feel like Jell-O afterward, like I'd held a toddler for hours, and they feel nothing like that now.

Just as I suspected, it's another box filled with wires. *Why do we have so many goddamn wires?*

I reach for another, able to tell right away that this is the one. Instead of dragging it nearer to me, I save my arms the trouble and crawl toward the box, wasting no time ripping it open.

I haven't seen this in months. Probably longer, actually. The last time I used it was when I worked at the library. We were each given laptops to do research, but they were small and I had trouble working with them, so I brought my own. I've had no use for it since I resigned, or since Jack suggested we give up electronics, or since I lost all desire to write that book of mine.

I press the power button on my old HP Envy, but the battery is dead. I don't know why I thought it wouldn't be.

THE NOISE

I tip over the previous box and sort through the web of wires in search of my charger, finding it intertwined with the cable for a television we sold four months ago. After plugging it in, I watch the screen light up blue, then black, and my old icon appears above a loading sign.

I'd forgotten about my icon. It's a picture of a star in honor of my favorite poem by John Keats. I memorized it for an assignment in Romantic Literature when I was an undergraduate, where I had to recite it in front of the class. My peers sighed as I spoke each line carefully. Most of them had chosen Wordsworth, Shelley, or Byron. To me, Keats was, and always will be, the epitome of romance. I can still remember the words now, words which often echo in my head like a catchy song—*Bright star, would I were stedfast as thou art, not in long splendour hung aloft the night and watching, with eternal lids apart, Like nature's patient, sleepless eremite—*

The home screen loads, presenting me with the wallpaper I'd chosen on my first day of work—an old wooden bookcase filled with blank spines. I was so eager back then. I came in two hours before my shift just to clean and organize my desk. I hung inspirational posters, put out fresh flowers, set up my file folders, and added the library's most important bookmarks to my browser. Then I fiddled with the color theme and screen saver, making sure everything was perfect.

I remember my password without even trying—Keats1990.

ALLISON A

The noise pummels the floor above, but I can't worry about that right now. I need to do this before Jack gets home. If I can do this without him knowing, then it's no harm, no foul, no matter the outcome.

I click the Wi-Fi icon, realizing I don't even know if we have Internet. I remember Jack saying he was going to bundle it with the landline, even though we don't have a television or a computer, because it was cheaper.

I hold my breath as the screen loads, praying for the bundle.

I'm relieved to see "Blau" pop up as a possible connection, but disheartened when I'm prompted for a password. I would consider searching for the router, but I know Jack well enough to know he would have changed the password to something more personal.

I try the password he used to use for Netflix.

It doesn't work.

I try the password he used to use for online banking.

No good.

After a pause, it hits me.

I enter: LappuLappu

As soon as Chrome loads, I waste no time being grateful for his sentimentality and instead begin typing, my fingers flying over the keys as if they knew no time apart.

I enter: "Bright Future Hidden Heights." That's as much of the headline as I can remember, and it's more than enough. The screen populates with pages of results. I don't need to sift through all of them. A preview of the first result contains keywords I remember from the newspaper, such as "homecoming queen" and "AP chemistry." I click on it.

My mouth slaps shut with so much force that a crack screams from my jaw. Her sea-foam green eyes are unmistakable.

I rub away the pain in my mouth as my heart booms inside my chest. It *is* her. It has to be. There's no other explanation. I really did see this girl in our living room the night she passed. And, if that's true, then...

I type: "Hidden Heights deaths." It's a ridiculously basic search, but my fingers are in a race against the clock and my brain struggles to catch up.

The search yields nothing of value, though I knew it wouldn't.

I try again. "Deaths in Hidden Heights, NJ."

It's been a long time since I've researched anything, and I've clearly lost my edge. There could be, and are, hundreds of results for this low-level search.

I take a deep breath and lay my hands down flat, enjoying the coolness of the keys on my fingertips. There's so much potential bubbling up from the keyboard, if only I could remember how to harness it.

The term Boolean shoots out of my memory.

I type: "Hidden Heights AND Woman AND Death," then proof-read the words before tapping enter. I'm encouraged to see a slightly filtered list of results, though the leading articles are mostly about a woman who passed in her sleep, or another woman who passed after being stung by over a hundred bees.

I try again. "Hidden Heights AND NJ AND Woman AND Death AND Mayo Park."

RAINSTORM SENDS CAR INTO MAYO PARK, WOMAN TRAPPED INSIDE UNTIL SHE DIED.

I open the article.

There are no pictures of the accident, nor of the woman, but the precise location of the crash is mentioned. It happened beside the swings, which is exactly where I saw the woman digging.

I return to the previous page and skim through the rest of the results, hoping for a photo of the victim, but I find nothing. I brainstorm other ways to word this search, but I come up empty. I had more details for the young girl—Lacey, her name was, *is*—but all I have to go on for the woman in the park is just that; a woman in the park.

I move on.

"Hidden Heights AND NJ AND Woman AND White Roses."

I didn't expect much.

I try again, this time using the cross street where she was standing when she stomped on the flowers.

THE NOISE

Still nothing.

Next. "Hidden Heights AND NJ AND Mechanic." I don't know if he was a mechanic, but he was working on a car, and I figure it's worth a shot.

Nothing.

"Hidden Heights AND NJ AND Riverside Drive AND Death."

Bingo.

RIVERSIDE MAN COMMITS SUICIDE AFTER LOCKING HIMSELF INSIDE RUNNING CAR

I don't bother reading through it, because the picture of the deceased is more than enough. I was too far away to see his face, but I could never forget his curly silver hair. It's a little shorter in this picture, but it's him.

A woman who passed in a car accident in Mayo Park, in the same spot where I saw the woman digging, the same woman who came into our house in the middle of the night. A man who committed suicide at the same house where a strikingly similar looking man was beating his head until it bled. This is proof. It's all real, all of it.

But why? Why have I been seeing these spirits all over town?

The noise crashes overhead.

And in my own home, I realize.

ALLISON A

I compose myself, place my hands on the keyboard once again, and type: "Hidden Heights AND NJ AND 905 Prospect Drive AND Death." Just as I hit enter, the noise stops.

I look up to the ceiling. The noise has stopped. The house is quiet. Quieter than I've ever known it to be. It's so quiet that I can hear the blood rushing to my head like waves lapping at the beach.

Feeling dizzy, I lower my gaze back to the laptop and try to refocus. The screen is flooded with results.

I see a title I remember from the articles Jack brought home, and I know I'm in the right place. My eyes spin from one article to the next.

WIDOW LEFT REELING IN THE WAKE OF HUSBAND'S DEATH

BELOVED MAN MURDERED BY BURGLAR

HOME INVADER SOUGHT CASH, TOOK WHAT HE COULD FIND

I don't know which article to click first, so I choose randomly, opening the one titled, NEW YEAR BEGINS WITH TRAGEDY ON PROSPECT.

The noise resumes with such fervor that my neck snaps toward the ceiling on impulse, instigating an immediate pain to

THE NOISE

flourish at the base of my skull. All I can do is stroke the back of my head, trying to ease the pinching vertebrae, while I stare at the smooth white ceiling above. As I watch dust trickle down like tiny waterfalls with each thump, it occurs to me for the first time who it could be.

How could I not have realized this before?

If everything else is real, then why wouldn't the noise be real, too? And, if it is real, then who better to haunt the second floor than the man who lost his life there?

He hasn't just been haunting the second floor, I realize. He's been haunting my episodes, too.

I remember seeing the back of his head in the window reflection during one of my episodes. I remember the wound running red with blood that matted his hair. I remember the purple marks around his wrists. I remember the strange cross-hatch bruise encircling his neck, a bruise that very well could have been made by a chain.

It's been Charlie this whole time.

Is this what my dad meant when he told me to pay attention to when the noise starts again? Is Charlie trying to talk to me?

"Charlie?" I call. "Is that you?"

The noise stops.

"If it's you..." I go on, "I'm so sorry for what happened. I can't imagine what you've been through." I take his silence as in invitation to continue. "I'm sorry if we've upset you with the renovations. We never meant to replace any of the memories you had here." A thump prompts me to rephrase, "*Have* here." It's quiet once again, and I feel emboldened by his responses, like I'm finally grasping at the truth. "Charlie, I want you to know that—"

There's a knock at the front door.

I'm sure my irritation is showing as I wrench the handle back, ready to scream at a lonely old man.

"I'm sorry to interrupt. Do you have company?" Arlo asks as he pokes his head inside. He must have heard me speaking to thin air moments ago.

"Can I help you, Arlo?"

"I brought you these," he says, offering a bouquet of white roses. "You and Jack liked the last ones so much."

A black truck rounds the corner and my heartbeat quickens at the thought of Jack coming home to find Arlo here. He would think I broke my promise, or that I haven't been as forceful with Arlo as I should have been. But I have been forceful. I know I have because of how upset Arlo was when he left yesterday, which he doesn't even seem to remember now.

The truck drives past the house, and I realize it isn't Jack after all. Still, I'm reminded that the clock is ticking.

"You can't come around here anymore," I tell him, watching his face harden the same way it did before. "Please leave."

THE NOISE

His eyes go black, or at least it seems like they do. He looks like a demon standing on my front porch, eyes glistening like onyx.

"You have no idea what's happening right in front of you," he snickers. I try to push the door closed, but he catches it with his fist. He's much stronger than any man his age should be. "Jack is lying to you." He tilts his head to one side. "But you know that already, don't you?"

"Get out!" I use all my strength to close and latch the door, leaving only a barrier of thin glass between us.

I stare into his dark eyes and furrowed brows, and that strange familiar feeling rises up again. I know him.

THIRTY-SIX

A window shatters above, sending my pulse into a frantic state of unrest.

Cold air whooshes in, funneling down the stairs and encasing me in a threatening frost. As I rub my arms to ease the goose pimples, I consider fleeing the house altogether, but then I remember Arlo is still outside, and I realize I'm trapped.

I look through the porch windows, checking for where he might have gone. I don't see him, but I latch each window regardless. He's stronger than I expected, and I don't know what he's capable of anymore.

I lock two more windows in the living room, then check the door again, pulling on the handle to make sure it's fastened.

Another shatter comes from upstairs.

Then a bang, so loud a drinking glass shakes itself free from the drying rack and smashes into the floor.

THE NOISE

Without thinking, I rush to the steps and climb five of them before an even louder crash stops me in my tracks.

"I know that's you, Charlie," I call up to him, and the noise stops. "You have to move—"

Before I can get the last word out, the noise picks back up, louder than ever before. I've angered him.

Through the slamming and banging and shattering glass, the phone rings. I barely have a second to wonder who it could be before something else is thrown above, something heavy enough to shake the ceiling.

"Please stop," I beg, taking one more step up.

"Jack, it's me," my mother's voice echoes from the kitchen.

Charlie throws old ceramic pieces from the second-floor bathroom, sending tornadoes of dust down the stairs.

"I know I said my last phone call would be just that—my last—but I needed to call one more time and tell you that I really hope you find happiness, like I'm finding here. I really like it here." She sighs, as if this is hard for her, when she's really basking in the fact that she has a better relationship with Jack than she does with me. I bet she's even hoping I'll hear this message and that it'll hurt me. She's so petty and childish. "I've been thinking a lot about you, you know?" *Fuck you.* "Oh, before I forget, I'm going to text you the link to that dating app I was telling you about."

My head fills with fog, making me dizzy. I'm afraid I might pass out. I clutch the railing to keep from falling down the stairs, but I'm so lightheaded that my fingers barely wrap around the wood. I sway back and forth, reaching out for support with my eyes closed while begging for this to stop, for him to stop, for her to stop.

"Visit anytime, okay? Good luck, my son. I love ya. Goodbye."

Hot tears burn my cheeks. Jack never mentioned anything about a dating app. *Is that what they discussed when my mother came to visit, while I was crying into my dad's shoulder?*

No, he would have told me.

Maybe they've spoken since then.

He wouldn't.

He *has* kept things from me before.

Did he keep this a secret because he doesn't want me to be hurt by my mother's suggestion, or because he plans on actually using the app? Have I pushed him that far away?

Slamming, banging, and shattering from above. The noise. The message. The noise. The message. Jack. The noise. It's all too much, and before I know it, I'm screaming. The shrill pitch of my voice bounces off the staircase walls, creating an echo that consumes anything in its path.

I've tried my best to be a good wife. I'm not perfect, but I've given Jack everything I have. I've tried to do everything I can to make him happy, everything within my ability. Sure, I've slipped up here and there, but I've tried my hardest. *This is what I get in return?*

THE NOISE

"I've had enough!" I yell, snatching the railing as I prepare to take back what's mine. For once, I'm going to get what I deserve. I've had it.

"I've tried to help you, but you don't want help. This is *our* house! Get out!"

The only response is more noise, and my feet take me to the next step as I prepare to face him and tell him to get the fuck out of my damn house.

The stairs creak beneath my feet and I realize I'm more than halfway up. I haven't climbed this high since we first moved in because I thought, because *Jack told me*, I would fall through. *But I haven't fallen through, have I?* In fact, aside from a few creaks, the stairs feel sturdy.

I take another step. Nothing.

I put all my weight on the stairs. Nothing. I grab the railing with both hands, lift myself up, then let my body pounce down hard, ignoring the pain shooting up my spine. Nothing.

He lied.

Just like Arlo said.

The articles, the dating app, the stairs...

The labels.

ALLISON A

THIRTY-SEVEN

Using every bit of adrenaline coursing through me, I manage to tip the garbage can on its side, but I find the adrenaline is no match for the sharp pull in my lower back.

I drop to the ground in agony. The more I move, the more it feels like my spine is being rung out by a phantom hand, determined to make sure I don't find these labels. But I won't let it win. I make use of the anger I'm harboring, exploiting it as a means of pushing myself toward the mess. I claw through the wet dirt as I drag my body, dirt that fills my nails and clumps through my hair. I don't care. I start digging.

I couldn't find them last time, but maybe I missed them. Maybe they were wet from the rain and somehow bonded to the back of another piece of paper. All I know is I have to try, because the garbage will be picked up tomorrow, and this is my last chance.

THE NOISE

I bite through the pain as I pillage, unable to tell what's wet dirt and what's disintegrated cardboard. Whatever it is, it sticks to my hands like cookie batter, making it difficult to pull apart any pieces of paper I find.

This is good. I was too careful last time. Too delicate and too fearful. Not this time. Now, I'm determined to uncover his lies, and I'll dig through whatever mess I have to. I'll do whatever it takes. I don't care anymore if he sees me. I know I'm right. I know what's really happening, because I—

I can't help but laugh like a madwoman as I peel a silky sheet of paper from the back of last month's water bill. I'm lying on my stomach in wet dirt surrounded by garbage, but I'm the happiest I've been in a long time.

I'm finally holding the labels in my hands. They were real all along.

I think back to every time it turned seven o'clock, every time Jack dropped whatever he was doing to get my medications, every time he stood there and watched me take them. He always refills them before I get the chance, which I thought was because he was being a good husband, a loving husband. I thought he was being proactive so he could unburden me. I thought he cared about me.

The errors, the smudges—I can see now what I couldn't see before. This is a poor attempt to create labels that look like they came from the pharmacy. He no doubt noticed his mistakes and hid them out here in the garbage where he thought I would never find them because, of course, I do nothing around here, and I certainly can't manage to take out the trash. He's been creating these labels to cover up the fact that he's either giving me the wrong dose, or the wrong medication altogether.

I stick my fingers as far back in my throat as they'll go, choking on my knuckles until I vomit chunks of banana all over the muddy grass. I catch my breath and go in for another round, wanting to expel whatever it is I've been taking.

My spine lurches with each forceful gag, until it's numb, until I can hardly feel my own legs. If I don't get to my feet now, I never will. He'll come home and find me here, vulnerable, among the labels and the vomit, and I'll stand no chance.

I scream through the agony as I lift myself to my feet, standing hunched, but standing nonetheless. I wipe spit and puke from my chin and catch my breath as my eyes fall to the house, wondering what my next move should be.

Through the windows, I see our brand-new kitchen gleaming. Jack worked so hard to give me the kitchen of my dreams, down to the smallest details, like the old-fashioned wrought iron handles on every cabinet. He drove two towns over to get them, even after I swore I was okay with brass. He's always done everything for me. He's always been the perfect husband.

Or so he's wanted me to think.

THE NOISE

Beside the brand-new kitchen, I see the stairs.

I don't know how he could have done this to me, but he did, and whatever the reason is, it's upstairs.

ALLISON A

THIRTY-EIGHT

I wretch the door open before just as soon grinding to a halt, my heels practically digging into the hardwood. I can't seem to catch my breath. *It can't be.*

Arlo is inside my house.

I would recognize those tufts of curly white hair anywhere, floating like clouds around the sides of his head. He's wearing the same exuberant smile he greeted me with the first time I met him, one made brighter by his twinkling blue eyes. I'll never forget seeing him standing there in the kitchen, talking to Jack. I thought he was just a friendly neighbor. I believed everything he said. But he is none of those things.

His arm is wrapped around Charlie's wife's waist at what looks like a New Year's Eve party—I can tell by the glittering silver hats on each of their heads and the cobalt blue whistles in their mouths. They're here, in this house. I know because of the all-too-familiar staircase behind them. Only there's a television off to the right, an old one, and rich chestnut cabinets to the left.

I opened the article, I remember, and then the noise stole me away. I never got to look at it, or the image the writer chose. But it's him. It's Arlo. He's inside this house with Charlie's wife, posing for a picture that turns my stomach. Charlie was attacked this same month. He was probably in the hospital when this picture was taken, recovering from a beating he took to spare his wife's life. Yet, here she is, hosting a party and smiling for the camera with his friend's arm wrapped around her.

They were more than just friends, I can tell. My gut is telling me that, and I'm listening, because I've learned to trust my gut. God, have I learned to trust my gut.

I think back to the conversations I had with Arlo. He swore Charlie's wife didn't love Charlie anymore, and I assumed he knew that because he was such close friends with them. Now, I'm wondering if he was privy to this information because *he* was what came between their marriage. The more I think about it, the more I realize he never spoke much about Charlie. His attention has always been fixed on Charlie's wife.

Something in the lower left corner of the screen steals my attention.

It's small, but it glints in the light bouncing off the streamers, like a single ember. I look past his grin, past his blue eyes sparkling beneath his festive hat, and I zoom in on the hand resting on her hip, to a gold Claddagh ring.

I already know the answer. Or, my gut knows, because it churns as I close in on Charlie's wife's left hand now. Her dainty fingers are wrapped around a flute glass, and I realize this picture wasn't taken the year they were attacked. It couldn't have been, because Charlie was at this party after all.

There, on her ring finger, is the same Claddagh ring.

How could I not have realized it before?

I was wrong about everything.

It isn't Arlo in the picture. It's Charlie.

Arlo *is* Charlie.

My neck snaps toward the ceiling.

I understand now why Arlo looked so familiar. Arlo, who worked at a hospital *up north*, who lives *a few houses down*, is the same man who's been tormenting me at night with episodes and nightmares.

I look at the door, at my futile effort to keep him out. He's been inside all along.

He's been upstairs.

I hear the noise.

He *is* upstairs.

I struggle to think of a reason for why he's been coming after me. I've heard of spirits growing angry when you move into their home, even angrier if you renovate, but I'm not the one doing the renovations. Jack is, and Jack hasn't seen or heard anything.

It doesn't make sense. One minute, Charlie is a gaunt monster trying to kill me, and the next he's a sweet old man bringing us flowers.

I think about the storm clouds I've seen rolling in over his blue eyes. He has another side to him. A darker side.

He wasn't always like that, though. If my nightmares are any indication, he was strong, brave, and loving when he was alive. He took the brunt of that beating without so much as a whimper. Yet he comes after me for asking him to leave my house? Something isn't right. Something must have happened to him, after the home invasion.

I take a step toward the stairs, toward his noise.

I'm afraid of him. I'm petrified. My heart is thundering and my vision is blurry from the anxiety rising inside me. Yet I step closer still, because there's nothing else to do at this point. He knows how to get to me. He's done it before. He's been inside my mind and in my dreams. If he wants to hurt me, he can. But he doesn't want to do that. At least, not right now. He wants me to come to him.

What does he want to show me?

Jack has been hiding a secret. Whatever it is, it's bad enough that he's lied to keep me away from the second floor, to keep me from discovering the truth. Maybe Charlie is trying to help me.

ALLISON A

My body shakes with each step, fear mounting over what I might find at the top.

Will I find the same gaunt and unnatural version of Charlie I've been seeing in our living room at night? Will he lunge at me with his claw-shaped hands? Or will it be sweet old Arlo, kind and helpful?

The yellow wallpaper adorning the second floor appears on the horizon, hanging from the dried-out plaster like shavings of rotten peaches.

Behind me, the front door opens.

THE NOISE

THIRTY-NINE

"What are you doing?" Jack yells, his voice full of panic.

"You lied," I tell him, setting my lips in a hard line.

"The stairs aren't safe," he says, to which I respond by stomping twice.

He nervously scans the room, as if searching for another reason I should come downstairs now that I've seen through his ruse. I watch his gaze fall on the dirty labels I left on the counter, beside the roses.

"You've been lying about everything," I accuse him, watching tears build up around the rims of his eyes. *Why is he crying? What does he have to cry about?*

"Angela..."

"What have I been taking every day, Jack? *Twice* a day?" He starts to answer, but I know it'll only be more lies, so I cut in. "How many times have you spoken to my mother without me knowing? And a dating app? What the fuck, Jack? Do you even volunteer at the animal shelter? Who *are* you?"

"I'm your husband. I always have been," He answers, his voice firm as he takes a step forward.

"Stay where you are," I demand, and he does.

"Please, just come down. I promise I'll tell you everything." He looks so sincere that I almost believe him, but I catch myself. I don't know him at all, and I can't trust him. I never expected he could lie to me like this, and I no longer know what he's capable of. A terrible thought pangs in my chest, that maybe he's even capable of hurting me. I take one more step up.

"It's not what you think," he says, urgency in his voice as he presses his palms out, begging me to stop. "I'm protecting you."

"You've been *drugging* me to protect me?"

"Come down and I'll tell you everything."

"You can tell me from here."

The noise resumes overhead and I catch Jack looking at the ceiling. He doesn't even try to hide it, because he has nothing left to lose.

"You hear it," I say. "You've been making me think I'm crazy this whole time, but I'm not, am I?"

"I never wanted you to think you're crazy. Please, Ang, please believe me."

"Why should I believe anything you say?"

THE NOISE

"You're wrong about everything. Please come down."

I take another step up instead, only walking up the stairs backwards is causing pain in my lower back, like my lumbar spine is jutting upwards into my stomach.

"Okay, yes, I hear it," he admits. "But I only just started hearing it a few days ago. I swear."

"Liar."

A bang overhead ushers Jack two more steps toward me.

"Stop!" I yell, and he does. "Tell me what you're hiding up there."

He says nothing, so I threaten him with one more step. It's just one more step, but the pain in my back is too great. In an instant, it shoots down my leg and into my foot, numbing my entire limb and causing me to slip.

I remember bursting through the door, soaked from rain and sleet, but shaking more from anger than from the cold. Jack wasn't home. He was at the shop working on a grandfather clock.

I was still crying from what my mother said. I couldn't stop crying, and I couldn't see through the muddled haze dripping from my eyes. I had to feel my way around the house, and I ended up at the foot of the stairs. I was still used to the stairs in our apartment, and I was on autopilot. I climbed to the second floor without thinking, found my way into the bathroom, and stepped over the broken toilet bowl to get to the shower. It was only after I turned on the faucet and saw soap scum dried on the walls, and black mold forming in the corners of the tile, that I realized I was in the wrong shower. But I also didn't care.

I curled into a ball among the shattered bits and I cried harder. I cried for how unloved I felt, and for how devastated I was that a person who gave birth to me could be so heartless. It must be because I'm not worth loving, I thought. That must be why my dad passed, too. I started hitting myself again, harder this time, so hard that I threw up. I laid there for an hour, sobbing and smelling my own puke, until I had nothing left to dispel from my body.

Except for one thing.

I reached for one of the broken shards and held it to my wrist.

I wanted to stay with Jack. More than anything, I wanted to live a full life with him, but I also knew what that life looked like. It looked exactly like how it turned out. My body is pathetic. It can't do anything, and it will only get worse. I knew that then. I knew that, for the rest of his life, he would have to take care of me. That wasn't fair to him, no matter how much I wanted to stay. I knew he loved me, or I thought he did. I thought he would do anything for me, even sacrifice his best years to adhere to my new normal. Who was I to make him do that? Someone who was clearly not worth loving, according to my mother. Maybe she was right after all, I thought. Maybe I should go live with my dad.

THE NOISE

I dug the shard into my wrist. Not deep enough to kill me, I later learned, but deep enough for blood to begin pooling faster than I had expected. As I watched red mix with vomit and tears, I quickly realized I wanted it to stop. I hated the sight of it, and I wished I hadn't done it. All I wanted instead was to be clean and dry, wrapped up in Jack's arms, with his fingers brushing through my hair. I wanted to sit by the fire with him, kiss him, and smell Endymion wafting off his clothes. I wanted to cook with him, laugh with him, and make love to him. But I made sure none of that would ever happen again.

I tried to pull myself up from the floor, but I was dizzy from blood loss and I'd been lying there for too long, so long my bones were stiff.

I didn't have a towel to wrap around myself, because we hadn't put anything in that bathroom. There was nothing but shards and rubble. I crawled along the floor, sopping wet, reaching for the stairs, hoping Jack would arrive home in time to help me. I sat there for five excruciating minutes, waiting for him and trying to move, but he didn't, and I couldn't.

After another two minutes, I managed to stand. I didn't know my wet body left a puddle on the landing.

It happened so fast. I remember standing for barely a second, hunched over, head spinning, reaching for the railing for support, and then I remember spilling down the stairs in an avalanche of brittle bones before crashing at the bottom. I

ALLISON A

stayed there, splayed out and in excruciating pain, until Jack finally opened the door and stepped inside.

I remember meeting his eyes, and I remember the second it took for him to process what had happened before he ran toward me.

Just like he is now.

THE NOISE

FORTY

Jack fell down on the floor beside me, eyes frantic as he looked me over to see where the blood was coming from. His panic only grew as he discovered the source, or sources. My wrist was bleeding, but so were my nose and ears. I know, because I saw him pull his hand away after touching me, fingertips colored red. He wrapped his arms beneath my legs and carried me to the couch. Then he left me.

I tried looking for him, for where he'd gone, but I couldn't turn my head.

I heard a dial tone. I heard him giving someone our address. And then...

And then...

And then what happened?

"Stop!" I yell, grabbing the railing in time to catch myself from falling.

ALLISON A

He comes to a halt five steps down from me, eyes frenzied, skin pale.

The alarm on his face that night, not unlike the alarm he's wearing now, is one of the few things I can remember clearly. Everything else seems fuzzy, but I remember that look. I can't unsee it.

What happened after I saw his face like that?

Did an ambulance come? Did I go to the hospital? Did I spend a few days lying in bed recovering?

And then what happened?

I feel myself trembling on the verge of tears. *Why can't I remember?*

All this time, I've been blocking out what happened that night because it was too painful to deal with. It seems I've been so successful that I can't even remember it now.

Or, I consider, I've forgotten because of the drugs Jack has been feeding me.

"Tell me what I've been taking every day, Jack."

In a calm voice, he answers, "You've been taking Meloxicam, Sulfasalazine, and Flecainide."

"No. No, you've been giving me something else," I press him. "That's why I can't remember, isn't it?"

That familiar look of worry is his only response.

"Don't you do that. Don't give me that look like you're worried about me. *You* did this to me. You're why I can't remember." I start to cry. I can't help it. "Why can't I remember?" I beg through my sobs as the noise taunts me overhead. "Please tell me why I can't remember," I wail over the thuds and bangs, growing uncertain whether it's him who can't be trusted, or me.

Through the hazy vapor of tears, I can still see his face, and it doesn't look like the monster I've made him out to be. He doesn't look like a man who has, or would ever, endanger me. He looks like he's suffering as much as I am, which only makes me angrier.

"Tell me!"

He takes in a deep breath, releases it slowly, his lip quivering. "Okay. I'll tell you everything."

"Why did you really hide the articles from me?" I start at the beginning.

He pauses, and I can't tell whether it's because he's thinking of a suitable lie or because the truth is too difficult for him to admit. "I was afraid they would lead to something bad happening."

"What does that mean?"

"I was worried about how they would affect you."

"Because you think my mind is fragile," I state.

His face twists as if my comment stung. *But that is what he thinks, isn't it?*

"No. I was worried it would lead to something you weren't ready for."

"Just tell me what you mean."

He hesitates to answer, but I deserve to know the truth, so I push on. "You told me you only found those articles. But you found more, didn't you?" I say, piecing the puzzle together.

"I found a few more articles online, yes," he answers.

"New Year's Eve?" I ask, and his skin sinks to a lighter shade of white.

"How did you..." he starts, his head spinning like a windmill as he looks for an explanation. His search ends with my open laptop.

"I let you talk me into giving up our electronics. I thought you actually believed in that shit, but what you really wanted was to isolate me."

"That's not true at all. That's not why I —"

"You knew he was a ghost." I stop him, dots stringing together in my mind. "That's why you didn't want Arlo, *Charlie*, visiting anymore, isn't it?"

"Yes," he admits, cringing at the word ghost. "That was part of it. Please, please come downstairs."

"Tell me why we can see him."

"I don't know. That's the truth."

I move to take a step up, prompting him to add, "But I think it's because we talked about him."

"What?"

"I don't know. I don't. I don't understand any of it. That's just what I think."

THE NOISE

I squint my eyes at him, as if it will somehow help me see the truth.

"And my dad? Have you seen him too?"

"Your dad?" He asks, wearing a sincere mask of surprise, eyes red and bulging and desperate.

We've been seeing a deceased person, talking to him even, but my dad is out of the realm of possibility?

"And my episodes?" I move on, losing patience. "You've seen what I've seen, haven't you?"

"I've never seen any of it. I swear."

"The woman in the park?"

"What woman?"

"What medications have I been taking?" I ask again, anger coating my voice.

"I haven't changed your medications. You're taking the same ones—"

"No," I stop him. "You've been switching them."

"*No*, I haven't."

"Why do you always refill them? And *always so promptly*," I mock him, smirking as if I think I'm on the verge of winning.

"I'm so sorry, Ang. I never meant for this."

"Tell me what you're hiding!"

"I don't refill them!" He yells so loud that I take a step up on impulse. He breathes out and softens his voice, shoulder slumping. "I *can't* refill them."

"Because you're making the bottles from home, and slipping God knows what inside them," I say, filling in the blanks for him while thrusting my finger at the labels on the counter. "That's why you always remember when it's seven o'clock, because it's important for me to take them and stay drugged up. Is Charlie even real? Or am I hallucinating because of what you've been giving me? It's why I can't remember, isn't it? And why I've been seeing all this crazy shit. You're trying to make me think *I'm* crazy."

"I always remember because I don't want anything to happen to you. I don't know how this works, okay? I don't want to lose you."

"So you drugged me to keep me here with you, to keep me nice and insane?"

"Jesus Christ, Ang. No. What do you think of me?"

"Tell me the truth!" I shout at him, sputtering tears and snot into the air.

"Okay, okay." He pauses. "I refilled them once, four months ago."

"Get there faster, Jack."

"I had to refill them at five different pharmacies, using a different script each time," he spits out. "I forged the scripts, okay? But then I almost got caught, and I had to stop, so I could only get a five-month supply in total. I've been trying to figure out a way to keep getting them. I even tried to convince your rheumatologist that *I* have AS." He shakes his head. "I

THE NOISE

made the labels so you wouldn't notice the old dates on the other bottles. I promise you, Ang, I haven't changed your medications."

"I don't understand."

"I know you don't."

"Where do you really go every day? To more pharmacies? Why do you have to use fake scripts, Jack?"

"I go to the shop, and the shelter," he answers. Before I can interject, he adds, "But, there were a few times when I went to your mother's, before she moved."

The betrayal stings. "Why would you go there?"

"She needed someone to talk to."

"*She* needed someone to talk to?"

"*And*," he stops me, "I've been building something for her."

"What are you building for her?" I ask, almost in a whisper, my voice calming, sobering.

Tears fall from his eyes and build in the corners of his mouth. He tries to answer, but a small hiccup is all he can manage.

"What are you building for her, Jack?" I press on, my voice falling flat as fear bubbles in my gut.

He's lying to you again. Make him tell you the truth.

He releases a breath, then looks up at me. I've never seen his eyes look so sad, so hopeless. "A bench."

"The memorial bench?"

"Yes."

"Why now? My dad passed fourteen years ago. My mother has never even cared," I say, shrinking from my own willful ignorance.

His skin grows splotchy and his eyes can't seem to stop watering.

"Why now?" I insist, my voice cracking beneath the sobs. The less he says, the larger the pit in my gut grows, filling up with the truth. "Why can't I remember what happened that night?"

Tears cascade over the sharp apples of his cheeks.

A knock cuts through.

I can make out a haze of purple through the porch door.

"Fuck, not now," Jack says to himself, wiping his face with the hem of his shirt. Looking up at me with softened eyes, he says, "She asked if she could come by today, and I said yes. I didn't know *this* was going to happen. I thought she would make the noise stop. At least, for a little while."

Another knock urges Jack to explain faster.

"The first time I heard it was the night I brought the ladder home. I heard it after you went to sleep. Then Charlie's wife came over the next day, and it stopped for a while. That's what made me research the house. I knew you were right all along. Something *was* happening. But I couldn't tell you because I didn't know if it would change things."

THE NOISE

I remember it stopping after she visited, I realize, but I didn't know why. And then it started again, and I still don't understand.

Another knock at the door, then a smash upstairs puts Jack on edge, forcing him to pick up the pace. "Arlo never spoke to you when I was there. I didn't know he could. When you told me he visited when I wasn't home, I realized he couldn't be a living person. He had me fooled. And then his behavior was so odd. That's why I told you to stay away from him. But then I felt bad, because you're stuck in this house with no one, and I wanted to make sure I was right about him. So I went back to the library and did some more research, to be sure, which is when I found his picture."

"Hello?" Charlie's wife calls through the door.

"I'm going to answer it," Jack says, backing away slowly.

As soon as Charlie's wife walks over the threshold, the noise stops and Jack looks at me as if it explains something.

I finally leave the stairs and walk toward her, toward the woman whose face was beaming with happiness in that New Year's Eve photo.

If what Arlo, *Charlie,* said is true, then she didn't even love him when that picture was taken. She was so convincing, though. If I didn't know any better, if I came upon that article by happenstance, I would have thought she was happy to be with him. I would have thought his death destroyed her world. Knowing otherwise makes me hate her now.

ALLISON A

How can people be so good at pretending to love you?

"I know you said I could come by around four, but something came up and I wondered if now's a good time?"

"Now's fine," Jack answers, keeping a close eye on me.

"I'll never get used to stepping inside this house, you know?" She asks, as if this is normal. Nothing is normal, and I hate her for not realizing what's happening. "But I wanted to come back one more time."

I hobble across the hardwood floor, hearing the heavy thud of my own feet, but she doesn't pull her gaze away from the smooth tile backsplash.

"I wish we had this when I lived here. We had wallpaper instead. Very hard to clean."

As I tread closer, I tell myself he's wrong. He's filling my head with lies. Any minute now, he's going to stop me before she greets me and I prove him wrong. But he doesn't.

He watches me with that familiar look of worry as I get closer and closer. I stand in front of her, impeding her view of the backsplash. She doesn't even blink.

I scream, shout, wave my hands in the air. I even try to push her.

That's what happened after.

I died.

FORTY-ONE

"I really do love the backsplash. I know I keep saying that, but it's beautiful. If only Charlie or I had the know-how to do this when we lived here, the place would have looked a lot different," Charlie's wife says, as if there isn't a distraught girl screaming two inches from her face.

I don't exist to her. I mean nothing.

"Oh, before I forget," she goes on, pulling something from her purse. She retrieves a lavender envelope with a floral border and hands it to Jack, who awkwardly accepts it.

"What's this?" Jack asks, eyes flickering to me. I can see the burden plaguing his face, because as much as he wants to, he can't comfort me in this monumental moment. He can't, because it isn't okay for the living to see the dead.

"It's just a card with a little housewarming gift inside," she answers, smiling broadly. "A housewarming gift, but also a thank you for letting an old lady come see the house she once lived in."

I realize now why Charlie's wife never spoke to me. It wasn't because she didn't like me, or because she felt it only necessary to speak to the man of the house—it was because she felt it only necessary to speak to the living.

My memory whirls to the woman with the bangs who pushed her stroller past our house. The one who reminded me of my mother. I waved at her, and I thought she couldn't see me through the tint of the porch windows. Now I know why she really couldn't see me. I think back to every townsperson I *thought* ignored me. But also, haven't they been ignoring me?

All except for Charlie, who's just like me, and just like my dad.

Why can't Jack see my dad?

That familiar look of worry distributes itself across Jack's features, and I understand why I've seen this look so many times. He wears it not because he's worried about me, but because he's worried about losing me. I think back to each time I saw this look, most of which occurred when I told him about the things I'd seen. He didn't disbelieve me—he was worried I was seeing these things *because* I am deceased. The more I saw, the closer he thought I was getting to the other side, away from him.

How could I have stopped trusting him?

THE NOISE

All the suspicions, all the hideous thoughts I've harbored, I was wrong about all of it. He does love me, so much in fact that he can see me.

I remember the conversation I had with my dad the day we walked by the river. He told me he felt all his ailments at first. He still felt alive. And it dawns on me that this is what Jack meant when he told me he doesn't know how this works. He doesn't know why I'm still sick, and he always makes sure I take my medications so my illness doesn't take me from him, again.

I was worried it would lead to something you weren't ready for, Jack told me when I asked him why he'd hidden the articles. If I knew what happened in this house, then I would dig and make connections—just like I *did* do—connections that led me to uncover the truth about myself. He didn't want me to know, because he doesn't want me to leave him.

Jack's stormy blue-gray eyes water, which Charlie's wife doesn't notice through her ramblings over the appliances and precious wood countertops. But I notice. I notice the way his tears glisten in the soft yellow glow of the kitchen, like there's a tangle of Christmas lights behind them. I remember the day we got married. I remember when we exchanged our vows, and how his eyes sparkled just like this.

It was a simple ceremony. His family is small, and I didn't have enough living relatives to warrant a large reception. We covered an autumn-bare tree with golden lights and asked our friends to marry us beneath it. Those in attendance, aside from us and our friends, were Jack's parents, his aunt and uncle, my mother, and twelve seemingly empty white chairs. Adorning each chair was a picture of the person, or animal, who it was saved for.

The living in attendance didn't understand the chairs and saw it as morbid and depressing, but I felt surrounded by love and warmth. Seeing those chairs added power to my vows when I told Jack I wouldn't love him until death do us part, because death isn't the end. Instead, I promised to love him forever and all eternity. He repeated the same sentiment back to me, his watering eyes sparkling under the golden lights. Then he smiled, and said, "I'm sure," and I knew I would never be alone again.

Charlie's wife doesn't hear the noise upstairs, but Jack does, and as he raises his eyes to the ceiling, I realize I still don't know what's up there, or why he hasn't wanted me to see it.

"How long did you say you and Charlie lived here?" Jack asks.

"Oh, almost sixty years, I would say. We moved in a few years before he went off to serve."

"When did he come back?"

"Mid-sixties. You know, we were lucky to hold on to the house while he was away. A lot of others lost everything. We were especially nervous because he was just a laborer back then. He wasn't a doctor yet."

THE NOISE

"No?"

"After what he'd seen, he returned with a passion for helping others, and he studied hard. I was so proud of him. It wasn't easy, bills-wise, as he was going to school, but we managed."

The silence overhead helps me understand what Jack meant when he said he thinks having Charlie's wife here will make the noise stop. Charlie just wants to be heard, like I do, like we all do, by those who are supposed to love us. He just wants to be remembered.

Is this why Jack can see me? Because I'm anything but noise to him?

I made sure my dad wasn't just noise either. After six months of blocking him out, I welcomed him back in, and then I saw him, like Jack can see me.

The porch door creaks with a timid knock, and my head snaps toward it, expecting to see Charlie.

"I hope you don't mind, but the real reason I wanted to come by again was to show my husband the house. I lived a whole life before him, and I thought it would be nice for him to see some of it."

"I didn't know you remarried," Jack answers, his voice trembling.

"Of course," she laughs as she opens the door.

He's a short man, about my height. He steps inside and kisses Charlie's wife.

ALLISON A

Every cabinet in the kitchen rips open, sending plates and dishes hurtling through the air and splintering into a confetti of ceramic shards.

FORTY-TWO

Jack raises an arm to protect me from the debris flying through the air, while Charlie's wife covers her face in her hands and burrows into the corner of the wall.

"Are you okay?" Jack asks me.

"I'm fine," Charlie's wife responds. "What the hell was that?" She asks, touching a finger to the trickle of blood cascading down her chin. Her new husband, who had bolted for the door, now rushes back to her side, wrapping his arms around her to shield her from the blast that already occurred.

Before Jack can answer, a window breaks in the living room, followed by another, and another.

"It's happening again," Charlie's wife stammers.

"What's happening again, dear?" Her news husband asks.

"It's Charlie," she says, her voice quivering. "He's come to take me with him."

Charlie's wife's new husband pulls her close, as if she's the one who needs protecting. "That's ridiculous. Charlie is dead."

"I've seen him. That's why I moved from here. But I thought it was over. When I came to see the house, I didn't notice him. I thought he was finally gone. But he's not. He's here, and he's angry with me."

"I won't let anything happen to you," her new husband assures her.

"I want to leave. Now."

With his arm wrapped around her shoulders, Charlie's wife's new husband ushers her to the door. He shoots Jack a look, as if this is his fault.

"Coward," a voice says from the stairs.

Charlie's wife stops in her tracks. She knows the voice. She'd recognize it anywhere.

She untangles herself from her new husband and steps forward, eyes wide and bright as bulbs as she points a shaky finger at him, at Charlie. Only he doesn't look like the version of Charlie who brought us flowers, the version we've come to know as Arlo. He looks like the ghoul who's been haunting my nightmares.

His face is unnatural—gaunt and twisted in a way it wasn't when he was alive. I know enough by now to say this with certainty.

Decaying gray skin hangs from claw-shaped hands as they stretch into the stream of light shimmering through the

THE NOISE

curtains. A pebble of light flickers within his deep-sunken eyes glaring from the bottom step where he's crouched.

He lets out a small noise. A kind of guttural growling.

"I didn't know this would happen," Jack swears to me.

"Wha—what are you? What is this?" Charlie's wife's chattering jaw causes her to trip over the words. She breathes in, steadies herself, and finds the nerve to harden her voice. "You shouldn't be here. This isn't right."

Charlie swings his rotten arm at the vase of white roses on the counter, heaving it toward the ground.

Pain swarms my chest, sending me to my knees. It feels so heavy, so all-encompassing, and I can't breathe. I can't catch my breath. My heart palpates and races, then slows to an almost unnoticeable pace before picking back up again. I feel lightheaded. I'm going to pass out.

"I shouldn't be here?" Charlie towers over his wife and her new husband as they sink down to their knees. "I've *been* here. You knew I was here. But I'm just noise to you. Noise you can't stand to hear, so you silence me," he accuses her, his eyes flaming.

"You were supposed to be in a better place," she tells him. "You were supposed to move on, and so was I. I didn't do anything wrong."

"Who says?"

"I…I—everyone says."

"Everyone who's never seen this *better place*," He mocks her. "There's only here. There's only this."

"Try to breathe," Jack tells me, cradling me with one hand while his other hand desperately cups my cheek. "It's going to be okay."

"I was lonely," Charlie's wife whimpers.

"*I'm* lonely. *This* is what lonely looks like!" He shoves his gray skin in her face, and she turns away, repulsed. "You can't even look at me. You did this to me, and you can't even look at me."

"I didn't do this," she cries.

"No?"

"No!"

"Leave her alone," Charlie's wife's new husband stutters, hiding his face in her shoulder.

"You," Charlie sputters the word like it's not worth gracing his tongue. "What kind of man marries a woman whose husband died? Do you think that little of yourself?"

"We fell in love."

Charlie scoffs.

"You have to let me go," Charlie's wife tells him. "I don't deserve this. I stayed by your side through everything. I did everything right, everything I was supposed to do."

"Everything except for the most difficult thing of all." He inches closer to her, his stale breath blowing against her scarf. "Guess what? There is no death." He smiles, barring his black,

THE NOISE

corroded teeth. "The only death is what you've sentenced me to. You left me here to rot, and soon I'll turn into one of those things," he points to the window, to the town outside. "They don't even know who they are anymore."

I gasp to get air in. It's as if I'm breathing through a straw. My lungs feel heavy and swollen. I know I'm suffocating, and I can't do anything to stop it.

"Angela, stay with me. Breathe, just breathe," Jack begs.

"Life is *so hard* for the living, isn't it?" Charlie ridicules his wife. "You have to lose people, and grieve, and move on, while *we* are lost, and afraid, and wither away. You're selfish and weak."

"I loved you."

"*Loved.* I'm still here!"

"No, this isn't you. This isn't the Charlie I remember."

"You *don't* remember me!" He yells, his voice so loud it shakes the floor.

"I…I do. I do remember," she says, half-heartedly. "But this is not who I remember."

"You're right. This isn't me. This is what you did to me," he says, his coal-black eyes narrowing in on her. "You tell yourself you loved me, but you don't know what love is. That's why you moved away. That's why you forgot me. Because you're not capable of love." He pulls away, but his eyes remain fixed. "You don't even understand, do you? Oh, but you will. One day, when you're on this side, you'll realize what love is because you won't have it, and you'll want it. You'll want it so badly. One day, maybe even today."

He reaches out with his claw-shaped hands and wraps his long fingers around her throat. For the first time, Charlie's wife and I have something in common.

I watch through gulping breaths as her body lifts from the floor, feet twitching, starving for oxygen. Neither of us can breathe, but there's one difference—Jack is by my side. Her new husband hasn't moved from the floor. He only stares in mute horror as his wife's eyes bulge from her head.

"He won't save you after you're dead any more than he's saving you now," Charlie tells his wife. "Look at me. Look at what you will become," he demands. "He'll forget you. He'll move on. Just like you did to me." He tilts his head to one side. "Let's find out, shall we?"

"Arlo!" I manage to call to him, surprised when he turns to me. I want to tell him to let her go, that she isn't worth it, that I'll remember him, but I've used all my energy just saying his name.

"Sh," Jack tells me. "Don't try to speak. Save your breath."

I may not be able to use my voice, but Jack can. I pull him into my gaze, silently asking him to do something, say something.

"I don't care about anything else but you right now," he whispers to me.

THE NOISE

I want to tell him I love him, and that I'm sorry. I'm so very sorry for doubting him. I couldn't have asked to be loved any better than how he has loved me, and I almost ruined it. I hope he can forgive me. I don't want this to be his last memory of me.

"You don't have to be sorry," he tells me, as if my thoughts are audible to him. "You didn't know. But you do now. You know now how much I love you, don't you?" He asks, tears forming in the corners of his eyes. I shake my head up and down. I do know. I know he loves me. "I will *always* love you," he swears, his voice cracking. He believes this is the end. "I will never do that to you. I will never forget you."

Charlie's eyes deepen as he glares at us. I see the threat, but Jack is unaware. I want to tell Jack to stop, that he's angering Charlie, but I can't.

Charlie drops his wife to the ground, her fragile bones letting out a loud crack as they smash into the brick. Her new husband reaches for her, supporting her right leg as she screams in pain. She can't walk. It's broken.

Her new husband picks her up, something Charlie would despise, if he was paying attention. His eyes are glued to us now.

His wife's new husband carries her to the door, taking only a quick glance back to make sure they aren't being followed before escaping down the porch steps and fleeing outside. Just like that, they're gone, never to return again. Charlie will never see his wife again.

"I'm sorry we told you to leave," Jack tells him. "Please stop this. I remember you. Angela remembers you."

"She can barely remember herself," he says, spitting the words as he steps toward us.

"I…do," I manage. "I remember."

"Maybe so, but it won't help you. You'll be noise, just like me."

"I'll never let that happen," Jack swears.

"That's what my wife said," he tells Jack, his beady eyes gleaming in the light. "I heard her, the day I passed. I was standing in the room when her sister told her it was okay to be sad. She said it was okay because, one day, when she's ready, she'll move on and she won't feel sad anymore. My wife swore she could never love anyone else." A manic laugh shakes his loose jowls. "It won't happen suddenly, you know. Each day, you'll get lonelier and weaker, and you'll start to entertain the advice you pushed away before, that you should *move on*, that they would *want* you to be happy. Then you'll wake up one morning, and everything you experienced with Angela, everything you ever felt for her, it'll be in the distant past." He turns to me. "As vague as the memories of your nightmares in the daylight."

"That *won't* happen," Jack tells him.

THE NOISE

"The kindest thing you can do is let her go now. Spare her the pain of having to watch you let go slowly."

"I…see you, Charlie. Even if…she doesn't," I say.

He steps closer to me and leans in. "Do you remember my thirty-first birthday?" He asks, his voice ragged as if he's losing the energy to speak. "Do you remember when the balloon popped so close to my ear that I couldn't hear for the rest of the night? Do you remember my wedding day, or the day we moved into this house? Do you remember the train set we gifted my niece for Christmas, or how we drank hot cocoa and laughed as she played with it until midnight? You know me now, you can see me now, but you can't hold on to me. Only one person can do that," he says, looking at the door.

"Don't hurt me," I ask him.

"I don't have to hurt you. Just like I didn't have to hurt her. I belong with the others. She sentenced me to that. You belong there, too, and we'll both see her there, one day. It's a fate worse than death." He walks to the stairs and takes a step up. "I'll see you soon, Angela."

"Dad?" I manage to ask through my diminishing breaths.

I can't believe it's him. He's there, in Charlie's wake on the stairs, basking in a light that has no natural origin. I never thought I'd see him again. I thought I cast him out forever. I can't believe he's here.

"Angela?" Jack asks, searching the room for my dad and finding it empty. "Please don't leave me. Please stay with me."

ALLISON A

The noise resumes overhead as Jack lays me down on the hardwood floor. Then he leaves.

I turn my head and watch him fall to his knees beside the broken vase as he struggles to collect the scattered white roses.

He gives up and drops the mangled stems before fleeing through the porch door, and I wonder whether I will ever see him again.

Just as my vision shrinks to a small pinhole of light, my dad's voice echoes in my head. *When the time comes, that will depend on Jack.*

THE NOISE

FORTY-THREE

I'm standing, facing the stairs. I look for Jack, expecting him to tell me to stay away from them, but he isn't here. I'm alone.

I take in a breath, anticipating my lungs will fight back, but they don't.

I breathe in and out, in and out, in and out, testing myself. My chest effortlessly expands, then falls, then expands again. I can breathe.

As I breathe, I notice I can't smell anything. The air is blank. I can't feel anything, either. There's no scent of burned wood coming from the fireplace. No sawdust. No white roses. No gust of cold wind on my cheeks from the broken windows. No heaviness in my chest.

I lift my hand to my face to see if I can feel my own skin, and it moves as slowly as a raindrop trickling down a windowpane. I turn my head to the side, and it, too, lingers in its movement. Everything has slowed down, I realize, watching a breeze idly sift rose petals across the hardwood floor, a breeze that is indifferent to me.

I sluggishly turn back toward the stairs, toward the sound of a footstep.

"Dad?" I ask, noticing my words aren't slow like everything else. If I don't move, then it all feels normal.

I'm relieved to see a warm smile broaden his face, but I know I don't deserve it. I never thought I'd see him smile again, certainly not at me. I thought I ruined our relationship forever.

"I'm so sorry," I waste no time apologizing. "I'm so sorry I left. I never should have done that, least of all to you. I'm so sorry dad. I'm so, so—"

"None of that matters now," he says. His voice is calm, too calm.

"Are you here to take me?" I hesitate, only now realizing what must be happening.

"Yes," he answers. "But not yet. First, we need to talk."

"Where is Jack?"

"If you want to help him, then we need to talk."

I may not be able to sense the surrounding atmosphere, but the shaking of my chest from the nerves creeping up inside is unmistakable. I know what he wants to talk about. I've been putting things together ever since the stairs. But hearing these

THE NOISE

things out loud is different, because I'm not sure I'm ready for what will happen once it's all been said.

"It's your turn," I tell him. I can't bring myself to start.

"Jack held onto you. You know that now, don't you?" He asks, and I nod.

"Then why am I still like *this*?" My arm slowly sweeps over my ailing body. "Why am I still sick? Why aren't I like you?"

"Because it wasn't only up to him. You needed to hold on to yourself. You needed to remember."

I think back to all the times I hated myself and my body, to all the times I saw myself as worthless, as a nuisance, as noise. He's right. I have blocked myself out for a long time.

The world doesn't think kindly of disabled people, no matter how much it tries to convince itself it does. Whenever I used to leave the house, people would stare. They stare because I'm different. Because I'm not normal. I'm sick. My life is less than theirs *because* I'm sick. They stare because they're thanking their lucky stars that they don't need support in order to walk. All I do by ambling past them is give them the gift of appreciating their own bodies.

After I fell down the stairs, any self-worth I had remaining was gone. I didn't want to remember what happened, because it was devastating. I tried to slit my own wrist, yes, but I failed, and I wouldn't have died if I didn't have AS. I wouldn't have died if my pathetic body hadn't frozen stiff on the shower floor. I wouldn't have fallen down the stairs if my body was like everyone else's. I didn't want to think about how different I am. I wanted to block it out, like everyone else blocks me out. And I did.

"Do you remember all those times you caught sight of your reflection?"

I remember lightning illuminating the room, revealing my reflection in the window. I couldn't stand to look at myself, twisted and hunched like an old hag.

I remember seeing myself in the living room window and stepping back, mouth gaping at my appearance. I looked just like her—the deranged woman in the neighbor's house—hunched, hair unbrushed, eyes sunken from lack of sleep. I ran my hand through my hair, smoothing the wild red strands as best as I could, though it still looked untamed. My skin became hot from friction as I rubbed at the winkles in my cotton shirt to little avail. I straightened my shoulders and took another look. I couldn't do anything about my sunken eyes, and the wrinkled clothes were relentless, but I no longer saw her. Not fully, at least.

I remember seeing myself in the hallway mirror. I looked unkempt. That was a nice way of putting it. I'd forgotten to brush my hair that morning, let alone my teeth. Suddenly, the stench of coffee was unbearable even to me, and I was embarrassed that I'd been spewing it at Arlo the entire time. Deep circles clung to my eyes, emphasized by my paler than usual complexion.

"Yes," I say.

"You were seeing what you were turning yourself into." He looks through the windows, at the town, and I understand.

"They're real?"

"They're real to you," he repeats the same answer as before. "No one else believes in them. No one else even knows they're here. Then you came along, and you gave them hope."

"How did I do that?"

"You remember me, Angela. You've held onto me. That's all they want. They're being forgotten, and they're desperate. They think you can help them too, but you can't, just like you can't help Charlie."

"Why *can't* I help them? It's not fair that they have to turn into those...things."

"Charlie was right. You can't help them because you don't know them. You can't hold on to memories you don't have."

"I don't understand," I say, gulping down the realizations. "If all they want is help, then why are they trying to hurt me? You told me they can't hurt me if I don't look at them," I remind him. "What did you mean by that?"

"It's not them. It's what they've turned into. As time goes on, as their loved ones forget them, they disintegrate, in a way. Who they once were disappears. They're desperate, and desperation can make you do ugly things, especially if you aren't even yourself anymore. I know it's cruel, but if you don't look at them, they think you can't see them, and their desperation turns elsewhere." He pauses before adding, "My turn."

I concede.

"Your mother."

"I don't want to talk about her," I stop him, but he persists anyway. "You have a right to be angry," he says, lowering my guard. "She left you those messages from a distance. She was remembering, but not holding on. There's a difference."

I nod, tears spilling from my eyes.

"But she *was* leaving you messages," he goes on. "She misses you, Angela. You have to know that now."

"That bench says otherwise."

"I think you should accept what your mother is able to give you."

"Would she have seen me if I didn't hide the day she visited?"

"Probably, but only temporarily. By being here, in your house, where it happened," he says, and I cringe, "she was reminded, but she still wasn't holding on. It's the same reason Jack was able to temporarily see Charlie, and why Charlie's wife saw him for a brief time, too."

"Because remembering is different from holding on."

He smiles at me.

"Why can't Jack see you? I've talked about you a lot over the years, so much that he says he feels like he's met you."

THE NOISE

"I didn't want him to see me. I didn't want to frighten him, or make him think I was here to take you away."

"That's why you always visited at night, or when he wasn't home," I say, making sense of things.

He nods.

"Okay. Your turn."

"Do you have any idea how proud I am of you?" He asks, instigating more tears.

"What do you have to be proud of?"

"Angie," he says, stepping toward me, leaving a leisurely trail of colors in his wake. "You may have forgotten yourself for a little while, but you did something not many people can do, and you held onto me. You found that strength. You taught Jack how to have that strength, too. You made a difference in this world."

My chest swells with appreciation. For the first time, I don't see myself as weak and pathetic. I see myself as a strong, resilient woman who not only fought against the daily pain of my own body, but the pain of my own heart.

"Are you ready?"

"I still have questions," I tell him. "The rest of them, they're left here to turn into *that*?" I ask, my head slowly turning first to the stairs, then back to my dad. "Why can't they cross over too?"

"They can, but they won't."

"Why won't they?"

"For the same reason you didn't," he points out. "The same reason I didn't for the first six months either, and the same reason Charlie thinks this is all that comes after. Underneath all the rage and discontent is fear that, if they cross over, if they leave their loved ones, they'll be forgotten completely and disappear. By staying, they think they can somehow beg them to hold on."

"But the living have no idea."

"I wouldn't say *no* idea. The living catch glimpses of those who've passed more times than they realize. Brief shadows darting around a corner. A passing reflection in a television screen. Disembodied footsteps. Small cries of a person long since forgotten. They ignore it, or they find rational explanations, then go about their days as if they won't soon join them."

"They're just noise," I say.

"Noise the living learns to tune out." He steps toward me. "It's time."

"The episodes," I say, desperate to prolong the inevitable, but also desperate for an answer to this fourteen-year-long mystery. "What are they?"

"They're no different from the spirits you see during the day. It's just easier for them to get to you at night, when your guard is down."

"Down how?"

THE NOISE

"Do you think we're supposed to walk through life without ever seeing those who've passed? It's natural to see them. But, over generations, we've learned to put up walls, we've learned to block out the pain and fear. We don't want to see what we think we've lost, and we don't want to see what we will become. At night, though, when you're sleeping, those walls are lowered, and they can fit through the cracks. Tell me, why do you think they always leave when you tell them to get out?"

"I don't know. It's just always worked."

"It's because they realize you don't want them there. They realize there's no hope for them," he answers, and my stomach sinks. I want to cry for them, for how I've made them feel because I was afraid. *They* were afraid, and I could have helped them.

"You couldn't have helped them," he tells me. "You can remember them, but you can't hold on to them."

I swallow the despair I have for them, feeling it sink into the bottom of my stomach. "What will happen to Charlie?"

"It'll take years," is all he says.

"I don't want that to happen to him. He doesn't deserve that."

"None of them do, but you can't stop it."

"How can I cross over and leave him, leave all of them?"

"Jack will tell your story. You have to trust that. He'll show others how to hold on, because *you* showed *him* how. Not everyone will listen, and some will mock, but a few will understand, and it'll make a difference. That's how you can help."

"How do you know he'll hold on to me?"

"You have to put all your faith into what you aren't sure of." He reminds me. He extends his hand. "Are you ready?"

I look to the porch door where Jack ran out of, then back to my dad.

FORTY-FOUR

Jack runs past me. The rose pieces and shards of glass cascade across the floor in his wake. A tiny storm of debris.

He eagerly searches through an open cabinet, looking for something Charlie likely sent crashing to the floor. He yanks open another, then another, until he finds what he's looking for—a chipped drinking glass. He fills it with water and throws the freshly cut white roses into it.

"Jack," I say his name, not knowing if he can even hear me anymore. But he does, and he turns, eyes wide, to find me standing before him.

"Are you okay?" He asks as he rushes to me, cupping my face in his hands, searching for any lingering proof of pain or ailments.

I breathe in to show him I can. I feel no pain at all. There's no soreness in my joints, no stiffness in my hips, no aching, burning pain in my back, no racing heartbeat. I feel nothing, and everything.

"I'm so sorry I lied to you," he cries to me. "I never meant to do this to you."

It breaks my heart to watch his face crumple like this, to watch his beautiful skin turn red from the pain bursting to the surface. "It's okay," I tell him, but he shakes his head.

"I love you so much, Angela. I would never do anything to hurt you. I just didn't know what to do," he pleads. "You died, and I missed you. I missed you so fucking much. And then I started bringing your favorite flower inside," he says, spinning from one thought to the next. "I brought white roses inside for you, and then you appeared, and I didn't know how, and then you were still sick, and all I could think about was keeping you here with me. I couldn't let you use the stairs. I couldn't let it happen again. I'm sorry I lied to you. I thought if I told you what happened, you would somehow disappear. I never wanted to make you doubt yourself. I'm so sorry, I'm—"

"Stop," I say, placing the tips of my fingers on his lips. "I know, and I love you. I love you so much, Jack. More than anything."

He tries to speak, but tears stop up his throat.

"I know," I say again, but he only cries more, because he knows I have to go. We both know.

THE NOISE

And, just like that, a light appears at the top of the stairs. My dad steps out from it and onto the landing, where he waits for me.

"This isn't goodbye," I tell Jack. "I know that now, more than I ever understood it before. It's see you later."

"No," he begs as he brushes his shaky fingers through my hair one more time.

"Listen to me," I tell him. "I'll always be here. You just have to hold on to me, okay?" I say, crying as I fight to push down the lump in my throat.

"I will. I'll never let go. I'm sure. I'm sure," he repeats.

"I'm sure too. Forever and all eternity, right?"

He clutches my hand, and as he runs his fingers over my knuckles, over the creases in my palm, over the scar just below my pointer finger that I got from a broken glass when I was little, I know he's wondering when will be the next time he gets to touch my skin.

I remember the first time we held hands. I was walking him to his truck after we spent the evening watching movies in my bedroom. He slipped his hand into mine at the last minute, as if he'd been working up the courage to do it all night, and my stomach soared with butterflies.

You never think about the last time you'll hold someone's hand. You never think about all the times you took advantage of being able to touch your loved ones, and how much you'll miss it one day. You don't think about it, because it's sad to think about death. But that's only because we've been trained to see it that way. I'm convinced now that if we always think about the day when we won't be able to anymore—the day we won't be able to hold hands, won't be able to embrace, won't be able to kiss, won't be able to argue, won't be able to make-up, won't be able to laugh—then we would appreciate our loved ones more. That appreciation would grow to be so strong that it could hold us up during the time we're apart, so that we can hold on to them.

Together, we ascend the stairs, toward the warm yellow glow waiting for me at the top, where I finally see what Jack has been keeping from me.

In the first room on the left, I see it.

Sitting beneath the window, where I imagined my desk would be when we first toured this house, the desk where I thought I'd write my great manuscript, is a small chestnut box with an etched rose design.

"I'm sure," he repeats.

As I gaze at my urn, at the proof of what he's endured, I understand how his love for me allows him to endure still. He has loved me more than I ever thought possible, and more than I ever thought I deserved.

I turn to him in time to catch his lips on mine, which will be the last time, for now.

THE NOISE

"I love you." He pulls away to look at me, and as I sink into his stormy blue-gray eyes and take in his familiar scent of Endymion, I tell him, "I love you too."

"It's time," my dad says.

I savor every remaining sensation of my fingertips slipping from his until my hand drops.

"I'll see you later," I say, and step into the light.

ALLISON A

FORTY-FIVE

I drape my winter coat over my shoulders and arrange my sheepskin hat so it covers my ears, then head out for firewood. I should probably just close the living room windows rather than go through the effort of starting a fire. At eighty-five, it's become more difficult to carry in log after log from the woodpile. But I've grown to enjoy the fusion of harsh winter cold and reassuring warmth. She taught me that. To appreciate one, you must endure the other.

Before making my way outside, I stop by the bookcase to choose my next read, or re-read. I'll start it later, maybe by the fire while I have dinner.

I built this bookcase after she crossed over. She always said a built-in bookcase looks more colonial, but she has so many books that I think she was really just worried it would topple over if it wasn't fastened to the wall. It's the one thing I'd

THE NOISE

never built before, and I couldn't help but laugh each time a plank wouldn't fit because I measured incorrectly, or when a stripped screw refused to fasten. I laughed, and I thought about how I wouldn't have spent so much time building something for anyone else. For her, I would do anything.

I stand back to admire the smooth white paint—paint that took days to dry between each coat because of the humidity in the house. It was worth it, and I admit she was right about the color. I wanted forest green, to match the kitchen, but white showcases the neatly lined book bindings. They're all horror stories, with mostly black covers that pop against the snowy wood.

I'd never been a fan of this genre, and yet I've read each of these books more than once. They've helped me understand her better. I think that's why people listen to the songs their loved ones used to play. In some way, it invites you into their thoughts and their ways of being, and you get to see what helped make them the person you love. Through knowing her, I understand the ghosts in these books much better. The same ones who made me jump before now make me sad. I'm sad for them, and I'm sad for those who miss out on them.

These books have helped me understand how to write about ghosts, too. After she passed, I became consumed with the things she never got to do, like write a book. She always talked about doing that one day, but her disease took her before she had the chance. It wasn't a conventional way of writing, I'll admit, but it worked.

I pull *The Noise* from the shelf, admiring the cover and smiling at the name etched below the title. I may have typed these words, but the story came from her and her alone.

I slip the book back into place and take the one beside it—*Voices in the Snow*. It's the book she was reading when she passed. I leave it on the arm of the couch, then tip my hat at her dad's urn resting atop the fireplace.

I pass by a wall of pictures on my way to the porch. There's the one we took at Double Trouble, back when we first started dating, with my red plaid shirt and her matching red hair blowing across her face as she smiled down at the camera. Her hair smelled floral, I remember. The one with her sitting on my lap that one Christmas Eve we spent with her family. I was looking through a cookbook I'd gotten as a gift, but all these years later, I'm only looking at her. That's all that matters in the end. Feelings, not things.

Or the one I love the most, the one of us on our wedding day. I never get tired of seeing her in that long-sleeve, lace wedding dress, red hair tied back in a French braid that spilled over her shoulder like a sunset over pure white snow.

And, of course, Charlie. I couldn't help myself. I framed the newspaper clipping of him, hoping that, by me seeing it every day, it would somehow help him cross over. But the noise

THE NOISE

perseveres upstairs, even now, even at this moment, just as it has for over five decades.

I see others, too. I see them all around town. At least, I see them until they disappear forever, soon replaced by other poor, forgotten souls who will succumb to the same fate. The worst part is that I can't stop it. I can't do for them what Angela taught me to do for her. I can only hope others will listen.

Charlie's wife passed forty years ago. I don't know how. Probably old age. I only know because there was a sign for an estate sale in her front yard. I don't know where she is, either. Maybe haunting her new husband's grandchildren with the small hope they'll rescue her from the same fate she sentenced Charlie to. Or maybe she's haunting the house she passed in, causing her own noise that the new owners and their children, with their bright, hopeful futures, just want to stop.

I never had children. I've lost count of how many times I've been told to move on and find someone who makes me happy, or that just because Angela passed doesn't mean I have to miss out on one of life's most precious moments. What people have never understood is that my memories with her *are* my life's most precious moments. Everyone told me the way I'm living is sad, like I'm living in a mausoleum. But I'm just living the same way I would if she was here, because she is here, because dead doesn't mean gone.

No one bothers me anymore. They haven't for a long time. Now I'm just a useless old man. But I used to tell them the same thing I tell myself: you don't move on, you carry on, toward the reward of true love that will last an eternity. Everything else is just noise.

After four trips spent bringing in logs for the fire, I finally get it going and strip off my coat and hat before dropping onto the couch. I never liked coffee before she passed, but, like her books, it's been a comfort for me. I sip from the warm mug I made for myself, enjoying the taste of cinnamon on my tongue—her favorite.

I go in for a second gulp, taking time to admire fresh sparks glittering in the dim light of the living room, then grab my journal from the end table. After fingering through dozens of memories, I land on a clean page.

I date the top right corner for today, February 4th, 2075.

Today's memory: the toilet paper tubes.

While we were living in our apartment together, she had a habit of leaving empty toilet paper tubes on the roller. She never felt the need to replace them. Until, of course, she had to go to the bathroom, and then she'd call for me to bring her a new roll. It drove me crazy. I brought it up in conversation one day. We spoke about it, then moved on to cook dinner, I thought. Next thing I knew, she came out of the bathroom, laughing to herself. I didn't know why, until I went in there and found an

THE NOISE

empty tube sitting upright on the toilet lid, wearing a smiley face drawn in red lipstick. She thought it was the funniest thing, and she left them everywhere after that. I'd find them under my pillow, inside my shoes, on top of the television, poking out from a cabinet. One time, she even put one on my forehead while I slept.

I read the entry over again, laughing to myself as I recall other places where I found the tubes. Once in the middle of the kitchen floor. Another time in the mailbox. In the utensils drawer. In the medicine cabinet. On my steering wheel. It was ridiculous, and I miss it. I miss it so much. I miss the way she would keel over, laughing so hard she could barely breathe.

That's what these entries do. One memory spurs another memory, spurs another memory, and she keeps breathing.

I down the rest of my coffee, and decide I'm ready.

I throw my coat and hat on one more time and make my way through the porch and down the steps, returning a short while later with a bundle of those which made it through most of the winter.

After shaking water from the stems of the old ones, I lay them on a towel to dry out so I can add them to the potpourri pile later on.

ALLISON A

I rinse the vase in the sink, dry it, then take the time to admire the way it sparkles in the light before dropping fresh white roses into it.

I close my eyes, breathe in, breathe out.

"Jack," she says, and I turn around.

A smile creases my lips at the familiar sight of her vibrant red hair that hasn't aged any more than my memory of her.

"I'm still sure," I tell her.

THE NOISE

IT'S NOT THE END.
IT'S SEE YOU LATER.

Acknowledgments

I want to thank my soulmate, Thomas Angell. You are my best friend and the love of my eternity. I wouldn't know what true love is if not for you. Thank you for always being so patient and supportive, and for encouraging me throughout this journey. You believed in me when no one else did, and you lifted me up in my darkest moments. This book wouldn't exist without you.

I want to thank my dad, Andrew Nazzaro, for making the greatest sacrifice of all. Your passing led me to discover my purpose in life, which is to be a writer, and to write this book in particular. You are my lighthouse, and you have always guided my way. I hope this book casts a beacon on your memory, allowing the world to remember you the way I do.

I also want to thank my step-dad, Wayne Tarus, for spending hours sitting at the kitchen table while proof-reading early versions of my manuscript.

Thank you to my mother, Lynn Nazzaro, for wanting to grow with me.

Thank you, Billy, for snuggling with me while I write.

Thank you to my loved ones on the other side: Buddy, Ginger, Sparky, Betty Nazzaro, Angelina Malchiodi, Louis Malchiodi, and Jefferey Murray. Thank you for the endless signs I've received from you all. You are always there when I need you. I hope I've made you proud.

Finally, thank you, MCR, for providing the soundtrack to my life.

Made in the USA
Columbia, SC
30 November 2023

7fc62460-c4a3-47f6-921d-7c6590d93c3cR01